COME BARBARIANS

COME BARBARIANS

TODD BABIAK

HARPERCOLLINS PUBLISHERS LTD

Published by HarperCollins Publishers Ltd

First edition

"Three Is a Magic Number" from the show *Schoolhouse Rock!* was written by
Robert (Bob) Dorough.

HarperCollins books may be purchased for educational, business,
or sales promotional use through our Special Markets Department.

HarperCollins Publishers Ltd
2 Bloor Street East, 20th Floor
Toronto, Ontario, Canada
M4W 1A8

www.harpercollins.ca

Library and Archives Canada Cataloguing in Publication
information is available upon request.

ISBN 978-1-55468-441-0

Printed and bound in Canada
WEB 9 8 7 6 5 4 3 2 1

COME BARBARIANS

PART ONE

ONE

Rue Trogue-Pompée, Vaison-la-Romaine

FRENCH TODDLERS CHOOSE A SINGLE STUFFED TOY AND CARRY IT
wherever they go, a *doudou*. They remain devoted to the dirty, fading
mound of dyed polyester until they reach elementary school. Then, in
a ritual that changes from family to family but usually involves tears,
they divorce themselves from it, an education in fidelity and loss.
"Soft," in French, is *doux*. A *doudou* is a "soft-soft." On Lily's first day
of kindergarten, in 1992, when they were still a family, Christopher
Kruse was sure he had heard the letter *r* in there. "I sleep," in French,
is *je dors*. Kruse heard "*dors-dors*," and he convinced himself it made
sense: a sleep-sleep. Even when the child says a public goodbye to her
stuffed animal, at five or six or seven, the *doudou* can stay in bed with
her for years—for the rest of her life.

At Lily's school there was a wicker box just inside the classroom door
for the damp-with-slobber cats and monkeys, bears, crocodiles, terri-
ers, and fleece blankets with hawk and chicken heads. This was training for the eventual separation. In kindergarten, a three-year affair in
France, the *doudou* and its consolations wait until the end of the day.

3

Lily had been a serial monogamist with stuffed animals back in Toronto: Ray the polar bear led to Goo the flying squirrel, to Anty the ant. In Vaison-la-Romaine she chose a blue dishrag of a turtle from her collection and, with her mother's help, named it Marie-France.

Marie-France forever.

When they ordered him out of the house Kruse asked for a moment and tried to close the door. A gendarme in uniform blocked it with a heavy boot and a baton. In Kruse's business the jokes about cops carried a single truth: these men, certainly the men, join the force to make up for some lack or agony, an unexpressed roar in their guts. Someone mistreated them at home. Too few people said I love you. The gendarme stood with his fellows behind, longing for and fearing at once, Kruse supposed, what might come next: hit the scar-face with the baton and stomp him with these shined black boots and bend over him and shout whatever they shout in French to make a man feel less than a man.

Kruse didn't move. The gendarme's breath quickened and he planted his back foot, lifted the baton.

The squat lieutenant in a grey sweater, the same sweater he had been wearing last night, elbowed the young gendarme out of the way. It was early in the morning, an hour after dawn. The smell of baking floated down from the plaza, diesel from the delivery trucks, sulphur and tobacco from the lieutenant's freshly lit cigarette. Blood on the cuff of his old sweater had dried black. What was it? Seven, seven thirty. "Out of the house, Monsieur Kruse."

"I need something first."

"What?"

"It's a private matter."

The lieutenant had a large moustache and small eyes. He was five foot seven with a thick, boyish mess of grey-black hair that added an extra inch. His consent was a sigh.

Kruse led him across the main floor, a hard white tile that had destroyed Lily's porcelain tea set. She was nearly four and dropped things out of a lack of focus more than clumsiness. It was not a forgiving wooden floor like the one on Foxbar Road. All she had left after six months in France were two cups, one for Daddy and one for Marie-France. Lily had been taking her own pretend tea from a miniature sugar bowl.

The stairs were marble. It was originally a horse stable, this dark little house on Rue Trogue-Pompée, attached to other horse stables behind a bourgeois street. In the early years of the twentieth century the French stopped riding horses and a researcher discovered a Roman city under a hill behind the stables. Vaison became Vaison-la-Romaine and an unnamed back alley became Rue Trogue-Pompée after a first-century historian, Gnaeus Pompeius Trogus, born in one of the Roman houses. Then came the barbarians. When the tourist industry launched between the two wars, every horse stable on the block transformed into a *maison de village*. The haylofts became second floors with two generous but poorly insulated windows, marble stairways, and boxes of red gladiolas, overlooking two-thousand-year-old statues of dead emperors.

"I've been in here before." The lieutenant waited for him at the threshold of Lily's room. Fluff and plastic and torn bits of cotton lay on the floor—whatever he had not repaired with tape and glue. Kruse had planned to clean it up. Now it was evidence of something. The lieutenant bent over a moment for a better look. "You did this?"

"Yes, Monsieur."

The lieutenant stood up and adjusted his sweater, stared at Kruse for a moment and hummed. "When we were kids, Jean-François had a party and invited me. I was a few years older but he was rich. His parents were rich, and his parents' parents. Did you know that about him?"

"No."

"A Frenchman knows. We once knew. Today it's more difficult, as we're all pretending."

"Pretending?"

"To be richer, smarter, more important than we are."

"I suppose, Monsieur."

"We were in here, drinking wine and singing, celebrating I can't remember what. Maybe his engagement to Pascale. The early sixties, before everything went to shit. She was the prettiest girl in town, that black hair. That skin."

Kruse waited until the lieutenant was finished and picked up Marie-France and stuffed it in his front pocket. He had not eaten and he had not slept, but he didn't want food and he didn't want sleep. The lieutenant walked down the hall to the master bedroom. One of his feet pointed in and he walked with a slight limp. Childhood polio, maybe. It was tough to imagine any force hiring a man like him today, but last night in Villedieu the younger officers had deferred to the lieutenant. He seemed to know blood better, and politics.

"You know why we've come to see you this morning, Monsieur Kruse?"

He did not know but he knew. "No."

The lieutenant looked out over the gladiolas, which needed water, and the ruins. He was nearly finished his cigarette. It was cloudy and warm, a gentle mockery of a morning-after. Kruse looked out the other window. Some of his neighbours, the Moroccans and their children, gathered on the street and on the limestone gravel path that led to the cathedral and Lily's school, École Jules Ferry, to stare at the gendarmes. It was a small town. They would have heard. They remained far enough away to avoid what the renovated horse stable now carried in its old walls, whatever virus or curse. It was a haunted house now. The Moroccans watched the gendarmes and the gendarmes looked up at the lieutenant above the gladiolas, waiting perhaps for a signal.

On the other side of the gendarmes there was a black iron fence and beyond that statues of great forgotten men, half walls and pillars and latrines, the remains of a commercial street and a sewer, the bones of a two-thousand-year-old mansion.

The lieutenant looked at his watch. He had introduced himself the night before in Villedieu, city of God, the village down the road, but Kruse had forgotten his name. It started with a vowel. "Approximately four hours ago, someone stabbed your landlords to death in the salon of their farmhouse." He turned slowly to Kruse. The lieutenant's mouth was nearly always open, just slightly. He did not have the eyes of a policeman.

It was a test and Kruse received it in that spirit. The image came with a pulse of nausea but little more. He was a ruin too.

"Where were you last night, Monsieur Kruse?"

"Here."

"All night?"

"When we left Villedieu we went to the hospital. The morgue. After that we came here."

"At what time, please?"

"Before midnight."

"You've been up there before? The farmhouse behind the château?"

"Yes."

"Many times?"

"A few times."

"You were involved in politics in some fashion, I think."

"Not me."

"Madame Kruse."

"Yes."

"And Madame Kruse isn't here?"

"No, Monsieur."

"You said 'we.' She came back here with you, after the hospital. You destroyed your daughter's toys and clothes. You. Yes? And then she went out, if I may presume. When did she go out?"

Kruse wouldn't answer that. Not yet. They looked at each other for some time, the exhaustion and lies between them like a bad odour. The lieutenant put the cigarette out in the soil of the window box and tossed the butt into the cobblestone street. It landed and bounced a foot away from Madame Boutet, the other gendarme from last night, his partner. Neither of them would have slept much.

"You have what you need? Your something?"

Kruse reached into his pocket, touched the *doudou*. "Yes, Monsieur."

For some time the lieutenant remained at the window. "How did you know about this place?"

"This house?"

"Vaison-la-Romaine. Before you arrived, from America. How did you choose it?"

"It was in a book."

"There is a book, in English, about Vaison. And people in America can read it. With pictures, I imagine, of this. Come to our village." The lieutenant gestured out at the ruins, the swipe of his arm a bit of a flail. Come, barbarians, to our village. Burn it down.

• • •

It was warm and cool at once, like a Great Lakes September morning. He sat on the new sidewalk against the fence and Madame Boutet leaned against the horse stable, watching him. She looked down at Marie-France's head and one of her legs, poking out of his front pocket. The cigarette butt the gendarme had thrown out the window sat half a metre away, a pinched wet thing speckled with soil.

His body betrayed him: coffee. Kruse didn't want to want. He wanted to brush his teeth. Her blood remained under his fingernails and his throat was sore from shouting. The fatigue had a metallic edge, a taste. All of the shutters were closed on Rue Trogue-Pompée at this hour. One of the renovated horse stables was a jewellery store, locked down

with a metal garage door. It was November 1. Tourists had fled south
to the coast, where it would be somewhere between warm and hot for
another month. The crowd of Moroccan men and their sons continued to grow. Where were the girls and women? The sons, between fifteen and twenty-five, had variations on the same haircut—shaved close
with razor patterns above their ears. Adidas was their brand of choice,
and on a normal day their overall statement was "go fuck yourself," an
import from American hip hop. On a normal day they were tough and
worldly men, *le football* and angry music, chins in the air. This morning they were boys. None of them smoked in front of their fathers.
They were boys fascinated and embarrassed by Kruse, by the real thing
that had happened to him last night in Villedieu.

Inside the horse stable, the phone rang. There were six gendarmes
on the ground floor, all but the lieutenant in uniform. Those he could
see, in front of the open window, froze. The lieutenant told everyone
to shut their mouths and walked to the phone, picked it up. Evelyn
would not phone. She was no idiot. Madame Boutet stepped through
the open door, to listen. Kruse could not hear, from the sidewalk across
the street.

Madame Boutet walked back out with cigarettes, Gitanes, and
offered him one. Kruse shook his head no and she pulled one out. She
used it to point inside. "A journalist."

What if he stood up and ran around the corner, up Jules Ferry and
into the graffitied alleys? Madame Boutet would scream his name and
pull her gun with a shaky hand, bend her knees. Sweat would flash over
her shoulders, and if she gathered the courage to pull the trigger she
would miss.

TWO

Place de la Libération, Villedieu

THE GENDARMES PRESENTED HIM WITH A LIST OF WHAT THEY HAD
taken: four of Evelyn's notebooks, family photographs, all three
passports, and some photocopied magazine articles about the Front
National that Jean-François had given them. Madame Boutet and her
partner with the moustache allowed him back inside and ordered him
to be at the gendarmerie that afternoon. Once all the imported detectives from Avignon and Arles and Carpentras were finished their work
at the bloody farmhouse behind the château, someone would be in
charge of the investigation. Kruse stood at the window in the master bedroom, watering the flowers. This had always been his job, in
Toronto and here, and today he received it like a gift. If Evelyn came
home and the flowers were dead it would say too much.

Two German couples in shorts wandered through the ruins with
pamphlets. They were regular people with regular marriages, Sunday
night dinners with their grown-up children.

Sleep was impossible. Everywhere she had been, he went. Kruse

walked the narrow streets and through all the rounded, miniature pla-
zas of the medieval upper town. He climbed to the ruined château,
walked around it with some teenagers and, from its vantage point,
looked down. Back in their neighbourhood he sat for ten minutes at an
outdoor café along Place Montfort, watching for her. He took a coffee
and some sparkling water on an empty stomach. The table was polka-
dotted with dew. He had seen historical photos with the carved stone
fountain, water flowing crookedly and splashing into a pool on one
side, and the giant plane trees. The centre of the square, now a parking
lot, was once a place to talk politics and children and play *pétanque.*

From the café he could see the bakery, dark now, dark indefinitely.
On the exterior rock walls, on each side of the bakery's front doors,
were political posters. They were identical: a photograph of handsome, long-nosed Jean-François de Musset with the three colours of
the French flag behind him. Below the flag and his photo were the
words "Front national pour l'unité française" and the initials "FN."
Jean-François looked off heroically into the distance; no politician in
Canada would dare such a thing, to stray from friendly and competent.
The poster on the right had been marked. Someone had written *fasciste*
over his face in black, and in defiance Jean-François had not taken it
down.

"If I take it down I acknowledge it hurts me." They were in the bakery on a Tuesday morning. The sun had not yet come up. Jean-François
was teaching Kruse how to fold the dough during fermentation.

"It doesn't hurt?"

"Of course it hurts."

Kruse walked through the fallen leaves and the horse chestnuts,
into the cathedral. The three of them had visited the twelfth-century
church many times as it had been on the way home from École Jules
Ferry, though they had never taken up the priest on a Sunday mass.
Evelyn was a conservative but not that sort. There were tiny blue flowers in stone vases in the middle of the cloister. One hot afternoon,

after school, Lily asked her parents to identify them. Neither of them knew much about flowers but they were pleased she had asked: it said something about a kid, that she was curious about flowers. Evelyn had picked her up, kissed her.

"What, Mommy? Why?"

She kissed Lily some more. Not one child, at École Jules Ferry, had said a word about her lip. At least nothing Lily could understand. Giant bees had flown lazily from vase to vase that day in early September, occasionally bumping into one another. There were so many first-century artifacts, in and around the church, that they had been stacked along the walls. On the way back to the horse stable Kruse had lifted his daughter to his shoulders and she had picked ripe figs from the branches overhanging the path. It was hot but not in the cruel manner of August. Someone had stepped on an enormous snail that morning; the shell was cracked and the meat of it was drying out in the sun. Kruse pointed at some birds landing on a chestnut tree, so she would not notice the snail.

There had been a magnificent shock of blood on her face when she was born. They didn't let him see her immediately; the doctor ignored his questions and one of the nurses took him aside, to the window next to Evelyn's bed. Lily and Henry were the names they had chosen. The doctor, and now another doctor, called the tiny thing Lily before he did. Kruse wasn't sure this particular baby was his. It was not at all as he had imagined things. Maybe they could start over?

Some part of him, in these bewildering early moments, wanted to walk out of the hospital and keep walking.

"What's wrong with her?"

"Mr. Kruse, this is important. Look at me: nothing is wrong with your child."

"Then what are they doing?" When he tried to look over the nurse's shoulder she moved to intercept his gaze. She was short and nearly jumped. It would have been comical.

"They're making a determination." Hospital light reflected off a film of sweat on the nurse's upper lip. How we take our upper lips for granted. She glanced at the warming table and back to him. "What you have here is a very special girl."

Given his choice of career, he had made an art form out of keeping his temper: to lose it was always to lose. Evelyn mumbled. He held her hot left hand. None of this had been part of their birthing class curriculum. Finally, Lily was wrapped in pink felt and he kissed Evelyn's hand and they placed the baby in his arms. He had no idea how to hold her. Now at the end of her long screaming fit she slept with heaving and tinny breaths that were, they assured him, entirely normal. Nothing seemed normal: he had never seen a child born with what they called a unilateral incomplete cleft palate. The obstetrician, with a British accent, took him aside and delivered a speech. Kruse's parents had died suddenly when he was a teenager, thousands of kilometres from home, and he was young enough that he had never heard any bad news directly from a doctor. In the years since his parents had died, doctors joshed him in the examination room, reassured him about his cuts and fractures, complimented him on his fitness, his commitment to clean living. There would be a series of surgeries, the obstetrician said. Upper-class British accent or middle-class? He had learned the difference for a client, a risk assessment, but he was both exhausted and radically awake at once. What was he supposed to focus on? Would she live? Would her face heal? Why was she crying so much? Evelyn called out for him and he moved toward her with the baby, but the obstetrician stopped him. Kruse had competed for a couple of years, in his teens and early twenties, and if he took a punch square in the face the referee would look at him the way the doctor looked at him now. Was he fit to continue?

In the end, the doctor said, Lily would look and sound extremely close to normal. How long was "in the end"? The word "extremely" sounded extreme, a fib, a plea.

It would take years.

"In my experience, having a child like this, a child with uncommon needs, brings a husband and a wife closer together."

"Uncommon needs?"

"Emotionally and otherwise, Christopher, it's hard work. You feel ready for it. Already you love this little thing more than yourself, yes? Yes." The doctor stepped in closer. He held Kruse's arm, to prevent him for another moment from presenting Lily to her mother. "But be aware: sometimes it doesn't bring a husband and a wife closer together."

• • •

On November 1, All Saints' Day, the day of the dead, one of the priests in the cold cathedral recognized him. The afternoon papers had come out. No, the priest had not seen Madame Kruse. He delivered a short sermon about how this might seem to be about his daughter and his wife and Jean-François and Pascale de Musset. But it was really about God.

Kruse interrupted the priest to tell him the truth, as calmly as he could manage: none of what he was saying made the remotest sense. He spoke rubbish for a living. The priest listened and agreed. Where had sense brought any of them?

Evelyn was nowhere that made any sense so he searched the hair salon. She wasn't at the swimming pool and no one had seen her at the fitness centre. The museum was closed. The rented Renault was still in its parking spot next to the post office. Buses departed from a bar-tabac on the other side of the Roman ruins. Had anyone seen her? The men and women in the bar-tabac, tucked into their noontime pastis, usually keen to talk to *l'étranger*, shook their heads with something like shame. The room smelled of licorice and smoke. Only two buses had departed this morning, one on the north route and the other on the south. Kruse looked at the map. Each route had between fifteen and twenty stops.

It was peculiar to use air conditioning in November. He drove to Villedieu, past the farmers in their tall boots. A man and a woman walked on the side of the departmental highway with rifles. The sky in the east and the north carried an ominous, ghostly green. He parked in the lot and walked up to the square past the lime and the gravel still stained with blood. The waiter from Café du Centre was wiping tables. All the tricolour balloons Evelyn had tied for Jean-François had been tossed into the corner, against the village hall. All of the Front National posters and banners had disappeared, along with the political strategists from Paris. Most of the helium had leaked out of the balloons that remained, yet he still had an urge to bring one home for Lily. The waiter looked as though it had happened to him too. He had just shaved and his skin shone. One of his eyes was smaller than the other, as though it were infected. No, he had not seen Madame.

"Would you take a drink with me?"

"I don't think I can."

"Please, Monsieur Kruse."

"I have to keep looking."

"You won't find her. Not now." The waiter placed his tray on an adjacent table and sat down. Kruse pulled out a hollow silver chair and sat across from him. The waiter adjusted the table so it would not wobble. "Is it true, what they're saying in the newspapers? And on the news?"

Kruse still hadn't seen or heard any of it. "You were here last night."

"It's not really about what happened here, the things they're saying."

If it wasn't about Lily, about the end of his family, what the hell was it about? There was a faint roar in the air, a storm in the distance or an airplane. He wanted, like a boy, to go back in time. He wanted to pick up one of these chairs, five of them, and throw them as far as they would go. Down the hills, through the windows.

"The police were here again, today."

"Asking about my daughter?"

"Different police. I've never seen police like these before. Not like on

television. They asked about your wife and J.F. and the Front National."
The waiter's accent was strong, a country accent. His voice took a turn
when he said "Front National," as though it were the name of an ill-
ness. "They showed me pictures of men. Did I recognize any of them?"

"What men?"

"I didn't recognize them."

"What did they ask about Evelyn?"

"What she did for the party, your party."

"It isn't my party. It isn't Evelyn's party either. We're foreigners."

"They say it's her party."

When she was a teenager and a competitive athlete, Evelyn fell in
love with Benjamin Disraeli. He had been dead nearly one hundred
years, but at the end of her family's wealth and in the humiliation
that came with it she discovered and embraced the politician, who
had grown up outside power, who had endured financial ruin, and
who had embodied a careful and romantic sort of conservatism. While
some girls had posters and photographs of Barry Gibb on their bedroom walls, Evelyn had an 1878 photograph of the sad-eyed Earl of
Beaconsfield on hers. He wore a top hat for the picture and carried a
newspaper on his lap. When she had spoken of her love affair with a
dead man, Evelyn didn't smile: her admission contained just as much
wayward passion as screams for the Bee Gees. She memorized whole
speeches Disraeli had delivered. From time to time, at dinner parties
or at the intermission of the symphony, she would quote from them to
prove a point. Evelyn insisted Kruse read a short biography of him, so
he might understand. He couldn't finish the book and she caught him
out. She believed, as her childhood mentor had believed, that individu-
als are the source of all that is beautiful and transcendent and noble in
the world. The role of the state is to create a safe environment for them
and to get out of their way. Success is the child of audacity. Kruse could
never really understand, or even remember, why these strange heroes of
hers—first Disraeli, then Chateaubriand, then Edmund Burke—were

conservative instead of liberal, or where one word bled into the other. She never wavered from that early love and where it took her, even as it seemed destined to stall or cripple her career in the academy. Her time would come, as Disraeli's time had come. She merely had to dress well and wait patiently for her Queen Victoria.

Her Queen Victoria was Jean-François de Musset.

"What else did they ask?"

"About J.F. and Pascale. Questions I couldn't answer. Honestly, I didn't know her, your wife. I served her wine. The party had meetings here and I barely listened to what they said." The waiter rubbed his bare arms. He hadn't done a push-up since leaving school. He shouted to be heard over slamming shutters. "I don't know about politics."

It was called the mistral, this wind.

Before the wedding and again when Evelyn was having her troubles he had read a book about marriage: "You can never really know her heart."

"Are you a professor, like Madame?"

"No."

The flimsy silver chairs were beginning to topple over now, *crash* after *crash*.

"I asked you for a drink but I didn't get us drinks. What would you like? We'll move inside."

Kruse thanked the waiter for his kindness and for his offer and walked the way he had walked with his daughter. Leaves collected in the shallow stone gutter. Dust whipped into his eyes. He was fifteen minutes late for his meeting at the gendarmerie, seven kilometres away in Vaison-la-Romaine, but he didn't hurry.

• • •

Farmers had been burning grape wood in the valley below the village. Smoke hung and swirled in a deep green bowl. A moat of phantoms, Lily called it, in French: *un fossé de fantômes.* When they had arrived in May to repair themselves, this little family, Lily could hardly say hello and goodbye in her second language. After four months in the playground and two months in school she corrected her parents' pronunciation. She had pulled him to the edge, the plateau, the perch, to show him this: the dark green valley meeting the blue sky and, at the bottom, the moat.

Kruse's almost-four-year-old daughter had inherited his need for occasional stillness. Either that or she pretended to need it, to please him. She watched him and traced the scar that ran down the left side of his face. She leaned against his hard arm and looked out thoughtfully, imitating him. Autumn flowers bloomed. The wind changed and they could smell pizza from the plaza of Villedieu.

On Saturday, October 31, Lily wore a fairy costume. Evelyn had sewn it with swatches of baby blue satin from a shop on Cours de Taulignan, Vaison-la-Romaine's main street. It would have been unimaginable a year ago: Evelyn with the time, the patience, the joy, the matrix of priorities to sew a Halloween costume.

They would have to leave early to make Lily's seven o'clock bedtime, so they had arrived at three thirty to help out. It wasn't a Halloween party because they did not celebrate Halloween in Provence. It was something else altogether. Evelyn had helped tie blue and white and red helium balloons to little bags of silty stone. Two men from Paris fixed a political banner over the arch that led to the church: "Front national pour l'unité française." Orange lights had been strung from the branches of a wilting plane tree some years ago and many, most, had failed. Earlier that afternoon the mayor of Villedieu had ordered his sons to replace them.

"It's starting, you two." Evelyn stood under one of the arches separating the square from the edge of the hill.

Kruse had planned to watch from afar or avoid it altogether. Some of the villagers, he had heard, were appalled: the Front National in their public square. "Maybe we'll stay over here."

"The TV people want us in a group, so the crowd looks big."

"I don't want Lily on TV, at a political rally."

Evelyn closed her eyes for a moment, as though it required every cell in her body to remain calm. "Please, Chris. I'm not asking for much. No one you know will see you."

It wasn't that. But it was a little of that.

Lily insisted they each take a hand and bounce her back down the path, to the smell of hot dough and the music. There were two restaurants in Place de la Libération, one specializing in pizza and the other in galettes. On Halloween-not-Halloween, Café du Centre added its own tables and chairs near the fountain. A France 2 television crew had set up in front of the village hall and some print journalists in wrinkled jackets sat smoking and waiting at corner tables, alone. The mayor and his sons carried five picnic tables from the courtyard of their own house.

Mothers sipped pastis. Ruddy men in soiled shirts, the grandfathers of the village, studied their cigarettes. A fancy ghetto blaster sat in an open window with impossibly blue shutters. It was Callas singing the Habanera: "L'amour est un oiseau rebelle." Love is a rebellious bird. Evelyn had bought Kruse an opera appreciation class two birthdays ago. With opera, a small library of essential books, two serious magazine subscriptions, and a Woody Allen box set, she had resolved to make a man of culture of him, change him, inspire him to be someone else, someone in Europe who recognizes arias.

Autumn was the finest season, everyone said so, gentle enough even at sunset that Evelyn hung her thin sweater from the otherwise-ignored No Smoking sign next to the stone fountain and sat nearby. The fairy was not inclined to sit. Creatures in need—bugs mostly, and birds—demanded Lily's attention, her special powers and her kind heart. The magic wand, *la baguette magique*, was made of bamboo.

Evelyn's long legs were bare, crossed just above the knee. One of her black slip-on shoes swung from her unpainted toenails. The gay man who had fitted Evelyn for her wedding dress had called her legs exquisite. It was not a word Kruse could use but he carried it around, and her legs were no less exquisite with the red welts on her shins: evidence of recent nighttime attacks from continental insects. He did not understand her obsessions, she did not understand his, and nothing—not even a year in France—was going to repair that. But he was nearly finished his first glass of wine. Her skin was unusually tan and pretty in the late-day sun. She spoke to a man and woman from Nyons and caught him watching her.

This was why they had crossed the ocean.

The waiter walked out of Café du Centre with a full tray of beer and muscat, and knitted around the tables and feet and baby carriages and dogs. Kruse made the briefest eye contact with him, to call him over without calling him over. The waiter raised his eyebrows and nodded, just like that. They had only been here a few months and already it was just like that. It was about calm now, and beauty, just as she had planned. Kruse drank wine among strangers. He had his own *levain*.

Jean-François and Pascale de Musset entered the plaza from the path that led to the church and the château. Two or three of the Front National organizers from Paris—men and women with pressed shirts and dresses, designer eyeglasses, cellular phones, pinched accents, and a lot of perfume—shouted and gestured like circus masters and everyone stood to applaud. A small group, two women and a young man, booed. Those around them cheered more loudly, stepped in front of them. Lily wanted Jean-François and Pascale to see her fairy costume so she jumped and waved. Kruse tried to stop her but it was too late. The de Mussets were a childless couple and had become once-a-week babysitters and regular gift-buyers. Jean-François stopped and picked Lily up, laughing, as the applause around them continued. He was a tall man with an enviable pile of grey hair and a long nose that made him more distinguished if less handsome. The television cameras caught it.

Lily shouted, in French. "What am I?"

Jean-François smelled her. "A bowl of soup?"

"No!"

"The president of the republic?"

"No!"

"I know: a wild boar."

"No, no, no, Monsieur."

"You're a princess, it's evident." Jean-François put her down and pointed behind him. "And that is your château."

He continued along and someone handed him a glass of champagne. Their newly famous landlord and best French friend entered the crowd and for the rest of the evening they did not speak to him. Instead they spoke of him as the next leader of the Front National, inheritor of French conservatism, rescuer of the French idea, true heir of de Gaulle. Lily was upset because she was not able to tell Jean-François that she and Maman had designed the fairy costume themselves. Why didn't anyone even know it was Halloween around here? She did not have to trick-or-treat because, after her pizza, Kruse ordered her a crème brûlée.

Pascale lost Jean-François. She asked Kruse and Evelyn to look around, if they didn't mind. It was becoming strange, his absence, all of these people had come for him. "He did warn me." Her hair, so black it appeared wet, was pulled back into a tight bun and she wore a blue dress with a white and red scarf: Madame Tricolore.

"About what?" Kruse held Lily so she wouldn't run back to the fountain with her new friends.

"That some of the Parisians would take him aside, discuss strategy, make recommendations: say this and don't say that, walk this way, be ambitious but not too ambitious. The movement has a leader, after all. One wouldn't want to seem . . ."

There were only two possibilities: up here at the top of the hill or in the bar-tabac at the bottom. Evelyn went down and Kruse stayed up. He and Lily walked through the pizza and galette restaurants, toured the alley, peeked in the old church, and returned to the square.

Lily danced with the other little girls, looked for beetles and spiders and scorpions, dipped her magic wand in the fountain. Just after seven o'clock, Lily's bedtime, Evelyn walked back into the square.

"He's down there."

"With Parisians?"

"Maybe Parisians. Two men in suits, and he's drunk. Plastered."

Jean-François drank wine but it was difficult to imagine him drunk. He was a courtly and careful man, vain in a crowd.

"I tried to speak to him, and the men, both of them, told me to fuck off. I mean, more politely than that but not much more politely."

"You want me to go down there and . . ."

"No, Chris, but thanks. My honour is intact."

Kruse led her across the plaza. "That's the thing with fascists. One day they're nice and the next . . ."

Evelyn squinted. "That isn't funny here."

They told Pascale he was at the bottom of the hill, leaving out his condition, and spent the next hour saying goodbye to her and to others, men in the party who had taken too much wine and wanted to thank Evelyn with hand-holding and multiple kisses and bits of devotional poetry they had memorized long ago. Lily hugged Pascale too long and too hard, one of those things she did.

Pascale did not seem to mind. "That all of this should come from a disaster. Good night. Good night, my little fairy."

Traffic enters Place de la Libération on four thin medieval roadways that snake into and out of Villedieu. Nothing here had been built for cars.

They walked past the fountain and toward a parking lot at the bottom of the hill. Kruse and Evelyn walked along the houses while Lily

skipped, in character, on the opposite side of the road. There was no
formal sidewalk here, but the cobblestones did end in a rough path of
gravel decorated with old trees. She swung her wand about and sang in
French and in English, turned frogs into princes. In the distance, the
sound of sirens. When they had first arrived, the French siren had been
exotic and glamorous. Kruse called her over but either she ignored him
or did not hear over the noise of the party and her own singing. He
started to cross the street but Evelyn pulled him back.

"Let her be."

Kruse would later wonder why he did not hear the engine sooner.
Where had the sirens come from? He watched Lily and he watched
Evelyn, her tan face and the veins on the back of her hand. In the plaza,
under the inconsistent orange lights, he had studied the unlit pockets
they created along the wall, the sloped path toward the broken château,
entrances and escapes, hiding places, covered positions, until he took
another glass of wine and forced himself to notice other things. Evelyn
had succeeded: his business was no longer his business.

The headlights were not turned on.

Lily stopped skipping. She saw it first, swerving toward her, and
froze. There would have been time, if Kruse had started at that instant,
to run across and snatch her up and pull her into a doorway. By the
time he started to run it was too late. The car roared up the old road, its
new tires slapping the cobblestone. Evelyn screamed behind him and
said no, as the white Mercedes of their landlord and best French friend
accelerated into their daughter.

THREE

Cours de Taulignan, Vaison-la-Romaine

SOMEONE HAD BEEN IN BOULANGERIE J.F. SINCE THE MORNING. THE poster with *"fasciste"* over Jean-François's head had been removed. Flowers were scattered about. Candles had been placed before the door, though they had blown out in the new wind. No one had left flowers and candles for Lily, not in Villedieu and not in Vaison-la-Romaine. Inside, the stone and stainless steel workshop shone in the faint light, most of the sun doused by stage one of the mistral: dust. Three nuns in their habits bent into it and either ignored him or couldn't hear when he offered to help with an arm or directions. Cours de Taulignan was deserted. The people of Northern Provence had hunkered into their dim little houses to make stew.

By ambition Jean-François de Musset was a regional councillor on his way to the palace. By trade he was a baker, as his father had been. He held the title of Meilleur Ouvrier de France—the best in the country. President François Mitterrand had bestowed the honour on him after a display of bread making, wine pairing, and historical speech making at a series of arduous competitions in Paris. He had been profiled in every major newspaper and magazine in France, and had merited a small piece in *The New York Times* in the eighties. These pieces had been fitted into wooden frames and hung on the interior walls of his bakery, where they were stained by the sun and warped by humidity. The converted horse stable they rented from Jean-François and Pascale was small but it was clean and safe. Morning baguettes from Boulangerie J.F. were delicious. The baker and his wife had been kind to their daughter. Through Jean-François, Evelyn had found something to study and Kruse had found something to make.

The lieutenant greeted him at the door of the gendarmerie in a clean shirt and blazer. "We were just about to send a bulletin, Monsieur Kruse."

"I was in Villedieu."

"Why?"

"Perhaps you've forgotten. Last night, a drunk man—"

"Yes, yes." The lieutenant's smile faded for a moment. "That crime has been solved."

"It must be gratifying."

The gendarme fussed with his moustache. He had a name tag: HUARD, Yves. Behind him, a woman in uniform sat on a raised chair behind a desk, smoking and watching them watch one another. Pop music played distantly inside the building. From somewhere else, a man's heavy and exaggerated laugh. All was ridiculous, the day after his daughter's murder.

"Have you found anything in my wife's notebooks?"

"Only one of us reads English, and he's slow about it. I'd ask you to translate for us but I fear you'd be conflicted."

"You're wasting your time. She's no killer."

"See? Conflicted. Follow me, Monsieur Kruse."

He never wanted to talk for the sake of talking. In the hallway he did. "You're married, Monsieur Huard?"

"Not me, no. I was and then I wasn't."

"Children?"

"We didn't make it that far, Monsieur Kruse. I regret it but I would have been a miserable father. I'm miserable at most things. Even interrogation, as you'll soon see." The lieutenant stopped and turned around, fixed Kruse in the eyes. "And how are you?"

There was no way to answer.

"And now the winds have come. Just think, if they had arrived last night the party would have been cancelled."

The interview cell was not the bare walls and raw concrete of his imagination. It was a conference room with potted plants and a white screen for overhead projections. There was a fax machine and, in the middle of the table, a speakerphone. Madame Boutet's hair was still wet. She stood up, in a thick black police sweater, to shake his hand.

"We hear you've been looking for her."

"She's my wife."

"Rather you find her than us." Madame's nose flared. "Is that it?"

The handshake had lasted too long. He retreated.

"You've eaten something since this morning, I hope."

"Not yet, Madame, but it's in my plans."

Lieutenant Huard clapped his hands. "Sous-lieutenant Boutet, how would you like to go next door and order us a lovely fromage-charcuterie?"

It was evident Madame Boutet would not like to do that. She paused a moment and stared at her partner, flatly but malevolently, and then she walked out.

"You're in for it now, Monsieur Kruse. She can't take it out on me but she can punish you. Please sit."

The chairs were mismatched but made of leather, with wheels on the bottom. Kruse sat and leaned forward over the table. "You interviewed him, your old friend, after he killed her."

"Killed? You mean Jean-François. I didn't mean to imply we were friends. He was a wealthy and powerful man, an artisan. Who am I?"

"What did he say?"

"He was destroyed, Monsieur. I promise you that. He had strong feelings for your daughter. He knew his future, his career and life as he imagined it, were as dead as your Lily. This one terrible moment. He said he didn't remember."

"What didn't he remember?"

"He was barely coherent and then as he came out of the fog, his drunkenness, it was as though he didn't know how it had all come to be. From late-afternoon to midnight: nothing."

"He was preparing his legal defence, no doubt. Evelyn spoke to him in the tavern at the bottom of the hill, or tried to speak to him, while he was drinking. He was with two men, from Paris I think, and they were rude to her."

"I would ask my old friend about these men." Lieutenant Huard twirled his soft, crumpled package of cigarettes on the table. "Their names and addresses. But someone stabbed him, you see. Do you know how many times? Did you read about it?"

"No, Monsieur."

"We are fragile creatures, aren't we?" Lieutenant Huard waited a moment, for confirmation. Then he winked and lifted a plastic bag from a side table, next to the coffee machine, and dug his hand into it. He pulled out a fragrant pile of newspapers.

"You haven't seen these yet."

"No."

"While we wait for Madame Boutet, why don't you take a look?"

There were two national newspapers, *Le Monde* and *Le Figaro*, and two regional papers, *La Provence* and *Le Dauphiné Libéré*. Each carried a version of the story on its front page. He skimmed the first few paragraphs of each.

France is not a violent country by American standards, but enough people are murdered that it isn't automatically news when a man in Toulouse strangles his wife or shoots his business partner in the head with a hunting rifle. It was news because Jean-François de Musset was a politician and, more recently, a national hero. This was the lead of all four stories. Lily was worth a sentence, a phrase. He pushed them aside.

"You didn't read far enough, Monsieur Kruse."

"I was in Villedieu last night. I know what happened."

"Read all of the stories until the end. It will lead rather elegantly into some of our questions."

A little more than a month earlier, Jean-François and Pascale had insisted the family spend a few days at their holiday home in Cassis, on the Mediterranean coast. Kruse had been volunteering at the bakery for two months, working as a free apprentice; if he was in France to change his life for Evelyn and for Lily, to learn how to make something beautiful, bread had seemed as beautiful as anything else. Evelyn was not one to work with her hands but she had been busy. She was studying Jean-François's political party but also teaching him. She participated in meetings and events, provided advice, gently steered them away from extremes; his conservatism was her conservatism, even though he had never read Edmund Burke or Chateaubriand. She and Kruse accepted the offer of a beach vacation and drove their rental car to the pretty little town on the sea. Evelyn lay on a beach towel and read about the meeting place between French art and politics: a publishable paper, at least one, was revealing itself to her. He and Lily dug holes and buried each other in the sand. Even in September the sea was warmer than any Ontario lake.

One night in Cassis, Kruse and Evelyn hired a babysitter through the tourist office and spent way too many francs on food and wine in a waterfront bistro. Back in the apartment they made love so well they woke up Lily. The next morning the heat that sustained them on the Mediterranean moved north and smashed into the cool from the mountains, and Vaison-la-Romaine formed the unlucky centre of the most intense rainstorms and the most devastating flood since the seventeenth century. The Ouvèze river overflowed, knocking out everything in its path but one of the oldest bridges in the world: the Roman arch separating the lower and upper towns. Over thirty people, most of them campers east of Vaison, were swept to their deaths. The man who organized the rescue and pulled several people out from trees and smashed buildings, in front of television news cameras, was a baker and Front National regional councillor named Jean-François de Musset.

Two weeks after the flood in Vaison-la-Romaine, the first Sunday in October, Jean-François was invited to Paris. One of the country's most famous television talk show hosts, Bernard Pivot, sat across from him in a bright studio. The show was called *Bouillon de culture* and the Kruses were invited to watch with Pascale, at the farmhouse behind the château.

It was a night of magic: Lily had never seen someone she knew on TV. The de Musset domaine was an enormous converted farmhouse between yellow and brown, with a faded almost-pink terracotta roof and a small vineyard, down a secluded road. They had dinner before the broadcast: a beet salad, bouillabaisse with aioli, tomates confites, and a roasted chicken with lemon and rosemary, every ingredient from their garden or a product of the Tuesday morning Vaison-la-Romaine market.

During dinner Evelyn said very little. Kruse caught her staring at Pascale, a tiny but beautiful woman with enough Italian ancestry to give her a permanent tan. She moved in a slow but lively fashion, as though she were always stopping herself from breaking into a run. If Kruse hadn't known that Jean-François was fifty-one and that he and Pascale had been lycée sweethearts, he would have had trouble guessing her age. She spoke to Lily almost all the way through dinner, formally and sincerely, about Lily's hopes and dreams, her mission in life, her favourite colour, favourite music, favourite food, favourite country.

La France, évidemment.

Kruse knew enough, from Evelyn, to understand that Jean-François's political party was in a curious spot. Young people were apt to deface a poster with the word *fasciste*, and the Front National's early incarnation had attracted men who were later outed as Nazi collaborators during the Second World War. The current leader had been caught on camera and on tape saying abominable things, and every few months the press found another anti-Semite or neo-Nazi member of the party, a skinhead or a Vichy man. But Vichy men were everywhere, embedded in every party and every institution in France, in its blood and bones, the architecture of its shame. The source of the Front National's growing popularity in the last five years was its frankness about North African migration: the Moroccans on the sidewalk.

This was Evelyn's port of entry into the Front National. She could help change its narrative, reposition it as the party best fit to return France to glory. Every great society in the history of the world has been a racist society by someone's definition. If there were true racists in the party, Jean-François's job was to isolate and remove them. But a culture needs coherence if it aspires to nobility, not a cult of fairness. Nostalgia is natural. Jean-François's political party was only unique in its honesty. The changes that European leaders had proposed were dangerous, culturally and economically, and under Mitterrand, immigration in France had exploded while job growth had stopped. A conservative party could be honest and fair and open-hearted at once. Evelyn had worked with Jean-François on what he might say to Bernard Pivot and, by extension, several million French voters.

Kruse asked what Pascale thought of the newspaper editorials that predicted Jean-François would soon lead the Front National.

Pascale answered first with a sigh. "I am not a political woman."

"No?"

"I am a woman who married a political man."

"Sure. I can sympathize with that."

Evelyn performed a long sigh. He knew what she was thinking in defence: substitute "political" with "violent."

"I know what people say." Pascale had hired a Moroccan woman and her son to cater the dinner. They silently filled the wineglasses. She waited until they were out of the dining room, back in the kitchen. "There are extremists in the party, crazies, but they're a minority. Maybe one or two percent. Crazy people are everywhere. The newspapers hunt them down."

"We have to remove them from the party," said Evelyn.

"Is that democracy?"

Evelyn felt the word "democracy" was flawed. It was all things to all people, Soviets and Americans and African dictators. "It's necessary.

"Jean-François did join the FN to transform it. The current leader, the man who must be replaced, is a clown and a buffoon. Please don't tell Jean-François I said that, but it is true. If he changes the party, perhaps these people will simply melt away and start their own. A party of genuine crazies, like they have in England and Austria."

"Clown." The chocolate dessert had jolted Lily. "Buffoon."

"What has France lost, in only a few years?" Evelyn could now talk politics in French the way she did it in English—with authority. "A powerful religion, the most rigorous school system in the world, genuine art by genuine artists, honour and strength and purity."

"Don't forget our spirit of individualism."

Evelyn had grown up in a family that had once been wealthy, an old shipping family. Her grandfather May had turned out to be a drunk and a gambler. He lost everything but his sense of distinction. It had formed her politics and her work ethic. And her machine of judgment. Evelyn had confessed she thought Pascale was pompous, a phony who had grown up poor and now carried herself like a baroness. "Individualism, after the Second World War? Please do tell me more about that."

To run off the cake and to avoid boring her with politics before a boring hour of television politics, Kruse took Lily outside.

Before the flood, they had a routine. On Wednesday and Saturday mornings, the Kruse family would walk to Place Montfort and visit the bakery for pain au chocolat, croissants, or maybe brioche with a spot of jam. The baker-politician-landlord would walk out from behind the counter to move a strand of blonde hair and kiss Lily on the forehead, leaving a trail of flour. Here, Kruse became comfortable with synonyms for "beautiful": *belle, jolie, ravissante, superbe.* Other mornings, Tuesdays and Thursdays, Kruse volunteered at Boulangerie J.F.

The de Musset garden was spread out and concentrated in pockets of the best sun: ripe tomatoes grew here, lemons there. The fig tree had produced lovely fruit that Kruse would carry home from the bakery, his payment, after his mornings around the oven. After only a month in school Lily understood everything and she was learning the singsong Provençal accent: *Bonjour-uh. Au revoir-uh.* School, she said, was *chouette-uh.* When she played with the toys they had packed for her, she made nasal sounds—French sounds—if not words. They hunted for cicadas in the shrubbery around the de Musset house and failed to find any. They played hide-and-seek, *cache-cache.* Lily could not remain hidden for longer than a minute without giggling or singing, betraying herself. Hiding in silence made her lonesome and scared. The heat of the day had collapsed into the cool of the early October night. They inspected the grapes, which were just about ready to be picked. In neighbouring villages, the big harvest party—the *vendange*—had already begun.

Lily wore a grey cotton dress with short sleeves and her arms were covered in goosebumps. Kruse took her hand and led her back into the house.

There was a musical introduction and then Bernard Pivot. Pascale had explained about the famous man: he was a socialist, surely, if not a communist, but a very smart and curious one. The moment the camera revealed Jean-François, Lily screamed and clapped. Evelyn gave her an ultimatum. If she did not remain quiet for this very important show she and Papa would walk home early together. Lily promised—if, if, she could have one more tiny sliver of chocolate cake.

Pivot put on and removed his reading glasses with startling honesty. Much of what they discussed was beyond Kruse, who knew little and cared little about French, or any, politics, but the theme was clear. Most thinking people would say the Front National, since its birth in 1972, has been a race-obsessed party with a limited view on who is and is not sufficiently French. Yet many of those Jean-François had helped rescue from the wreckage on September 22, often at personal risk, were North Africans and gypsies. Pivot contrasted the baker-politician's heroism with the reputation of the Front National as isolationist, anti-Europe, and anti-intellectual.

"Aunty?" said Lily.

Evelyn shushed her. "*Anti* is 'against.' We'll explain later."

On TV they spoke for twenty minutes about the soul of France and how it too might be rescued. Pivot, it turned out, was also a nostalgist. He remembered the thirty glorious years after the Second World War with as much affection, and melancholy, as Jean-François. They remembered growing up in this enchanted place, where French people were French people and where immigrants—there are good ones, after all—wanted nothing more than to be French. Bicycles, baguettes, berets. Yes, it was an international stereotype but there was great comfort in it, and unity. While he could not agree with the entirety of Jean-François's analysis, Pivot declared the Front National an utterly transformed if not simply misunderstood party. He concluded the program by calling Jean-François de Musset the most articulate and most attractive conservative leader in France.

Before the night was out, national organizers and fundraisers were calling to set up meetings with Jean-François. Kruse, Evelyn, and Lily sneaked out, quietly waving at Pascale, who would be on the phone for hours. Evelyn, walking down the hill into their Roman quarter, was so pleased with what she had achieved she briefly wept. The party in the picturesque central square of Villedieu three weeks later, on Halloween, was designed as Jean-François's national coming-out party.

There were quotations from *Bouillon de culture* in *Le Monde*, the first of the lieutenant's articles that Kruse read in its entirety. The cause and effect of what had happened Halloween night was clear enough, tempered with words like *présumé* and *accusé*. Jean-François de Musset, politician and hero, drank too much on the evening of his fundraiser in Villedieu. He ran over and killed a three-year-old girl. He was charged with the crime and released. The girl's mother, a foreigner, went to his home and murdered him and his wife in a fit of vengeful rage.

At the end of the story in *Le Monde*, after the turn, there were speculations from an anonymous source "close to the accused and the deceased." The foreigner, a Canadian woman named Evelyn May Kruse, was deeply involved in the Front National party and was carrying on an affair with Jean-François de Musset.

The lieutenant leaned against the back wall of the conference room with his arms crossed. Kruse read the paragraph once more to be sure he had understood. He had understood. His right hand went cold, as it always did before a fight—nerve damage in his shoulder, from an ugly job in Montreal. Madame Boutet returned with a smelly plate of cheese and cured meat, dried fruit, and two baguettes. The articles in *Le Figaro*, *La Provence*, and *Le Dauphiné Libéré* carried the same information from the anonymous source: Evelyn was deeply involved in the party and carrying on an affair with the most articulate and most attractive conservative leader in France.

• • •

It was dark when they dismissed him from the interview room, three and a half hours later. The wind had calmed but only barely; it whistled and whined around the corners and through the empty corridors of Vaison-la-Romaine. Already the air was cleaner. No more grit in his eyes, no more humidity. He had eaten some of the meat and cheese, but it hadn't oiled any of the ironworks in his stomach.

The trap he had set in the front door of the horse stable had been sprung: the book of matches sat half a metre inside. Kruse moved to the shoe cupboard near the door and slid his rattan fighting sticks out from their hiding place. No one was in here now. His teacher, mentor, and business partner, Tzvi Meisels, was a flawed religious Jew but an amateur spiritualist. Tzvi had convinced himself that if he followed his intuition without any doubtful mental chatter it led him correctly eighty percent of the time. In his work with the army and with Mossad, this confidence had saved his own life and the lives of his men. He had insisted Kruse hone his own sense of self-trust.

At the base of the stairs Kruse knew who had been in the house. He climbed up. Evelyn had sprayed her perfume into a silk floral scarf and had hung it from the door handle to Lily's room. The bottle itself and other toiletries were gone, with some of her clothes. So was Marie-France, the turtle *doudou*, and an envelope of family photographs. She had not left anything for him, not a note or a map or a denunciation of what he had read in the newspapers; only a spray of perfume in her least-favourite scarf.

The gendarmes had wanted to know how long she had been sleeping with Jean-François de Musset. It confused and muddied her motivation, which had seemed so clear: you kill my daughter and I kill you. Who was the anonymous source, close to the accused and the deceased? You can never really know her heart.

The great wind, her camouflage, shook car alarms to life. He turned on the lamp. There was still water in the glass on her side of the bed, next to the guidebook she studied every night. Evelyn had never been to Paris and she wanted her first time to be perfect, with the right hotel, the right restaurants, museums, and sites of execution. They had planned to spend Christmas in the city, three weeks. Eighteen percent of the time there was snow at the end of December, even if it wasn't cold enough to stick.

Twenty-four hours earlier, at the hospital, a bearded man in a rumpled seersucker suit had asked them to give Lily's organs to the state.

Unfortunate children across the country could use her eyes, her liver, her heart. Not everything in her had been ruined. All they had to do was sign the form. Evelyn listened carefully. She looked at Kruse, squeaked, and answered the administrator. "Why would I give anything of her to France? You stole her from me."

"Madame. You are refusing out of simple spite?"

La rancune, "spite." She turned away and stared for a moment, evidently at public service posters tacked to a billboard. Wash your hands. Watch out for lice and AIDS. Then she jumped at the administrator with a right cross. Kruse caught up Evelyn and led her to the sliding doors. Until this moment he had not wanted to leave, to give her up. He had been hoping, not consciously but in some waiting room of his heart, that a doctor would emerge from a hallway and take off his glasses, wipe his forehead, and tell them Lily was going to be all right. The operation was a success. It was a miracle. He helped Evelyn down the old stairs to the Grand Rue, floodlit and deserted at midnight, and when she collapsed against the outer wall of a lavender shop and wailed and cursed God and begged God and cursed God again, windows opened along the street. The Vaisonnais, men and women they recognized, looked down silently.

For a long time, ten minutes or an hour, they stayed on the Grand Rue. She couldn't move and didn't want to move. Neither did he. Kruse fantasized about crossing the street, running for Lily, carrying her on his shoulders, holding her hand. Always hold Daddy's hand on the road, *la main de Papa.* When she began to shiver Kruse bundled his long wife into his arms and carried her down to the converted horse stable on Rue Trogue-Pompée, his hard soles clacking on the stones. He carried her up the marble stairs and into bed, this bed. He drew her this glass of water.

Kruse had performed CPR on his dead daughter until Evelyn had taken her from him. His first and most powerful instinct, to rush into the crowd and find him and destroy him—all of them—did not weaken or fade. Some men in Front National T-shirts surrounded Jean-François, jostled each other, and delivered short sermons. The organizers from Paris remained at a distance, pale and sick. Kruse only saw Jean-François in flashes. Men and women held each other and led each other away. It was not a thing anyone should see. Music was still playing in the plaza, a German dance song called "Rhythm Is a Dancer." After his initial plea for an ambulance, all Kruse could do now was shout into the crowd that it would be really goddamn nice if someone turned that shit off. He only realized afterwards, by the looks in their eyes, he had been speaking English.

The police cars arrived quickly. He mentioned this to Huard and Boutet during the interview: he was sure he had heard the sirens before the accident. How could that be? And even before the cars arrived, Huard was there in his grey sweater. The lieutenant had run up the hill from his house at the base of Villedieu and stopped. It was difficult to spit out his questions, through his panting and the phlegm.

"A car hit her, Monsieur?"

"Yes."

"And she's dead?"

Kruse could not say the word. Yes.

One of the men in a Front National T-shirt met the gendarme, his hands up. "It was me. I confess. I was driving the car."

Journalists on the other side of the street shouted the man down. In his response to them and to the gendarme, he and his supporters said *les étrangers* several times. Jean-François de Musset was the next president of the republic. These, these, were foreigners. There didn't seem to be any risk of Jean-François trying to escape; he was sitting on the gravel now, against a tree, lolling sweaty and drunk. The men in T-shirts tried to prevent the gendarme from speaking to him, his old rich friend. It was an accident, *alors*. She came from nowhere, the wild little thing.

Jean-François wasn't arrested until the cars arrived. There was a harmless scuffle, between the men in the Front National T-shirts and the police. Television cameras hovered. One of the print journalists laughed out loud. Someone must have told the ambulance driver there was no great hurry. There was no great hurry. Evelyn would not let them take Lily at first. A paramedic asked for permission to sedate Madame. Kruse shook his head no.

They followed the ambulance to the hospital. It was the paramedic who told them Jean-François had been charged and released. A court date had been set. He was at home, in his faded yellow farmhouse behind the château.

Soft light from the street shone flatly into the horse stable on Trogue-Pompée. Normally, he would be tuned to Lily in the next room. When his daughter woke for a bathroom break or a glass of water, or when she startled herself out of a nightmare about cats, it was his job to tend to her. Evelyn dozed in the miserable silence. Like her daughter, she had blonde hair with a hint of natural curl and bright green eyes. They were closed now, crunched. Both of them had one dimple above and to the right of their lips, those crooked smiles. She was breathing too quickly. The French, who insisted on making these sorts of determinations, said both Evelyn and Lily looked Swedish. Maybe Norwegian.

Evelyn wasn't more than one-sixteenth of anything, a mongrel. Still, she preferred a coherent and traditional culture—a feeling of us, something to protect from them, *les étrangers*.

Kruse leaned over the bed to touch her forehead, the way he would have touched Lily's forehead if she were sweating and thrashing, to check for fever. She slapped his hand away and hopped out of bed, pushed him and stomped, in her T-shirt and panties, into Lily's room.

"What are you doing?"

She didn't answer and he didn't want to watch or stop her. For the next half hour Evelyn broke Lily's toys, ripped the pages from her picture books, threw her little clothes on the floor and stretched them and tore what she could tear. Kruse remained in their bedroom, the master bedroom overlooking the Roman ruins, where he had thought they were falling in love again.

FOUR

Avenue Frédéric Mistral, Orange

THE CONSULATE URGED HIM TO CREMATE HIS DAUGHTER. IN THE MIDDLE of these conversations, instead of listening to the young Québécois bureaucrats, he flipped through his choices. If only he had run for her. If only they had gone home at six thirty, as planned. If they had found another town, another house, another country. If they had learned to speak Spanish in school instead of French: Guanajuato or Seville. If they had saved their marriage in Toronto—another neighbourhood, maybe. The suburbs. Some fried chicken village in Quebec.

"Monsieur Kruse?"

"Yes."

"You're still with me?"

The nearest crematorium was in Orange, a small city thirty kilometres down the road from Vaison-la-Romaine. He toured the facility and, in the midst of a chat about receptacles for her ashes, he excused himself to run to the toilet and throw up. There was no one else in the unusually large room, designed for crowds. Every click and slide of his shoes echoed in the toilet. Kruse had checked the regional bus stops, thirty-nine of them, and had questioned hundreds of people: restaurant and café operators, hoteliers and owners of *chambres d'hôtes*. No one had seen his wife on the day of the dead or any of the four days thereafter. They had seen the newspapers. In their eyes he was a desperate cuckold whose wife had disappeared into the South of France. He knew Lily was gone, but in the crematorium, for the first time, he believed it. He was alone with his echoes. The funeral director knocked gently and opened the door. They could not wait much longer, as they had entered high season for death. The towns of the Vaucluse were full of retirees and many of them succumbed before winter, the anticipation of January air igniting and overpowering their imaginations. There were laws and rules and with respect, Monsieur, he did not have infinite space in his refrigerator.

Jean-François and Pascale de Musset's joint funeral came first. On the fifth of November, a cool and dreary Thursday, the cathedral filled quickly. Officials from the town rushed to set up folding black chairs behind the pews. Media from Marseille and Paris set up in the back. Several hundred people stood on the brown grass outside Notre Dame de Nazareth, in a murky spray that threatened to transform into rain. Kruse had come early, to look for Evelyn, though the smell of incense and the whispering around and about him was too much; he surrendered his seat to a retired woman in a veil he recognized from the Tuesday morning market. She did not thank him. The cloister where they had inspected the little flowers and the fat bees was inaccessible, so Kruse sat on the moist curb on Rue Saint-Exupéry, where he was close enough to hear through the outdoor speakers but far away enough that no one would be obliged to look at him. They did anyway.

Afterwards, the procession of black limousines and pedestrians crossed the Roman bridge. All the newer bridges had been destroyed in the flood. The de Mussets had a family crypt in the Saint Laurent cemetery; it had been there long enough that rain and sun had stained it black.

There was a substantial cross above, like two dull swords. Mourners filed into the sloped corridors between the dead. Small children and babies were propped up on the crypts of Vaison-la-Romaine's other prominent families. Graves were decorated with small stone and ceramic souvenirs, real and fake flowers, plaques and murky tablets declaring "*Tu seras toujours parmi nous*" and other truths. Older and richer families had tombs up in the shade, on the hill, many with statues and reliefs depicting both the lost loved ones and their saviour. The de Musset crypt was just below them. Dogs chased each other through the feet of the mourners as the sound system squealed and crackled. The spray turned to rain and, at once, hundreds of black umbrellas arose and popped.

He recognized Front National officials from the fundraiser in Villedieu and from outings with Evelyn: a meeting in Arles, a rally in Malaucène. The de Mussets had brothers and sisters but none who lived here. He stayed at the gates with two young cashiers he knew from the Super-U grocery, women in their twenties with long black-painted fingernails and dyed black hair, small-town goths, women who would always smoke. All that emerged from the speakers was an apology. Rain had made it too dangerous for outdoor electricity. Words were then spoken but none that Kruse could hear. The cashiers stared at him and spoke to each other until everyone in the small crowd around him was aware of his presence and properly distracted. A few men, with beer in their breath and strong accents, shoved him. He excused himself, for standing in their way.

Kruse walked around them all and climbed as high as he could climb. It was difficult to see, in the fog and the rain, with so many black umbrellas.

She had not come.

He booked an hour the following afternoon, the smallest room available in Hall 1E of the crematorium in Orange. It was outside the city core, set in the first wave of what would become the French approximation of a power centre. There were supermarkets, chain stores selling furniture, electronics, and shoes, and next door, a discount wine store.

Marigolds came with the cremation package, and under the fluorescent bulbs they shone like creamed corn. There were no guests. Lily's teacher might have come, or the parents of some of her little friends, the family from Nyons, the bartender in Villedieu, the banker, the woman from the cheese shop, but he didn't invite them. No higher authority was present, so Kruse said a few words about Lily, to Lily, in English; everything he had said aloud, since her death, to police and the coroner and the consulate in Nice, the insurance company and the municipal officials and the funeral director, had been in his studious French. It was not a speech worthy of his daughter's spirit. Speaking his own language, Lily's language, undid him.

After Evelyn had destroyed her toys and ripped her books, she had come back to bed, sweaty and shivering. This is what Kruse did not tell the gendarmes. The anonymous source, close to the accused and the deceased, did not tell the newspapers what she had demanded. Kruse had said, "Can I do anything?" and for two hours she did not speak. She mumbled and sighed, wept, said her daughter's name in a prayer to no one. Then, at 3:16 in the morning, Evelyn answered his question.

"Yes."

"Yes what?"

"You can do something." Light from the pedestrian street splashed teeth on the ceiling. "I think you know."

"Tell me what you want."

"He could barely walk."

"The gendarmes said—"

"He was drunk. Boris Yeltsin drunk. You well know what that makes it. Stop pretending."

"He's been charged."

"By his own friends in the police. The mayors. The political party. I've been studying these people and I know how it works. Don't tell me you haven't thought about this. I could feel you vibrating with it in Villedieu. Do it."

"We can't assume, Evelyn, just because—"

"He's a murderer. And his asshole friends, down in the bar, they're murderers too."

"Who were they?"

"One had long hair, one short. Men in suits. Men like you."

Kruse's hands ached from making fists. She was on her hands and knees now, on top of the sheets.

"You know what I want, Chris. I know you want it too."

"No."

"It's all I want. It's all you want. I take back everything I've ever said about what you do."

"About what I do?"

"The business you're in."

"Evelyn—"

"I love what you do. Go do it."

"It was an accident. We have to accept it as an accident, an accident, darling. Forgive him and continue. We go back to Toronto. We start over, and—"

"So you won't?"

Kruse stood up out of bed, walked again to the window and opened it. The air was cool on his chest. In the distance, garbage trucks were already running. Some towns in the south were populated by Algerian immigrants, others Tunisians. Vaison-la-Romaine was a Moroccan town. The garbagemen were Moroccans.

"Long as we've been together, you've done one thing. I never liked it or even understood it. Now, when I ask you to go and do your job for me, for Lily, just once, you're too good. Too pure."

"You told me to leave her."

"No, I didn't. Don't you say that again." He could hear she was up out of bed. "You owe me, Chris. You have to undo your mistake. You should have run faster and you should have run sooner. Go up that hill."

"And do what?" Kruse whispered it through the open window, a test, before he turned and said it out loud. "I don't hurt people."

"Bullshit."

"I protect people."

"But not your daughter."

His legs could barely hold him.

"All right." She pulled on a pair of imitation leather pants and the disobedient nipples of her small breasts peeked through the white cotton of her polo shirt. "All right," she said again, and walked out of the bedroom and down the hall, down the stairs.

Kruse leaned out the window and watched her glide up Trogue-Pompée in the pale street light. In her right hand she carried Lily's bamboo fairy wand. She swiped it once like a riding crop, whipped the air, and then she started to run.

• • •

On his way back to Vaison-la-Romaine from his daughter's cremation, he took the wrong exit from a roundabout and passed Gare d'Orange. A block later, he pulled over in front of a tavern decorated with a mud-splashed Père Noël from the previous Christmas. Orange station was the closest to Vaison, connected by the regional bus system. It was not yet five in the afternoon. His daughter's urn sat on the passenger seat, a silver box with her name engraved on the front. He briefly debated taking it, taking her with him. He pulled the emergency brake and left the car in front of the tavern, jogged to the station past the clipped and leafless branches of the plane trees that reached, tortured, for the sky. Lily, who so adored Halloween, called them witches' hands.

There were cameras in front, inside, and on the platform behind the station, a whitewashed mid-century modernist rectangle attached to a more substantial building in the back. An armed security guard stood near the door, his huge arms crossed. When they had renewed their passports, they were forced to buy six photos. Only two had been necessary, so the rest, of Lily and of Evelyn, were in his wallet.

The security guard suffered from the syndrome that affects all security guards: he daydreamed for a living. He barely looked at Evelyn's photo. Her hair in the photograph was newly dyed and especially blonde. She had not wanted to smile but both Lily and Kruse had tried to make her laugh. The dimple on the right side of her mouth seemed to be the only thing holding the frown in place. The guard invited Kruse to speak to the supervisor on duty, who had an office through the heavy metal door. All he had to do was knock.

"Harder," said the security guard.

The door opened a minute later and a somewhat less-bored security guard stood before him. Kruse asked for the supervisor by name: Madame Aubanel. Keys jangled as she walked out of her office and into the hallway. She was nearly six feet tall and shaped like a pear, a tawny-haired woman with glasses that magnified her eyes. He introduced himself, they shook hands, and he pulled out a photograph of Evelyn. Unlike the other security guard she listened to his pitch before telling him no, with a detailed explanation why. After six months in France he had come to see how bureaucracy had replaced Catholicism.

"I promise it won't take long, and I'll pay for my time."

"It's absolutely against the regulations, Monsieur, to show security footage to non-security personnel. I am forbidden." She lifted her right hand to her mouth, to catch a cough, and said with a whisper, "How much?"

"Whatever it takes, Madame."

She asked him to come back at nine o'clock and to bring five thousand francs.

The mistral had finished blowing. The sky and the air were blue and sharp. The quality of light now, as dusk began its long sigh over Orange, most resembled early May, the month of their arrival. Northern Provence wasn't nearly as fragrant or as green, as drunk with itself, as it had been at the height of summer. But now, in this season and through his fatigue and anxiety, every colour, every late-blooming flower and evergreen, every stained stone building, every man and woman and baby and bird was sharp with contrast.

It was not yet winter but the women dressed differently, replacing their white and off-white linen dresses with jeans and long-sleeved shirts, scarves. Lily's fourth birthday was in three weeks, so she would have had time to change her mind, but Kruse had already decided she would be a fashion designer when she grew up. For the figures she sketched, Mommy and Daddy and *la maîtresse* and her friends from school, Lily created flamboyant outfits. Often, in her drawings, Kruse wore a jacket that was also a live falcon.

The retired soldiers of the Roman empire had settled in Vaison and here in Orange. He walked from the station to the old city centre, with a hill in the middle of it and an enormous theatre turned black by two thousand years of weather. Retired couples holding hands, out for a stroll, were a minority. Tough boys in soccer suits stared at him.

Kruse paid the entry fee for the theatre and walked its dark corridors, waiting for his appointment at the train station. It was cold where the sun did not reach. In the auditorium there were hundreds of seats and, on stage, pillars and a statue. The lights above were modern; Elton John was set to play here in a week. There were only a few other tourists in the theatre. One of them, a handsome man in a navy suit, leaned back and appeared to watch Kruse. There was something familiar about him, so Kruse climbed the stairs for a better look. He was a friend of Jean-François's maybe, from the party in Villedieu. The man stood up and walked the length of the row and down and away without another glance in Kruse's direction. It was the slow and confident walk of an athlete.

At nine o'clock Kruse arrived at the main door of Gare d'Orange. It opened before he could touch it and Madame Aubanel rushed him inside, nervously chattering. The video cameras were off but eyes were everywhere. She led him down a hallway, her big feet pointed out like a cartoon ballerina's, and into a small room that smelled of sausage with three television sets attached to a video machine. It was already several years out of date so Kruse could not hope for much.

Madame Aubanel pulled nine tapes from the shelf, marked with the date and times. The recordings for November 1 started at 5:45 in the morning, roughly twenty minutes before the departure of the first train. There were only two possible directions: north to Paris or south to Marseille. There were several stops along the way but not for all trains. Madame Aubanel synced the three tapes at 05:45. Kruse helped press play on all three at the same time.

They watched at double speed. Madame Aubanel held one of Evelyn's passport photographs in her hand as she scanned.

"You had an argument?"

"Something like that, Madame, yes."

"Do you fear she has left you for good?"

To finish the conversation, Kruse nodded.

He was not successful. Madame Aubanel fixed her glasses. "You have children?"

"One."

"Boy or girl?"

"Girl. She's gone now, Madame."

"Gone where, with your wife? How old?"

"Nearly four."

"A baby. This is a crime, in France, to take a child from her father."

"She's dead."

"Oh. Excuse me. What was her name?"

"Lily."

"You're not . . . how did she die?"

Kruse told her.

"I read about her. About you." The French put the emphasis on the *y* at the end of her name. Madame Aubanel looked away from the television screen for a moment. "Lily."

No one who looked remotely like Evelyn had departed on the first four trains. They were now past five in the afternoon on the video, and the crowds in the station had thickened. The cafés were open for early dinner and passengers carried soda and snacks with their luggage. Trains arrived and Madame Aubanel slowed the tape. Watching in fast-forward was dizzying, so they took short breaks.

Evelyn appeared at the front of the station at 18:12 with a black bag. It was difficult to see her on the outdoor camera, as the mistral had blown up so much dust. White T-shirt, imitation leather pants, sneakers. She spent nine minutes in the lineup and bought a ticket.

"What is she carrying?"

He didn't tell Madame Aubanel: a fairy wand.

"Did she kill the politician and his wife? Is she guilty?"

"No, Madame."

Evelyn walked away from the ticket office and looked up at one of the screens showing departure times. She went straight out to the platform. The images were not perfectly clear but she was fidgeting with her ticket. She looked around constantly, not one of her habits.

"North."

"She went to Paris?"

"The 18:28 is a night express. There are only two possible stops, Monsieur: Lyon and Paris."

They continued watching until the express departed. The bridge was empty afterwards, but for a man in blue overalls pushing a broom.

Kruse pulled out his wallet.

"Just give me three thousand. You lost a child and, it seems, a wife. I cannot take five thousand francs from you."

"How about you take the extra two thousand for the videotapes? I'll buy them from you. You can say there was a technical error."

"I hope you find your wife. If she wants to be found." The woman ejected the tapes and gave them to him. She stuffed the money into her purse. "I wonder why the gendarmes haven't come, with the same questions."

The trains from Orange were finished for the day but he could drive to Avignon or Marseille. Even if he did, Kruse would arrive at four or five in the morning in a city of ten million people without a single clue. He wanted to take the train as she had taken the train, to see what she had seen: his best and only hope was some sort of psychological fusion, to enter her thoughts.

Madame Aubanel sold him a ticket for the first express of the day, departing before dawn. Would he like to pay with cash or with credit?

Kruse looked in his wallet and saw more than money. He came dangerously close to kissing the nearsighted supervisor for asking the question. "What, Monsieur? What?" She laughed along with him, missing the sarcasm.

"Do you have a telephone *cabine* in here?"

There were several, but Madame Aubanel had to lock up and leave. She was exhausted and a little nauseated, from watching the videos in fast-forward. Kruse drove around Orange, looking for a telephone, and couldn't find one in the dark. He drove twenty minutes to Vaison-la-Romaine and parked in front of the horse stable; it was the first time in weeks that he had found a spot on Rue Trogue-Pompée. Lily had been with him the last time. Evelyn had said she wanted to spend a few hours at the library, so Kruse had driven with his daughter to the top of Mont Ventoux. It was a sunny day, warm in town but cold and windy on top. They could see the Alps in one direction and the Mediterranean in the other. On the way back down they had stopped for a picnic. And there, just like in the Astérix books, a wild boar trundled out of the bushes, looked up at them, and ran away.

When he found Evelyn he would ask her: Were you really at the library that afternoon? Madame Boutet, the gendarme, had nearly spit out a mouthful of goat cheese when he told her that Evelyn is not the sort of woman who has an affair. Not with Jean-François de Musset or anyone else. Evelyn didn't believe in affairs, in that sort of weakness. She wasn't capable.

"But you said you had come to France to save your marriage."

"Our problems weren't like that."

"What were they like, Monsieur Kruse?"

He told her.

"So she couldn't be attracted to another man?" Madame Boutet looked at her partner for a moment and back to Kruse. "Your wife is really so different from every other woman in the world?"

There was a bank of two public phones at the bar-tabac that doubled as a bus station, at the limit of the terrace. He had bought a twenty-five-credit France Télécom card, but he didn't need it for the toll-free Visa number, which was fortunate. It took twenty minutes and he ultimately had to choose the "lost or stolen" option to speak to a human being at this hour. It gave Kruse time to punish himself for waiting this long.

It was early in the morning in Canada, though the operator did not sound tired. She wanted clarity: the card was not stolen or technically misplaced. Yet he had called the lost and stolen number.

"My wife has been misplaced, and we share a card."

"So you want to find her."

"Yes."

"Does she want to find you?"

"We were separated in error."

Her latest charges were for a train ticket, a hair salon, and two restaurants in Paris. She took money out of their account only once, in Orange. There was one request for a pre-authorization but the woman on the phone didn't have the location. Most pre-authorizations are from hotels. Kruse asked the operator if anyone else would have access to their accounts. Anyone in my position, she said. Certain law enforcement agencies, though she didn't have specifics: Interpol, surely. Did the operator have any way of seeing who had accessed their information, from among these organizations? Bankers, say, or police?

"Perhaps someone could see," she said. "It's all computerized. But I don't have that access. Anything else I can do for you, Mr. Kruse?"

He was tempted to cancel her card, so no one else could find her. Evelyn taught art history, which offered few opportunities to think like a fugitive. Her limit at the ATM was two thousand francs a day. At the same time, if he annulled her card he would lose his connection to her. Now that Lily was gone they shared nothing else.

FIVE

Rue du Champ de Mars, Paris

THE LAST TIME HE HAD BEEN IN PARIS WAS TO ACCOMPANY THE anxious son of a pharmacy magnate to ESCP Europe, the top business school on the continent, for an interview. His father, who also owned the Denver Broncos, had received death threats for something he had done to unionized workers. The most serious danger, on that trip, had been unpasteurized milk. The boy did not get into ESCP.

The man and woman he followed off the train fell to their knees on the concrete platform so abruptly he nearly tumbled over them. A little girl and a littler boy, perhaps five and three, in a dress and a suit, sprinted into hugs. An older couple, the grandparents, looked on. "Never go away again, Papa," said the girl, crossly.

The metro station at Gare de Lyon looked the way he felt. All but a few of the overhead lights were off and the tunnel was deserted apart from a security man smoking a cigarette, telling everyone who came around that metro drivers were on strike. The view from the front windows of the station was not encouraging: it was windy and raining heavily, and there was a long lineup for a taxi. He bought a sturdy black umbrella at a boutique on his way out, but the gusts were so strong along the river it turned inside out with a *pop*. Kruse walked the north bank of the Seine past city hall and the Louvre to Place de la Concorde, where they had cut off all those heads. He crossed the river at Pont Neuf and stayed along the quay, as Lily would have liked. She was the sort of child who would not have noticed the rain as long as there was something pretty to see, birds to identify, and enough to eat along the way. Maybe a hot chocolate in a little bistro. It wasn't the best day for distant views, birdwatching, or architectural wonders, as a dark cloud had collapsed over the city. She would have understood.

In the guidebook Evelyn kept on the bedside table, she ranked her chosen hotels from one to five. Her number one choice, on Rue Valadon, was impossible: it had been under renovation since the end of September. The neighbourhood immediately east of the Eiffel Tower was a hybrid of her interests: beautiful, chic, quiet, traditional, family-oriented, absolutely devoid of American chain stores. The streets were thin and in shadow most of the day, with a nearby market corridor full of bistros and grocery stores, fish and wine and cheese. There was nothing to do in this wealthy dreamland of Paris but live well. Less than a block away, on Rue du Champ de Mars, Kruse stepped into a pleasant but cramped lobby that reminded him more of a hotel in rural England than the seventh arrondissement.

The man behind the counter quietly exclaimed at the sight of Kruse, who was windswept and half-soaked. "I would not blame you for thinking otherwise, Monsieur, but the taxi drivers are not on strike at the moment."

"I like to walk."

"So long as you like to walk. Very good. Do you have a reservation?"

The lobby was designed and decorated like a cozy living room. Bookshelves surrounded a couch and chairs and a coffee table. Art and photography books were stacked carefully on the coffee table and all of it was bathed in warm lamplight. The noise of the traffic outside was softened by the thick front window. "I don't, Monsieur."

Monsieur put on his reading glasses and said, "*Alors,*" a few times. There was one room on the top floor, but the elevator was not working so well today. Technicians were coming. Would he terribly mind five flights of stairs?

As Monsieur spoke, Kruse scanned his workspace: it was cramped but orderly, with customized ledger books holding off the dread computer. The only piece of technical equipment was a central telephone router. The man was fifty, with a well-trimmed beard. Everything he said came off slightly ironic, as though he were playing the role of a hotelier to make a subtle point about hoteliers. His cards sat in an Eiffel Tower trolley: Guy and Dianne Balon. Monsieur Balon asked for Kruse's passport.

"I don't have it. I am a resident here."

"Your identity card."

"It has not arrived yet."

"Typical."

"Do you get a lot of Canadians?"

"A fair number, yes."

"How about a woman, on the first of November?"

Monsieur Balon squinted at him.

"Evelyn May Kruse."

"A popular woman, this Evelyn."

"In what way?"

"You are the fourth person to ask after her. A journalist was here. Then the gendarmes. And just after lunch today, another gentleman. I'm afraid I can only tell you what I told the gendarmes: I can provide no information."

"You took her credit card number but she paid with cash. Yes?"

The hotelier zipped his lips.

"She is my wife: Evelyn May Kruse." The consulate in Toronto had said, wrongly, that customs and the prefecture in Avignon would demand to see a copy of their marriage certificate. Kruse had folded it into his wallet. He opened it on the desk.

Monsieur Balon scrawled tiny notes next to Kruse's guest information—a sort of shorthand.

"What did the journalist want?"

"I run the hotel, Monsieur. That is all. The journalist, a woman, said she had a meeting with Madame at ten o'clock on the second of November. Our office opens at six but your wife had already departed by then. Madame Evelyn had left cash in our express checkout box." Monsieur Balon pulled out a white business card from a drawer and slid it across the desk: Annette Laferrière, *Le Monde*. "You can take this with you."

"What did Madame Laferrière look like?"

"Dark hair, thirty or forty."

"The man who asked about her after lunch . . ."

Monsieur Balon took a deep breath. "Yes?"

"Another journalist?"

"No. Or I don't think so."

"Who was he?"

"Not a guest. He did not identify himself. I thought at first he was another policeman but the gendarmes were from the south, clearly. Their accents were unmistakable. There was something more thoughtful about this one. He had time. He was refined, and his interest in Madame Evelyn, Madame . . ."

"Kruse."

"Madame Kruse. His interest in her had a kindly aspect."

"How do you mean 'kindly'?"

"He was seeking her to help in some way. And I remembered she had seemed sad, preoccupied. Downstairs, Monsieur Kruse, we have tables for our continental breakfast and, if you like, for a picnic lunch. I can learn a lot from a person by watching them eat. Your wife ate some fruit and cheese for dinner, when she arrived. I offered her a glass of wine. She said no. Normally, when a foreigner arrives in Paris—especially a woman—she is filled with delight. Madame was . . ."

"What?"

"Haunted. And this name, Evelyn, she did not use it. She called herself Agnes. It was the journalist and the police who used the name Evelyn. She registered as Agnes May, and since I had only taken her credit card number to hold the room . . ."

"Her mother's name."

"There you go, Monsieur. We long to be our fathers and they long to be their mothers."

Two guests, a retired couple, arrived at the bottom of the stairs and walked hand in hand through the lobby. Kruse could tell, before they spoke, they were not French. "Hello," they said, in American English, as they passed. They left the key with Monsieur Balon and he thanked them, also in English. When they were gone, Kruse continued.

"This kindly man who came to see her, did he represent anyone or anything?"

"He wore a well-cut suit. I remember thinking, as he walked in, he is much too wealthy to stay here. Not just the suit. He was a Four Seasons man. It was the way he walked and smelled, his tie, certainly the way he spoke. His accent was . . . do you know of the *grandes écoles*?"

"Yes."

"Like that."

"An aristocrat."

"Yes, Monsieur. Like that. An air of noblesse oblige. Perhaps that is why I had assumed he was seeking her to offer help."

"What did he want?"

"Like you: to see her. He asked several questions. Since he was not, like you, an immediate family member, I told him nothing."

"Can I see her room?"

"The room where she stayed? It has long been cleaned since then, Monsieur, and another guest is in there."

"Did she say where she was going?"

"She wasn't a talkative woman." Monsieur Balon arranged some papers on his desk. "Perhaps I should be phoning the police instead of checking you in. They did say others would come looking for her."

"And what did you tell them? These police?"

"Monsieur, please."

Kruse pulled out his collection of photos: the passport shots of Evelyn and Lily and another of the three of them at Niagara Falls.

"I was there once," said Monsieur Balon. "I took a ride in the boat, to get close to the falls. There was a wax museum as well. Tasteless, no?"

"Is there anything more you can tell me?"

"No."

"Was the aristocrat alone?"

"All right, this is peculiar. A second man stood outside, smoking, Monsieur Kruse. I might not have noticed him at all but he had no nose."

"No . . ."

"No nose, no nose. You see a lot of people with quirks, as an hotelier. This was the first time I had seen a man with no nose."

"Young man? Old man?"

"I will call the police. Together you can sort this out."

"Please, Monsieur Balon."

"Thirties, maybe early forties. Your age. Both men were trim, like you. You look like a small team of football players, you three together."

"No nose. And what did the aristocrat ask you, specifically?"

"When did she arrive and how long did she stay? Did anyone visit her? Did she make any calls?"

"And you didn't answer."

"No. Well, yes. I told the gentleman 'I don't know' to all of them, to finish the conversation. He was charming but persistent."

Kruse used the lobby telephone to call the journalist. She was out for lunch. The metro was not an option, with the strike, so Kruse asked if Monsieur Balon might call him a taxi.

"Taxi drivers are not on strike but I grant you they are difficult to find." He tried to phone and shrugged. "You see? Nothing. A catastrophe. But please, take one of the hotel umbrellas. They're much stronger in the wind."

• • •

The newspaper headquarters was a sloping rectangle of glass tucked between typically Parisian apartment buildings: stone and stately if not as imposing as the beauties along Avenue de Breteuil, the route he had taken. Kruse arrived too early. The receptionist on the main floor chuckled a bit cruelly at the idea that anyone in the newsroom would return from lunch before two. She handed him yesterday's edition of the paper and he went for a coffee and an inferior croissant at a busy café on the corner.

His parents, Allan and Nettie Kruse, had left half their insurance policy to a centre for poor immigrants in Toronto. They were pure Mennonites, by blood and by heart, and carried a special feeling for refugees and poor newcomers. Stories around the dinner table were stories of settlement and flight, settlement and flight, as bad politics and swords and guns had chased their great-grandparents and great-great-grandparents all over Europe for centuries. Nearly all his clients in Toronto had been conservatives of some sort, from the old families Evelyn so admired to the newly rich who had trampled on friends and laws and now simply wanted to protect what they had earned—or had stolen—with a low tax regime. He had liked his clients, or most of them, and he had admired his daring wife; it wasn't a normal woman's mission, to transform conservative politics in a foreign country. But the Front National, at least the one he read about in the papers, sounded a lot like the sort of party that would have either repelled his ancestors at the border or discovered a religious or legal reason to chop off their heads.

A block away from the offices of *Le Monde*, there was an eighteenth-century hospital for sick children. At one in the afternoon a smoky dusk had fallen over the city. Commuters were out on their belching scooters and little cars honked peacefully at one another, but with the metro shut down it was a day for pedestrians. Even in the rain the city was a riot of finely dressed professionals, elegant grandmothers, and courageous dog walkers. It was never an amiable place but the Parisians did look up at him. In France, especially in Paris, eyes rested on his scars longer than at home, where the possibility of offending a stranger hovers like a weakly-chained dragon over Southern Ontario. Kruse walked around the children's hospital after his coffee and croissant and settled on a park bench surrounded by hopeful, cooing pigeons. Now and then a mother and father would pass on the sidewalk, two umbrellas open, pushing their child in a wheelchair. One of the children, bald but for a few stray hairs, was so beautiful and so fragile Kruse could not look at her. Her tortured parents manufactured grins. He envied them. Nurses stepped out of taxis and walked through the hospital gates with determined sighs. There was an institute for children with blindness nearby, and they too were out for lunchtime strolls—arms linked or experimenting with a cane. Neighbourhood schools surrounded the hospital, an elementary and a lycée. The quarter was alive with laughing and crying children, exhausted parents, and tin-voiced adolescents and teenagers in the ripped jeans and flannel lumberjack shirts of Seattle.

Men in blue overalls had not yet picked up the shit from last evening's dog walkers. In the entrance of a shuttered magazine shop, a man in layers of wet clothes lay sleeping on a pile of cardboard boxes. From Foxbar Road or from her dreary office overlooking a parking lot in the stark northern reaches of Toronto, Paris was, for Evelyn, art and wonder. She had never been to Paris but it was her definition of conservatism, the way we once lived and the way we ought to live again; children and parents and public institutions and food markets and bistros and architecture in harmony. In the Paris of her imagination she walked Lily to school in the morning and said hello to the baker and the butcher, bought a coffee and proceeded to the Sorbonne.

The first time he had come to Paris, in the early eighties, the sight of graffiti on the side of a hand-carved and flower-gilded building made him long to have been born in another time. He saw Evelyn now, somewhere in Paris, similarly afflicted. The imperfections in the most beautiful city in the world were, at least partly, a relief from the terrible theory every child in Canada learns as they come into adulthood: that their parents and ancestors, who had chosen to settle in this wild place, had made a mistake.

For twenty minutes he walked around the Necker hospital again and focused more carefully, as Evelyn would, on architectural details, on art in bistro windows, on the confident manner of men selling newspapers and chocolate bars.

One mother pushed her son or daughter in a stroller away from the elementary school and leaned down to fix the child's jacket. The running shoes were as small as plums, lovingly tied with laces in an era of Velcro. The mother, a small, brown-haired woman dressed more for a cocktail party than an afternoon stroll, cooed and clucked and groaned in an almost sexual manner. Kruse allowed himself to think she was flaunting her good fortune. He went back early to Rue Falguière.

"I know I said it was impossible, Monsieur, but she has arrived. Before two!" The receptionist handed Kruse a badge and asked him to fill in his name and phone number, the company he represented. He had done this so many times, in the austere lobbies of Toronto and Montreal and New York, he wrote "MagaSecure" without thinking.

Kruse shared the elevator with two young women who had just applied perfume. The scents gave him a headache that passed when the door opened and he followed them out into the mostly deserted newsroom. Men and women were in offices, along the sloping front windows, but most of the desks were empty. The newsroom was a massive, open floor with interlocking cubicles. Every desk had a small Apple computer and a few had electric typewriters besides, holdovers of a dying era. Some of the beautiful women he had seen walking down Rue Falguière were here now, sitting at desks with newspapers, making notes, speaking clearly but quietly on the telephone. In the centre of the vastness was the only busy pod on the floor. Four men and two women sat writing or speaking on the telephone as police scanners bleeped in and bleeped out. Voices came and went, squelched away.

One of these women, who had perfected the art of intimidation, looked up as he passed. He asked if he might be directed toward a journalist: Annette Laferrière.

The woman frowned with her mouth but not with her eyes. With her eyes she was delighted. "Madame Laferrière is on this floor, but I don't know if it's correct to call her a journalist. Did someone tell you she was a journalist, Monsieur?"

"Not me. She told a man I know."

"Oh she herself says she is a journalist. Splendid." The woman stood up and flattened her skirt. Her legs were jarringly thin. She pointed across the newsroom to a cubicle against a grey wall. "That is Madame Laferrière, the great journalist."

"Thank you."

"No, no, Monsieur. Thank you."

Her hair was a dark and curly cascade over the arm that held up her chin as she read. Her skin was the fortunate colour of a lightly roasted nut. She sat hunched over her desk, reading from a long page, with an orange pencil. He stood over her for a moment. There was a hint of her citrus perfume above her: grapefruit. It didn't give him a headache.

"Madame Laferrière."

She dropped the orange pencil, startled, and looked up.

Kruse could feel people behind him, watching. His voice had been too loud. He had said the wrong thing to the thin woman. He leaned down now and whispered, "My name is Christopher Kruse. My wife is Evelyn."

Her eyes opened like a child's before a surprise birthday cake. She stood up out of her chair. It squeaked and spun away. "What are you . . . why?"

They shook hands and dealt quickly with pleasantries. Madame Laferrière said she was concerned he might have come here, all the way to Paris, to speak to her.

"The hotelier at the Champ de Mars gave me your name."

She reached up and slid an errant black curl behind her ear. "It's not yet two. The boardrooms will be open."

She led him down the aisle, her colleagues watching, and spoke like a tour guide. She pointed out the political editor, the cultural editor, the international editor, and they walked into the boardroom. She closed the door. One wall was glass and looked out over gloomy Rue Falguière.

"You spoke to Evelyn."

"Yes."

"Did she come here, Madame Laferrière?"

"No. No, not at all. She phoned."

"Why you?"

"I answered the phone."

"Where was she calling from?"

"A train station in the south. But she was coming here, to Paris, and she wanted to talk about the story. It was wrong, she said."

"What was wrong?"

"She said the story was wrong. That's all she said. To be honest, Monsieur Kruse, before I spoke to her I had not read the story. I couldn't probe."

"You made an appointment with her."

"At the hotel, yes. She was using a different name at the hotel, she told me."

"Agnes."

"Agnes May."

"And when you arrived to meet with her . . ."

"She was gone. Gone since the middle of the night, the hotelier said. Or at least very early in the morning."

"Have you pursued the story since then, Madame?"

"Yes. Yes and no. I—"

The door opened abruptly, no knock, and startled her. A man in a suit, bald on top but long on the sides and in the back, a classy hobo, stood up military straight and huffed as though he had jogged there. His black shoes, recently shined, were the sort that give a man an extra inch.

"What are you doing, Annette?"

"Monsieur . . ."

"Who, I wonder, is on the copy desk?"

"Five minutes."

"And this man?"

"A friend."

"It is lovely to have friends but this isn't a bistro. We need you on the copy desk. Speak to your friend on your own time, yes?"

Annette opened her mouth to respond but no sound came out.

Kruse would have been delighted to take a handful of the editor's preposterous hair and slam his face into his knee. Behind him, the thin woman and a few others stood watching. Proud snitches.

"Unless you're here because you have a story. Is that the case, Monsieur? You came with a story because Madame Laferrière represented herself as a reporter?"

"No."

The editor tilted his head and smiled. Even saying the word *non* revealed his foreignness. "Ah, American?"

"Yes."

Annette had gathered her papers. The editor stepped back so she could pass with short but quick, hectored steps through the door and into the newsroom. He remained close enough, with his haughty smirk, that as he passed, Kruse could smell his coconut shampoo. At Annette's desk he apologized, not for the editor's behaviour so much as for the inherent flaws in his gender.

There was a thin layer of moisture in her eyes and still she could not speak. She sat down in front of her computer with defiantly good posture. Her hands trembled. A young man in jeans and a T-shirt dropped some paper in a basket on her desk, his story, and walked away without a word.

Across the newsroom, the editor continued to watch Annette and him. Kruse picked up one of her notebooks and opened it to a blank page. He whispered as he wrote his name: "She is in trouble, and not only police trouble. Did she say anything that might help me find her?"

"I can meet you at the end of the day, Monsieur."

Annette wrote an address on the back of her business card. Under it, "19h."

• • •

It was no longer raining but the smell of it lingered as he walked out of the lobby and onto Rue Falguière. Cars lined the street and only one of them had passengers sitting in it, a window half-cracked as they smoked. Two large and homely men in a Citroën. There was a tabac and newspaper stand two doors away.

A shiny telephone booth had come with the glassy redevelopment of the newspaper office. Kruse inserted his calling card and dialed Tzvi. Immediately next to the phone was a frame set into the wall, with the words "*À la une aujourd'hui.*" Yesterday's *Le Monde* was inside. Kruse had read his own name in it. Tzvi answered breathlessly on the fifth ring, and the moment he heard Kruse's voice, for the first time in over six months, he launched a barrage of insults and indecencies—one of his talents.

Tzvi's official role in his life was business partner. It had not begun that way.

Neither Kruse nor Evelyn had been blessed with a normal family. Her father, Tom, had died shortly after their wedding, of lung cancer; he had worked in an asbestos plant in Quebec in the summers between university semesters. After a brief period of mourning, Evelyn's mother, Agnes May, dumped all of her old friends and clothes, lost fifty pounds, and took up marathon running.

Mother-daughter relations had soured since the marriage, especially since Tom May's death, and Kruse—the cause of this discord—had been an unlikely negotiator and peacekeeper. It fit. He was a Mennonite. His people had long been slaughtered, first for their faith and then for their stubborn refusal to slaughter anyone else. One morning in 1977, Allan and Nettie Kruse were on their way to volunteer at a leper hospital funded by the Mennonite Church when their small airplane crashed in fog that had gathered in the valley of the Paraguay River. Losing his parents at seventeen made Kruse the sort of man who declares "I love you" to his daughter three to nine times a day, just in case. He generally defended Agnes, as her attacks were born out of loneliness and sorrow and a variety of middle-aged mental illnesses that ran in the May family as Anabaptism and perhaps palate abnormalities ran in his.

Kruse was not wounded by Agnes and Evelyn's insinuation that Lily's imperfect face was his doing; he understood it to be spiritually, if not genetically, true.

On a Wednesday evening when he was fourteen, between Christmas and New Year's, Kruse tripped a larger, older boy named Matt Gibenus in the middle of a street hockey game. The boy skinned his elbows on the pavement. He roared and stood up and threw Kruse to the ground and, in front of several boys and girls—including one he fancied—jumped on him. Matt Gibenus trapped his wrists under his plump knees and slowly removed his gloves as Kruse squirmed and bucked, begged and cried. The kids around them called out, some for blood and others for mercy. Matt Gibenus leaned over him and spat in his face and rubbed it in with his thumb. He ordered Kruse to say things and Kruse said them. It wasn't the pain or the taste in the back of his throat when his nose exploded. It was the feeling of being entirely under someone else's control, the weakness and helplessness and humiliation. He knew what his parents would have said: submit.

Matt Gibenus had long dirty-blond hair. He wore a Black Sabbath shirt and cussed in the hallway. He hung around the automotive shop. Every day and every night Kruse thought about Matt Gibenus and others like him, out there ready to hold him down and spit on him, make him say things about his mother. The stories Allan and Nettie told at the kitchen table were stories of unfairness, of elevating moral victories above physical defeat and destruction. Kruse grew to despise these stories. He studied self-defence schools in the Yellow Pages the way other boys sneaked porn magazines and found one far from his neighbourhood. It was not a popular sport like karate or tae kwon do or judo.

Krav Maga was the hand-to-hand combat system of the Israeli army. He walked into the studio and felt it was more home than home. The white and black walls, the smell of bamboo, the punching bags and gloves and mats, rubber knives and pellet guns answered a question he had been carrying around ever since the evening Matt Gibenus broke his nose.

The bald man in a tight military T-shirt told Kruse to come back when he was eighteen. He did not like children and he could not teach children. But Kruse would not leave. He watched the bald man train for ten minutes, kicking and punching and sneaking about, sweating, stalking himself in the mirror.

"Go," said the bald man, when he stopped.

"No."

"I told you . . ."

"But I'm not a child."

"No?" The bald man bent over, panted. "All right. Come over here."

Kruse remembered he was a child. This compact man terrified him. He was unlike any schoolteacher or soccer or hockey coach he had ever encountered.

"Prepare yourself," said the bald man.

Kruse was in the middle of asking for a clarification—"Pardon?"—when the man slapped him in the face. A whip cracked inside his head. His eyes went hot and burst with tears. He backed away.

"Prepare yourself."

"Wait, wait. How?"

The man moved in quickly and swept Kruse's feet out from under him. He preferred this to the slap in the face, but he hadn't expected it and he landed on his right elbow.

"Prepare yourself."

Kruse stood up, lifted his hands. Far from his parents, at a friend's birthday party, he had seen *Enter the Dragon*. He did what he remembered Bruce Lee doing. This time, the bald man stepped forward and kicked him in the stomach. Kruse fell and gasped and rolled about until the air came back.

It took some time to recover, for the panic to subside. All he wanted now was to admit his childishness, the stupid dominion of Matt Gibenus, and return to his warm bedroom. But he stood again and lifted his hands, this time aware the bald man could attack his legs, his abdomen, or his face. Somehow he had to protect all three.

"Prepare yourself."

This time, instead of waiting for the next attack, Kruse stepped in with a swing. He had seen boxing on television but he had not really paid attention: he led with a wild roundhouse punch. The bald man dodged it. Kruse chased him in a semicircle, kicking and swinging.

Eventually, the bald man stopped hopping away and Kruse slammed into him, this rock of an ageless, happy man. He went for a clinch, a wrestling takedown. In gym class, wrestling was his best sport.

He could not budge him. With a *whoosh* the man tossed Kruse to the bright wood floor.

"All right, boy," he said, in his thick accent. "What do you want to know?"

"Everything."

"You have money, for classes?"

"No."

"Your parents?"

"No."

The bald man, Tzvi Meisels, leaned over and slapped him again, this time on the other cheek.

Allan and Nettie Kruse were outraged he would seek out and fold violence into his life, and they warned him of the consequences for his soul and for his humanity. When he argued that in learning to fight he would avoid fights—rhetorical advice Tzvi had given him—they pointed out the flawed logic of deterrence, which hadn't done much to prevent the proxy wars in Southeast Asia, Africa, the Middle East, and Central and South America. They could go on and they did, nightly, passive-aggressively, academically, the default mode of frustrated Mennonites. They brought ministers and theologians home for dinner, for philosophical and scriptural backup. Eventually, disappointed and dishonoured, they stopped talking to him about anything more substantive than dinner. They would wait until he figured this out for himself and returned to them and to God.

Three years later, after the crash, Kruse mourned his parents with the self-possession and formality they would have expected. Then he set about looking for Matt Gibenus, who had long since dropped out of high school. Kruse found him in Markham, sixty pounds heavier, working as an autobody mechanic.

In school Kruse had been careful around Matt Gibenus. His strategy was to seem accepting of fate, invisible, to believe as his parents believed. He had studied the ritual movements in and around the automotive shop in Markham, and waited until the other mechanics were on a lunch break. Matt Gibenus, as the lowest-ranking employee, was the last to eat.

The mechanic recognized him, or seemed to recognize him. Kruse had grown. He had trained two hours a day, most weeknights, and all day Sunday; he had imagined this moment, something like it, hundreds of times. Matt Gibenus squinted and asked how they knew each other, when Kruse stepped closer.

School, Kruse told him. They were old friends.

In the seventies, security cameras were scarce. Kruse had twenty minutes before the owner or either of the two other mechanics returned to the shop. He introduced himself and avoided a handshake, invited Matt Gibenus to take the first punch.

"I don't fight anymore."

"Not after today."

"I'm on probation for it. I can't."

Kruse reached up and flicked him in the forehead. "Now you can. I started it."

At first, he made it seem like Matt could win. Kruse prolonged the fight, ducking and parrying around the oil pans and the shop vacuum. Matt Gibenus swore and spit, came into his old self, called him a fuckin' pussy for wheeling about the blue Pontiac. Kruse saved his first strike the way he saved and coveted a chocolate-covered almond. A quick finger jab to the eyes. Then he began a slow but severe takedown.

The damage, the real damage, was an accident: Matt Gibenus, wounded and disoriented, stepped into an oil pan and slipped. He fell and cracked his head on the smooth concrete floor, convulsed, and lay still. For three months the man would be in a minimally conscious state. It was on the news, a robbery and vicious assault by a cowardly gang of youths, all for less than three hundred dollars in the till. Kruse donated the money to his parents' preferred charity, the centre for new immigrants. Matt's wife quickly divorced him and remarried.

Kruse did not follow his parents into the Mennonite Church or any other. Yet thirteen years later he knew his daughter was born with a cleft palate because of what he had done that afternoon in Markham.

The man who had been his father nearly as long as his father, Tzvi, was the only one who knew what he had done to Matt Gibenus.

"I'm coming to help."

"Tzvi, there's nothing to help with. I'm going to find her and bring her home."

"The cops have your passport?"

"Until she's proven innocent."

"She doesn't sound innocent. I warned you about this, didn't I? And who is this bastard without a nose?"

"A detective of some sort, maybe."

"The men she saw drinking with . . . what was his name?"

"Jean-François."

"Jean-François, the night he killed Lily. Do you know what these men look like? Who they were?"

"No."

"Can you find out?"

"Not before I find Evelyn."

"Before you find Evelyn! You have no idea what you're doing, Chris. You have no experience."

"Twenty years of—"

"Men like these, women, they're different. They're from hell. I didn't train you for this."

"Yes, you did."

"You're a goddamn sweetheart."

"I'm not a sweetheart."

"All they have to do is mistreat a kitten and you will surrender. It's a catastrophe."

"Tzvi."

"Fuck it, I'm coming."

"There's a car across the street. A couple of men in it, watching me."

"What are they doing?"

"Pretending not to watch me."

"Cops."

"Detectives maybe. They both have noses."

Tzvi gave Kruse advice and insisted he write down every word. Kruse pretended to write. The line went silent, so silent Kruse thought they had been cut off. He was about to hang up when Tzvi's voice rose again. "Lily," he said. "Our girl."

• • •

Kruse and Tzvi acted as bodyguards, analyzed and disrupted threats, and designed security arrangements for presidents and CEOs, paranoid billionaires, foreign celebrities, a few despots, and semi-retired gangsters. Clients hired MagaSecure to minimize the possibility of violence but it happened often enough; Kruse's opponents tended to be the recently fired, the cuckolded, the mentally ill, the drunk and drugged. Often they were convinced they had nothing to lose and carried weapons. Scars were inevitable. Kruse would come home with wounds on his hands and arms and face. He would call from the emergency room. While his work was dangerous, his most potent challenges came from his sparring partners: Tzvi and a small but active community of current and former Mossad agents living in the Greater Golden Horseshoe.

In the fall of 1988 Kruse showed up on the nightly news for preventing a physical assault on the incumbent prime minister during the federal election campaign. He and Tzvi had been on retainer, to guide and train a secondary detail of secret service agents. Neither the party nor the government had paid them to secure the rally in front of the gloomy county courthouse in Brantford, but the moment he and Tzvi arrived they understood the people who had been paid had done an abominable job. It was windy and raining and far too crowded. No one had been posted on top of the courthouse. Kruse and Tzvi abandoned their agents-in-training and escorted the prime minister and his wife through the crowd. Two large men who turned out to be drunken opponents of the Free Trade Agreement with the United States rushed the prime minister. Kruse was closest. In front of several television cameras, he took both attackers to the ground expertly and painfully. This had been spectacular for business.

Evelyn did not like it. She was eight months into her pregnancy. Until now the men and women who made decisions about tenure had been unaware of her husband's vocation. If they were invited to an event and he had a bruise on his cheek or a split lip or a swollen eye, Evelyn would either cancel or go alone, making an excuse for him. Now it was impossible to hide him, to lie about him. Black eyes did not go well with art openings, book launches, conferences in Chicago. Kruse didn't only work with his hands: he hurt people for a living, and after the television clip she could no longer explain it away as a boutique security service, an executive strategy company, white collar work. Kruse didn't see how it mattered but Evelyn did. This is how academic Toronto worked, how academic everywhere worked, and it mattered even more now as they were on the verge of becoming parents. They had met when she was young and not concerned about such matters, but advancement in the academic world had as much to do with dinner party conversations as publications.

Evelyn's interpretation of MagaSecure was, Tzvi assured him, emotional nonsense. It would fade after the pregnancy. Only it didn't fade. Lily's medical troubles didn't consume Evelyn the way they consumed him: her number one worry remained tenure, which was linked to an anxiety she never expressed aloud but one he felt so acutely it ached: she had married the wrong man.

Her revelation about the unearned sabbatical in France, to save their marriage and change their lives, had come at an imperfect time. When MagaSecure reached a point where it ran itself, with trained employees and a process that no longer needed him, it would make sense to take a year and travel the world. He lay in bed awake, debating with himself, as Evelyn mumbled in her sleep and kicked through her dreams. The winning argument was that if they did not try this soon, now, they would be in court within a year.

If twelve months away from MagaSecure and the house on Foxbar Road could save his family, it was worth any cost. He would swim to Europe with them on his back.

According to the pictures in *The Most Beautiful Detours in France*, which was published with a series of old poems, the most severe contrast to what Evelyn had come to see as North American ugliness was in the South of France. And of the Western European languages, French was the only one they could speak. If Lily wanted to be the prime minister one day, she would have to speak it properly.

Two days before the plane departed for Marseille, Kruse and Lily visited MagaSecure to say goodbye. Tzvi wore a suit for the occasion and stood in the middle of the office, on the shiny hardwood floor, hands behind his back, chest out, chin up, his usual stance—only he avoided eye contact.

Tzvi presented Lily with a stuffed pink chick. She hugged his legs and mumbled a nearly imperceptible thank you.

"I don't think he heard you," said Kruse.

Tzvi messed her hair. "Go play."

A quarter of the original studio remained, in the adjacent room, for clients who wanted to pay several thousand dollars for private lessons. Lily sprinted to the wooden man, a training tool they had purchased at a kung fu school's bankruptcy auction. She kicked and elbowed the man, shrieking with each strike, as they had taught her.

Tzvi had spent ten years fighting Arabs and another seven teaching close quarters combat and covert techniques to elite soldiers in the Israeli army; it had ruined him for subtlety. The office was decorated with his awards, citations for bravery, and signed photographs: Tzvi with Yitzhak Rabin, with Barbra Streisand, Tzvi and Kruse with Oprah Winfrey. Kruse had been Tzvi's student and partner and friend for almost twenty years; he had spent much more time with him than either of his parents. Tzvi had given him one of the scars and had fractured his cheekbone and had shot him four times, about the chest and shoulder, with a pellet gun.

"You come back for the film fest."

"No."

"Julia Roberts wants us again."

"It's one year. With the private clients and . . ." Kruse had said all of this before. It hadn't improved Tzvi's mood then and wouldn't now. It was ten thirty. "Let's go for a walk. We'll take you for lunch."

"I'm not hungry." Outside the window a man in several layers of grey clothing, muttering to himself, his hair soaked with sweat, or something like sweat, pushed a shopping cart full of bottles and cans. "Maybe I take a holiday."

"Yes, visit us."

"If I take a holiday, it will not be there. The Frogs sent two of my uncles to Auschwitz. You can have it."

"This might not work. If we arrive and Evelyn isn't any happier—"

"Stop."

Tzvi had already tried to convince Kruse that running away to Europe would do absolutely nothing to improve his family life. When you stand close to "beauty and truth" you realize it's just a bunch of old carved stone that some drunk fucker or gypsy has just pissed on. The stone is even older in his hometown, and Jerusalem is nobody's idea of beauty and truth. If Evelyn did not want to be his wife anymore, Kruse ought to write her a big cheque and let her go. He could take care of Lily himself. Uncle Tzvi would help, damn it.

They didn't have lunch together. Tzvi couldn't say goodbye.

• • •

He had walked around the Necker hospital enough that he knew where he might lure the men in the Citroën. He faked obliviousness and walked up Rue Falguière, toward the hospital and—if he went far enough—his hotel.

The car dieselled to life behind him, once he was half a block up the street, past the caviar shop and the Korean restaurant. Kruse stopped at a window of a travel agency, pasted with photographs of winter escapes, of Egyptian and Moroccan resorts, of Martinique, and of the Canadian Rockies—"ski champagne powder." On the corner, an asymmetrical intersection of four streets with an apartment complex driveway and a metro stop, Kruse took his time deciding where to go. The car rumbled and stank behind him. He chose a neighbourhood filled with shops, Rue de Vaugirard, and turned right at a peculiar street just wide enough for one car.

He rushed into a doorway. The Citroën screeched around the corner and over the interlocking bricks of the little street, Villa de l'Astrolabe. It passed him and Kruse stepped out. The car stopped and the passenger door opened. A large man, with a pillar of a torso, stepped out. He wore dirty jeans and a ripped vinyl jacket. A tattoo crept up to his puffy neck, the peak of it visible.

There was no one behind Kruse and none of the windows of Villa de l'Astrolabe were open. He removed his jacket to meet the big man. He was two hundred and fifty pounds at least, a brawler. The man, who carried time in prison about him, unzipped his own jacket and pulled a knife out of the inside pocket. He wasn't a cop.

And he wasn't French. The driver in the Citroën called out to the brawler sternly, in Russian.

Kruse said, in Russian, "You're looking for Evelyn?"

The brawler turned to his left and drew snot into his throat and spat, as though he had just discovered something poisonous in his sinus.

Kruse was close now. Everything about the brawler was ugly but his eyes, which were a ghostly, translucent blue. Whole neighbourhoods in Toronto looked just like him: Soviets. In the movies and spy novels, in his childhood imagination, this was the villain, the unknowable enemy of love and democracy.

The Russian was a wreck of muscle and fat, but he held the knife out in front of him and twirled it. Kruse thought briefly of that old Michael Jackson video. Maybe Kruse was a sweetheart but the man before him was untrained, a simple prison goon. With a frustrated shout, the driver leaned across and opened the passenger door. He held a cellular phone to his ear. The brawler called back and the driver held the phone aloft. It was an order. *An order!* Before the Russian was fully in his seat, the driver accelerated away. Kruse made a note of the licence plate number and jogged back to the intersection.

In Canada he knew what to do with a licence plate number. He had friends in police services. In France he had no friends at all, now that the de Mussets were gone and Evelyn was lost. He did have a business card.

The lieutenant told him he was not permitted to search for a licence plate number. His wife was a fugitive. For all the gendarme knew, Kruse was helping her.

"I am helping her. I'm trying."

"Describe the men."

Kruse told him what had happened, what they looked like.

"What did they say to you?"

"Nothing."

"What language?"

"Russian."

"Can you imagine why they're following you?"

"Yes."

The lieutenant laughed. "So?"

"They're looking for Evelyn."

"Why?"

"I don't know yet."

"When are you coming back to Vaison?"

"Soon."

"Come tomorrow. I have to discuss something with you."

"Discuss it now, Monsieur Huard."

There was a rather long silence, apart from the sound of heavy fingers on a keyboard. Then a sigh. "Will you come see me tomorrow?"

"Yes."

"Your Russians were driving a Citroën?"

"That's right."

"A family in Aix-en-Provence reported it stolen three days ago."

So far, the rain had not returned, so he walked to the national library on Rue de Richelieu, a secular hall with a cathedral roof, north of the Louvre and the Palais-Royal. A teacher's strike had been in the news, a companion to the metro strike, and he passed a parade of them in Place de la Concorde, shouting and singing. He recalled something Jean-François had said: if they're striking now, against François Mitterrand, just wait until someone who isn't a communist is running the country. Most of the chairs were taken in the Salle Ovale, but he found a desk and dropped the books and medical journals he and the reference librarian had found. No one spoke in a full voice, but the Salle Ovale echoed with whispers, rustled pages, high heels on the floor, sighs, coughs. He was overwhelmed by a feeling that had tormented him since arriving at the hotel: someone was watching him, and it wasn't the coolly flirtatious reference librarian who had guided him toward noselessness. There were over 150 Parisians at desks, reading books and magazines and comics, men alone and mothers with children, messy-haired students, and the elderly in bow ties and wool dresses.

No ugly Russians, no trim aristocrats in well-cut suits, no noseless men.

At his desk Kruse pushed aside thoughts of well-earned psychological imbalance, thoughts that had struck him on the night of Lily's death—he could not endure this; he would go crazy with grief—and concentrated. The eyes on him were Evelyn's. He would walk across the beautiful room, their last beautiful European room, and take her in his arms and forgive her and kiss her and lead her out of the library and into a taxi: Charles de Gaulle, *s'il vous plaît.*

There wasn't much to learn, in the medical literature, about noselessness. Cancer, usually. He found cases of motorcycle accidents, but in these it's usually more than a nose that has been lost. The photographs were hideous. For twenty minutes he pretended to search for more periodicals and watched the readers. Several walked out and several walked in, but none of them held his gaze. Tzvi had been a spy, though he didn't look like a spy. Kruse knew he would be unfit for the secret service, with his scars and what Evelyn had called his hunting little eyes.

He oriented himself toward the entrance and exit. As quickly and as gently as he could manage, he stood up and slipped across the floor. No one looked up as he passed and, when he reached his position and scanned the room, he recognized no one.

"Excuse me, Monsieur?" The reference librarian, with her playful half-smile, held a small envelope. She slid it across the desk and her hand rested on it a moment. She wore a wedding ring. "I was just about to bring this to you. Instead, you have come to me."

On the front of the envelope, in luxurious calligraphy: "Christophe Kruse."

"Who gave this to you?"

"A man."

"Did he leave his name?"

"No. Perhaps it is inside, Monsieur."

"What did he look like?"

The librarian had red hair and light freckles. She looked more Irish than French, but this was not her second language. She smiled and pointed. "I knew you'd ask, and after he left I realized I didn't pay close attention. He wore a suit, no tie. White shirt. Handsome in a clean and soft sort of way. He had a nose, if that's what you're wondering."

"Anything else?"

"Not a library man. I mean, not the sort we usually see. Neither are you, of course."

Kruse thanked her for her help on the subject of lost noses, and for the envelope.

"I did find one last thing, Monsieur." She handed him a code and told him where to hunt the stacks for a back issue of a glossy national magazine. "If it isn't there, it may be on microfilm. I don't know how long we keep them. Was anything else helpful?"

He decided to tell the truth.

"Check out this last one or don't. Perhaps it's the same as everything else. Good luck with your project."

With the metro system down, he was not sure how long it would take to get back to the offices of *Le Monde*. He was more keen to open the letter than hunt through magazine stacks for another story about the unfortunate woman whose dog ate her face as she lay passed out drunk on the floor of her apartment in Lille. In the garden outside the library the benches were damp. He sat anyway, under naked branches surrounded by slick and fragrant shrubbery. A knotty statue of a man in spectacles, leaning heavily forward into the wind or, perhaps, literature, stared at Kruse. He opened the envelope and pulled out a card. The paper was bright and thick and smooth, expensive. Inside, it read, also in calligraphy, "*Oubliez votre femme. Rentrez chez vous immédiatement.*" Forget your wife. Go home now.

Under that, in English, written in regular blue pen: "You'll be rewarded."

He walked out of the garden and across the Île de la Cité, in front of what he had come to see as his daughter's cathedral: Notre Dame. Five minutes could not pass without him thinking of her. First, the white Mercedes. Then something simple and wonderful, reading to her before bed or putting on her pyjamas or walking down some ugly wide Canadian sidewalk with her, holding her hand. Anything to hold her hand. Pushing her stroller through Queen's Park in a thunderstorm. Sitting with her on a hill, overlooking a moat of phantoms, as she traces his scars. Run across the road when your instinct is to run across the road. Ignore Evelyn. Snatch Lily up and run. Go get her. Just go get her and none of this happens.

Old music played inside the cathedral. The violin and harpsichord of Handel, who believed, echoed out the open door and into the courtyard of tourists with cameras. He had read about believers who held photographs of lost children or lost lovers and looked at them as they jumped off bridges and skyscrapers, the Eiffel Tower. He would jump off the nearest bridge, Petit Pont, with gravel in his pockets. He watched everyone now, every Parisian and every tourist, and studied men in suits. Aristocrats. Noses. He would surrender to it, soon become another of the wandering loons unrescued by faith. The sky darkened, a cool wind howled across the Seine, and it began to rain again, to lash his face. He opened his umbrella and then closed it.

SIX

Rue Santeuil, Paris

KRUSE WAITED ON RUE FALGUIÈRE FROM 5:00 TO 5:18, WHEN ANNETTE walked out the glass doors and came as close to jogging as any woman in Paris. In Toronto, New York, Montreal, and Boston he had followed bankers and lawyers, convicts, politicians, adulterous husbands and wives, mistresses, total mysteries. He had only been caught once, in the winter of 1986, by a clever woman who lured him through spooky Bryant Park and into the New York Public Library. He walked past the security man at the door and there she was, standing before him in the great hall with tears in her eyes. Kruse allowed her to slap him with the back of her left hand. The woman was rich, the wife of a less rich but suspicious man, and her elaborate diamond ring tore into his cheek.

Annette Laferrière arrived at an *école maternelle*, near Luxembourg Gardens. She looked at her watch as she entered the courtyard. There was a small playground in the middle and around it some colourful wooden tricycles and bicycles and cruisers, soccer balls, potted palm trees. A sign on the courtyard's tall metal door advertised the presence of scarlet fever with a round drawing of a sad face. Annette emerged holding the hand of a little girl in a blue winter coat and scarf, with the same black ringlets and slightly darker skin. When Evelyn had been in the midst of sewing Lily's fairy costume for Halloween, drinking wine and eating hard chèvre from a bowl next to the sewing machine she had borrowed from Pascale, she discovered her own French métier and the source of their pretend fortune: she would design children's clothing, jackets like the one this little girl wore, clothes that belonged in the forties and fifties instead of the vulgar nineties. He could hear Tzvi's voice: not a kitten, but close enough.

Mother and daughter walked through the wet leaves of Luxembourg Gardens in the early dark. Halfway through the park the rain stopped. The little girl wiped the rain from a swing and asked Annette for a push. There were times back home, agonizing to remember, when Lily had asked for a push and he said no: he was sitting, he was thinking, he was reading, he was eating a banana. Kruse had been here in Luxembourg Gardens on a hot day with the profane son of the pharmacy magnate, when the generous pool in the centre of the park was alive with little rented boats and children running along the side with sticks to find and push them and scream. Today it was too cold and too windy and too dark for a rented boat; the shack was closed up. The little girl ran all the way around the pool, shimmering with yellow light from the palace, and Annette checked her watch again.

It was another ten minutes up the slowly rising hill to the Panthéon. Men and women in business clothes gathered in cafés and bistros for an after-work apéritif. Paris is a northern city, like London, darker than Toronto at this hour and moodier in the mist and the rain. On the other side of the Panthéon, almost at Jardin des Plantes, Annette and the girl turned onto what was surely the ugliest street in this corner of the fifth arrondissement, Rue Santeuil, across from a humanities building of the Sorbonne. Ugly for Paris was somewhere between normal and vaguely attractive, by North American standards. The atypical apartment building had been built for students and belonged, poetically, to the suburbs of Paris more than Paris itself—the things one lazy mayor can do. Laundry and flags from former colonies—including a Maple Leaf—hung over balconies. Across the street, in the courtyard of the squat university building, some students in bog jackets sat on a patch of wet grass, one of them with a guitar. They sang a Bob Marley song.

Annette found her keys in her purse, finally, and opened the door for the little girl. He waited forty minutes under the awning of an entrance to the Sorbonne. The rain had come again and the student troubadours had fled indoors. She walked out at 6:45 in a dark blue dress with a crisp tan overcoat, high heels. Her hair was dry now and arranged. Annette carried a handsome polka-dot umbrella with a wooden handle but no daughter. Kruse followed her back up the hill to Rue Mouffetard, close enough that he caught the outer cloud of her citrus perfume. She stopped at a pharmacy window, before the plaza, and deftly tucked the umbrella under her arm. The not-a-journalist reapplied her lipstick and licked her finger, dabbed at her right eye, and then just stared at herself and breathed, whispered something into the glass.

A masseuse had set up a mini-clinic under a big umbrella next to the fountain at Place de la Contrescarpe. Under the umbrella was a special chair and a hand-painted sign: "Free Massages with donation." The old lanterns around the fountain had popped on. In the springtime, trees that bordered the fountain would blossom pink. Tonight the branches were bare and wet. Their shadows hung over the neglected masseuse, who was making eye contact with passing pedestrians like a lonely hound.

Café Delmas was designed as a library, with soft light and books on the shelves, leather chairs and an antelope's head on the wall. Annette went immediately into the washroom, so Kruse found a table for them. His seat backed into the corner, faced the room. Some of what he had heard, from travellers and Bugs Bunny cartoons and American comedies starring Chevy Chase, had turned out to be correct: the French are not afraid to smell the way men and women smell at six or seven o'clock at night, after a day of work. They are a musky people.

He stood up when she emerged and didn't quite know whether to offer his hand or kiss her cheek. Neither perhaps. Neither. Before she sat down she began apologizing for what had happened in the newsroom, her voice shaky and her words so jumbled together he had to focus completely to understand.

"When Madame Kruse phoned it was early in the evening and I was on the late shift, you see, and she asked for a journalist and I am a journalist—I am, truly—so I believe I did nothing wrong, nothing unethical. The reporter who had written the story, he was not in the office. He rarely is. I might have transferred her, of course, but who was in at that hour? Interns. Contractors. I am a journalist, as I said. It was very kind of you, this afternoon, to lie for me. But please understand I know how to do this, what I am doing."

"What would you like to drink, Madame Laferrière?"

"If you would prefer a journalist with a byline in *Le Monde*, a byline already I should say, it is only natural and correct. I will find someone for you, one of the *grands reporters*."

Kruse looked up and gestured the waiter to their table. Annette breathed, somewhat regularly, and ordered a glass of white wine. The courtly waiter turned and leaned down. "And for your husband?"

Annette blushed and stuttered her way through an explanation of what they were: colleagues, friends, acquaintances, hardly more than strangers, in fact. The awkwardness gave Kruse an opportunity to scan the room. There were men in suits, half-hidden by cigarette smoke, but no one who matched the hotelier's description of the Four Seasons gentleman. Finally, he was able to say what he wanted: a small bottle of sparkling water. When they were alone again, Annette closed her eyes in mock pain.

"I am sorry for that, for his assumption."

"My people are famous for unnecessary apologies, not the French."

"As I was saying, Monsieur Kruse, I would understand if you would like someone else."

"No."

"Thank you."

He was not remotely interested in another story in the newspaper, a correction or an elaboration. "Can you find out about this anonymous source?"

"In our story?"

"It was the same in every story. How anonymous can it be?"

"Monsieur, I think not."

"It was wrong. She could not have had an affair with Jean-François."

For the first time in their conversation, she allowed a silence between them. She looked down at her notebook but didn't write anything. Café Delmas was wild with conversation and laughter, curiously powered by the wind and the rain outside the sweating windows. Behind the noise, a woman sang sadly over a viola.

He would not say it again, or think it. The waiter arrived with their drinks and now he wanted a glass of wine. A million husbands and a million wives were sitting in bars, at this moment, telling themselves similar stories.

"I know for sure that Evelyn is incapable of murder, Madame Laferrière."

"Then why doesn't she present herself to the authorities? If she is innocent?"

"She was researching the Front National and working with them. It seemed everyone knew everyone, that they protected each other. I think she found this charming, at first, but if Evelyn . . . men are following me. Someone is threatening me."

"Many of them are Nazis. Not real ones but Vichy men, men who seek opportunity above all things. Their humanity. The party has tried, I know, to get rid of them. I wrote about them in Bordeaux. But if a thing is in your culture, does it not just sit and rot and smell forever? It was not so long ago."

"What?"

"The war. The great humiliation. We can still smell it and this has always been the problem for the Front National."

"Until Jean-François de Musset."

"You know he descends from a very old, very wealthy French family? A family of the last king's court? This would have been a big deal, if he had run for president."

"Evelyn thought she could fix the party."

"Who is following you, Monsieur Kruse?"

"Russians."

"Why Russians?"

He regretted telling her. Tzvi was right. "I don't know."

Annette looked up, at the thick cloud of smoke in the room, and down at her blank paper. "When we consider the murder of Jean-François and . . ."

"Pascale."

"Pascale de Musset, we can dream up reasons why others would want them killed. But your wife has two motives, or appears to. One, the man has just killed her daughter. Two, forgive me, Monsieur, they have had an affair. It went poorly, one might suspect. An emotional woman, one might suspect, mad with vengeance. She has nothing to lose. If I am an investigator, Monsieur Kruse, this does seem rather simple. Catch the furious woman. Maybe these Russians are working for the police or with the police. If you think your way through it, this is where you arrive. No?"

"No."

"How can you be so sure of her innocence?"

Faith, he nearly said, but that would not have been precisely true. *Oubliez votre femme. Rentrez chez vous immédiatement.*

Annette finished her glass of wine and ordered another.

• • •

Kruse walked her home in the darkness and the rain. On Rue Lacépède they walked down and against the flow of cars, but there was almost no traffic. Parisians were up in their apartments, before their fireplaces and television sets, drinking tea and wine, glancing occasionally at the rain tapping their windows. Annette's voice echoed down this street and the next, the narrower and older and utterly deserted Rue de la Clef. A fog rose up from somewhere and further obscured the way ahead, a faint decline.

She was born and raised in the southwest. A lot of her friends, growing up and especially in university, wanted only to be in Paris. Not Annette: she didn't think she would leave Bordeaux until she was already gone. After university, where she had studied political science, she started her career as a journalist. Her first job was with a newspaper called *SudOuest*. She became a well-read editorialist at a young age and fell in love with another writer. They married and had a child. Then she was fired for writing the wrong sort of article about Basque terrorists.

"What does that mean? The wrong sort of article?"

Her heels echoed in the corridor and she hugged herself in the wind. Kruse offered his jacket and she took it, wrapped it around her shoulders. "Families are connected by history, by marriage, by secret alliance. The president of the publishing group was somehow insulted or exposed."

"You never learned how?"

"Our own lawyers deemed it libelous and worked out a compensation package for a man I had named, a terrorist. Part of that compensation package was my dismissal. It doesn't normally work that way, in a nation with freedom of the press."

Annette admitted, after a few quiet steps down foggy Rue de la Clef, past a bakery and a flower shop, she did not take it well. There were emotional and psychological stresses. Her husband, her ex-husband, a man so withdrawn she never once heard him pee, was now the editor-in-chief of the newspaper. He had remarried a dancer in the ballet company attached to the Opéra National de Bordeaux.

Over 55 million people lived in France in 1992, but the community of journalists was small and intimate. Once a major newspaper fires a journalist for what it might falsely call libel, it is nearly impossible to find another job. As a writer, at least. This is why they treated her like trash at *Le Monde*.

Three blocks from her apartment on Rue Santeuil, Kruse felt it. Someone was following them. He held out his hand and abruptly stopped her. It was not one footstep, back in the fog, but several.

They continued along.

"What?" she said.

"Nothing. Tell me about your daughter."

"Anouk is her name. She is four. The same age, more or less, as—"

"Yes, Madame."

He carried a small knife in a holster around his ankle, a gift from Tzvi. He bent down and pretended to tie his shoe, unsheathed the knife. In the early days of the school, young men would come in and, though they did not say it aloud, he knew they wanted to fight because it was impressive. Impressive to women, presumably. Sexy, maybe. Kruse, who had been doing it since he was fourteen, knew it was something else. It was grotesque, when it really happened. It turned you into a monster at the gate of the village, an enemy of quiet nights in the warm apartment, in the rain, proof. Evelyn was right to worry about what her sophisticated friends might think. In the movies it's one punch and they're out. In real life it's ten and they're lying on the sidewalk, looking like steak tartare pecked by pigeons. They were still two blocks from her apartment. She had continued talking about Anouk, a serious and studious girl, a watcher, like all only children. Annette seemed on the verge of asking about his only child. Was she like that?

There were five of them, at least. Between five and seven. Heavy and inelegant steps. They were amateurs. Rue Santeuil was not lively at this hour, in the mist and the fog. He closed his umbrella. It would be in the way. At her door Kruse was relieved; the men remained at a distance. So far he could only see the outlines of them, their slick jackets. They too had closed their umbrellas.

"Monsieur, I will use my free moments to research this. First, to discover the identity of the anonymous source. I shall go where that leads me."

"Thank you."

"If I find nothing, please know . . ."

"I know. It's very kind, Madame Laferrière."

She returned his jacket and kissed him once on each cheek, lingering a moment on each side. The two glasses of wine had opened one of the windows between a strange man and a strange woman in France. With a good night, she was through both sets of doors and gone. He remained with his back to them, watched her wait for the elevator. Her ankles were bare, below her dress and her jacket. The elevator arrived and she turned to him again and waved and stepped inside.

It smelled faintly of fish on the street, a maritime rather than a restaurant smell. The men were on the Sorbonne side, still in a group. Their steps were even heavier now, cavalier; they knew he knew. He walked northeast, toward Jardin des Plantes. They crossed the street, in behind him, and he turned and walked backwards for a moment as they sped up, as they began the transition from a walk to a run. The ugly Russian with the knife was among them, walking with a cigarette in his mouth.

The Great Mosque of Paris was across the street, a white wall designed with castle ramparts, a minaret. He had been in there once; a client had said the best tagines on the continent were served inside—chicken and prunes and nuts over rice, he remembered well. His stomach stirred. Annette had already eaten something with her daughter, Anouk—a new name for him, Anouk—so she had not been hungry. Eating in front of her had not seemed correct and he was hungry now, walking briskly through the smell of slow-cooked meat. Tzvi would remind him to focus: every fight is a fight to the death.

He turned right, under a stone arch and into Jardin des Plantes. Now they ran. The gardens were lit up by flat yellow lanterns. "*Voleur!*" one of them called out behind him, with that accent.

The park was nearly deserted but not quite.

A bearded man in a sweatsuit, a vigilante jogger, stood waiting for Kruse in a splash of yellow light as he sprinted over the crushed gravel. Kruse dodged him and turned left, past the tulip field empty of tulips, and into the menagerie, which was closed for the night. Two men in suits stood in a clearing ahead, guards of some sort, so he stopped running and ducked into a grove of trees. The five who had been chasing him ran past and split up, turning around and cursing him. He was among the noisy animals now and the trees.

The ugly Russian who had stepped out of the car with the knife said nothing. One of the others spoke to the guards, who shrugged and did that thing with their lips that Frenchmen do before they say something other than yes. "*Mais non, Monsieur.*"

Kruse moved through the trees, watching them and then watching him. Others had moved east, deeper into the park, toward the Seine. The ugly Russian lit a cigarette and walked past the orangutan enclosure. It smelled of wet cedar, an unplaceable scent from his childhood. When they were far enough from the guards and the others, Kruse stepped out of the cedars.

The last time he was in Paris he woke up early each morning and ran through either Luxembourg Gardens or Jardin des Plantes. He sprinted in a direction he knew well, to the modest labyrinth of shrubbery leading to the gazebo at the top of the hill—the garden's small, open-air observatory—and hid in a bush. *Cache-cache.* There is no translation for "ready or not, here I come." Lily would say, "*J'arrive!*" The Russian ran up the circular path toward him, alone. By the time he reached the top of the little hill the Russian was breathing heavily, a cigarette still in his hand.

In one motion Kruse jumped out and kicked him in the stomach. The Russian bent and stumbled and fell backwards, heaving. The path and the gazebo up top were clear of observers. Kruse checked him for weapons and found two knives, the one he had been twirling on the street and another in his waistband. Kruse pocketed them.

"No gun, Monsieur?"

The Russian flailed for air like an overturned beetle. Kruse put his knee on the man's neck and torqued his arm. No matter how far he turned it, the Russian did not cry out.

"Who is paying you?"

Nothing.

"Who do you work for? The Front National?" He switched to Russian. "Why are you doing this?"

Kruse lifted his knee, to let him respond. The Russian dragged up some phlegm and spit at him.

Tzvi had a theory: to torture a good man is pointless. It will suck the humanity out of you, if you try anyway, and haunt your nights and turn you grey. But a man without honour will always talk. He had trained Kruse in the strategies and techniques, thoughts to think as your man screams and writhes, lies first and then tells the truth. The Russian seemed bewildered not by the substance of the questions but that they had been asked at all. Kruse did not break his arm or put a blade in his spleen or threaten to dig his eye out with a dirty index finger. There was only one thing to do but he had never done it. In the distance there were footsteps, a soft conversation. Kruse stood up off him, released him.

The Russian wiped the mud from his jeans. "*Lâche*," he said, and fixed his tiny blue eyes on Kruse.

Coward.

It was a one-storey drop to the street.

He walked up into the fifth arrondissement. When had it started to rain again? Where had he left his umbrella? The Great Mosque was open for dinner. If he had run for her or if they had left Villedieu at six o'clock, six thirty at the latest, they would be eating here some night before Christmas. Kruse would ask for a booster seat, though Lily now insisted she was too big for that.

He could not sleep at the Champ de Mars so he walked north across the river and stopped at a dark and smelly brasserie near Gare de Lyon, and ordered soup. A mother and father ate with a toddler at the next table over. There was some commotion, a squeal and a laugh, so the mother pulled down the boy's pants and the father had him piss into one and then another empty wine glass as though it were the most delightful thing that had ever happened.

At the station he bought a first-class ticket south, and the moment after the train departed he walked from one end of it to the other, car to car, looking for Russians and aristocrats and Vichy men and Evelyn. When he found none of them he reclined his chair and closed his eyes. He did not sleep for long, a little more than an hour, with a knife in his hand. He dreamed: he is splashing in the Ouvèze river with Lily and Evelyn on some hot day, and then the flood comes. He swims as hard as he can, but they twirl helplessly away from him and into the night water. All he can do is float.

PART TWO

SEVEN

Rue Trogue-Pompée, Vaison-la-Romaine

THE FRONT DOOR OF THE HORSE STABLE WAS OPEN. KRUSE CREPT IN and knew immediately that whoever had been inside had gone. Every drawer was emptied onto the floor. Paper and utensils and broken tchotchkes were on the tile, with cushions and pillows and the linens from the daybed. The remaining pieces from Lily's tea set were broken. He knew it was pointless, but he ran out and around the corner to the commercial route, Avenue Jules Ferry. The shops were open and pedestrians were about in their sunglasses, but none of them had just broken into his house.

Kruse inspected upstairs, the master bedroom and Lily's room. The intruders had gone through the folder of paperwork but had not taken anything, no bank or insurance documents, criminal record checks, social insurance numbers or customs declarations. Nothing was missing, not even her least favourite scarf sprayed with perfume.

Lieutenant Huard came alone. "They often find you, people like you, by your rental cars. It's in the licence plate numbers."

"They didn't break into the car."

He shrugged. "Money?"

"None."

"Liquor?"

"The de Mussets had some bottles of pastis in the cupboard."

"Not taken?"

"And we had no exciting painkillers. They might have stolen the television set, or the old stereo system, but they didn't bother."

"You were right not to leave any money lying around."

"They weren't looking for money, Monsieur Huard."

The lieutenant crossed his arms. He hadn't taken out his notepad. "What were they looking for?"

Instead of answering, Kruse tidied the room.

"What are you reporting missing?"

"Nothing."

"What are you reporting?"

"I wanted you and Madame Boutet to see this, to know. Evelyn's innocent. They're after her."

"They."

"Yes."

"Perhaps it was your wife who did this. Have you received correspondence?"

"No."

"Not even a phone call?"

"No."

"*C'est des conneries.*"

"If she had phoned, Monsieur Huard, would I be here? Or would I be with her? Protecting her?"

"Can you imagine why someone would break into your house and steal . . . nothing?"

"I'm not a policeman."

"What were they looking for?"

"Monsieur Huard, if you were to break into this house, today, you, the gendarme . . ."

"Yes."

"What would you look for?"

"I'm a special case."

"Why?"

"Because I have an interest in finding your wife."

"And so . . ."

"So I might seek traces of her. Postcards, a phone number lying on or in a desk."

Kruse tucked the covers around the daybed and replaced the pillows. He picked up the papers and brochures, all of them designed to help de Musset tenants find markets, routes, and pretty things in Northern Provence. He picked up the pieces of his daughter's tea set and just held them, light and cool.

Monsieur Huard watched him and then he looked away. "Did you have a postcard in here? A phone number?"

"No."

Monsieur Huard grasped Kruse by the arm and pulled him out of the horse stable and onto Rue Trogue-Pompée. It was a cool morning but the Atlantic storm had not followed him south. The sky was blue and clear and the dewy town smelled of cypress. A travel group of retired Brits in safari colours and hats were making their way along the black fence. The lieutenant waited until they approached the fence, smiled at each one and said, in his heavy accent, either "Hello" or "Welcome to Vaison-la-Romaine" in English. A guide spoke to them of Emperor Hadrian, who had been here in the Vaucluse. There were bigger towns in the area, like Arles and Orange, but this is where the super rich had lived. Some of the most luxurious houses in the Roman world were here. Why here? No one could say.

When the tourists were gone, the lieutenant's smile disappeared. He whispered, "Someone is hunting your wife."

"Yes."

"Who, Monsieur Kruse?" The lieutenant seemed to like saying his name: Kruse-uh.

"I don't know yet. The Front National?"

"Anything more from your Russians?"

Kruse told him about his encounter in Jardin des Plantes.

"You may be inventing this."

"I may be."

"So what, you think they work for the Front National?"

"Maybe they work for you."

"We can't pay ourselves, let alone mercenaries. Russians. I don't understand. Your wife knew Russians?"

"Not that I'm aware of. Why break into the house, Monsieur Huard?"

He fussed with his moustache. "Maybe you messed up your own place, to create a mystery, to throw me off your wife's trail."

"And where are you, precisely, on the trail?"

The lieutenant looked out over the ruins. He took in two deep breaths, like a yogi, and sighed them out. "I've been told to back off."

"To back off what?"

"Your wife. The murders."

"Someone else is handling the case?"

"No one from our bureau. No one from Avignon or Orange or Arles."

"What does that mean, Monsieur Huard?"

He pulled out a box of Gitanes and offered one to Kruse, who didn't have to decline. "I'm just offering to be polite. I know the food you buy, the drinks you order, the paths you walk. Where you run up the hill, to the château, and where you do your ridiculous sit-ups and push-ups." He lit a cigarette and pulled a speck of tobacco from his mouth.

"Who told you to back off?"

"My captain. But someone told him, the squadron leader I suppose. Maybe the colonel told him. And who told the colonel? One of the generals? Who told the general? Why?"

Together they leaned over the black fence.

"It's older than the revolution, the Gendarmerie nationale. Before the revolution they called it the marshalcy. You know why it wasn't disbanded? Even Napoleon just renamed it. You might say it's because we've always been devoted to law and order. That's what they tell you in school. The real reason is we're fickle. We're agnostic. We're natural collaborators. We follow the leader. If you tell us to do something, and you're more powerful than we are, we'll do it. It doesn't matter why, not really. I can ask why all I like but it's insubordination to ask it of anyone but myself. Or perhaps you."

"What do we do?"

"There is no 'we,' Monsieur Kruse."

"Help me, Monsieur Huard."

"I'm not married. I was married but I was no good at it. No kids. Most of my old friends are either dead or moved on, even the ones who still live around here. I'm nearly sixty. This is all I have."

The gendarme remained at the fence for a long time, without another word. Then he patted Kruse on the back, turned right, and limped slowly up the cobbled street toward the gendarmerie. Kruse watched him go and then he went back inside to face the mess of the horse stable alone.

In Paris his clothes had been rained on and slashed with mud. He emptied his pockets upstairs, in front of the mirror of their foreign bedroom, and found the looping, handwritten call number for a magazine article about noselessness.

• • •

The library in Vaison-la-Romaine was in a complex called La Ferme des Arts, next to the swimming pool, on a street named after a poet. He had been here at least once a week with Lily, reading Astérix books. Evelyn found them too violent and disapproved, so it was a bit of father-daughter intrigue. The library had a sunny outdoor courtyard; they would stack pillows on the stone bench and cuddle.

"*À l'attaque!*" the Gauls scream.

"*À l'attaque!*" Lily screams, and looks around to see if anyone apart from Papa heard, and nuzzles into him.

It was a small library but it did keep several years' worth of popular periodicals. The librarian was dressed for a night at the symphony, in a long red dress and white scarf, though it was not yet eleven in the morning. She led him to the call number. The correct edition of *Le Figaro* magazine, from February 1992, was near the bottom of the pile.

"You're the Canadian. The man who . . ."

"Just a curious man."

She tilted her head. "Well. I am pleased they are still making curious men." She wished him luck and left him to his magazine.

There was no one else in the library. He sat at a small table and leafed slowly through *Le Figaro*. It was a small, blurry photograph near the end of the magazine, in a section of miscellaneous feature news events. A funeral in Marseille. Two men were at the front of an entourage, carrying the casket of Paul Mariani, who had died of a heart attack in a seafood restaurant on the port. Kruse recognized the man on the left: Joseph Mariani. He was the athlete who had been watching him, in the navy blue suit, from the bleachers of the ancient arena in Orange. On the other side of the casket was a noseless man named Lucien Mariani.

He nearly toppled a stack of newspapers as he ran to the startled librarian's desk. "Who are these people?"

The librarian looked down, up at Kruse again, and down again. "What do you mean, Monsieur?"

"The Mariani family. Who are they? It doesn't really say. They're famous enough to be in a magazine, evidently, but how? Why?"

"The Mariani family is the Mariani family."

"And who are they?"

"Corsicans."

"That's it? Corsicans?"

The librarian looked around. There was no one else in the library. She whispered, "You honestly don't know?"

She led him into the stacks and pulled a paperback book from the non-fiction section. It was called *Le milieu: les parrains corses.*

"*Le milieu?*"

"Read the book, Monsieur."

It only took an hour with the book, as an entire chapter was devoted to *la famille* Mariani.

They were not like the mafia he grew up with. *Le milieu,* in the South of France, was a web of quiet and polite men. Where gangsters in Montreal and Toronto were ostentatious, like their cousins in New York and Chicago, like the movie versions of themselves, dating supermodels and showing up on the front covers of gossip magazines, the Corsican was invisible. He gained more from subtlety than from shouting about how many chicks he banged last night—one of the quirks of a semi-retired Mafioso who had hired Kruse and Tzvi in Montreal. The traditional French gangster was the man in the Mini-Casino supermarket at lunchtime, wearing a baby blue sweater tied over his white Lacoste shirt, buying a tub of yogurt and a bit of dried sausage.

There was an epilogue at the end of the book, about the assassination of John F. Kennedy. A British documentary had demonstrated that the Guérini and Mariani crime families, originally from Corsica and now operating in Paris and Marseille, had been approached about the contract to kill the American president in the early sixties. At that time, the head of the family was Paul Mariani, the father of the noseless one and the aristocrat. Kruse made two photocopies of the page and ran to Cours de Taulignan. The woman in uniform behind the counter at the gendarmerie said Lieutenant Huard had gone to Avignon. Kruse circled the photograph and in the margin he wrote, "Two of the men looking for Evelyn." He kindly asked the woman for an envelope, put the page inside, sealed it carefully, and wrote, "Huard: confidential" on the front.

At the post office he sent the other photocopy to Annette at *Le Monde.*

He bought a new lock system for the horse stable at the hardware store on Place Montfort, and installed it. He picked up everything that had been thrown to the floor, folded the clothes, and trashed the paper. He mopped the floor with a touch of chlorine and remembered trips to the Wallace Emerson Centre with Lily, who was nervous in crowded swimming pools, of the strange echo of eighty kids swimming in bleach-water. If Evelyn were to come back he wanted her to feel welcome in the horse stable, to appreciate what was left of its beauty. At six he phoned the gendarmerie and asked for Huard: he was back but too busy to speak, unless it was an emergency.

• • •

A man without a nose stood over him, breathing through his mouth. He wore a dark suit and a dark tie.

"Is he awake?" whispered a second man, in shadow.

The noseless man did not respond. Without looking at a clock, Kruse guessed it was midnight. He interrupted his body's natural response— panic. He relaxed his breathing and his thoughts. He was at work again and it came with a rush of pleasure. It would take ten to thirteen seconds to subdue the noseless man, Lucien Mariani, in absolute silence. But he could not hurt the man, even this man, unless it was in self-defence. There was another, a man in shadow.

"I have a gun, Christopher."

In the instant between this warning and the noseless man's first movement, there was only one response: blind him and dart out of the room, forcing the other to hunt him in a house he knew well. There was something in the noseless man's hand, a baton of some sort, and a wire. Kruse moved but it was too late. It came with a hum and a blast of light, sizzling on his chest. Every muscle in him flexed and

locked, and the headache threatened to explode. He had been electro-
cuted before, by Tzvi. This lasted longer. He was hot and then cold,
an instant fever. It had immobilized him then and it immobilized him
now. The noseless man, grunting through his open mouth, hot mouth,
turned him over and bound his wrists. He yanked him over, onto his
back again, and turned on the bedside lamp.

A man in a stylishly cut black suit and pressed white dress shirt, with
no tie, sat in a dining room chair in the corner of the bedroom. Joseph
Mariani opened and closed his eyes slowly. If he said anything, in the
first while, Kruse did not hear it. He drifted out of and back into con-
sciousness, and the man's echoing voice solidified.

"Good morning, Christopher."

It was not midnight. It was shortly after five in the morning. Kruse's
first thought was of a priest or, given the accent, an Anglican minister
from Oxfordshire. It took a moment to realize the priest had spoken
English. His noseless brother Lucien backed up and stood against the
wall between the windows. He held a cattle prod or something like it,
a police baton with two metal tips at the end. The baton was attached
by wires to a small battery pack Lucien carried over his shoulder like
a purse. They would have killed him if they had wanted to kill him. A
Glock pistol rested on the priest's lap. He introduced himself and his
brother.

"Are your muscles settling? I do apologize for Lucien and his toys.
My preference was to knock on the door at eight in the morning, hat
in hand."

Kruse watched them and briefly despised himself for pausing when
every instinct had said attack. *À l'attaque.* His wrists were well bound.
Lucien took his wallet from the bedside table and handed it to Joseph.
It looked like Joseph took something out of it, but Kruse was having
trouble focusing. He thought of the gladiolas outside the windows;
when had he last watered them? A week ago? Two weeks? How long
ago had Lily died? The aftershocks wore off with a throb of nausea.

"We won't bind your feet, because neither of us wants to carry you. You're a big fellow. Strong!" Joseph lifted his gun as if it were a dirty dishrag. "But if you kick us, or try to run, I will shoot you—or Lucien will. And not with an electric stick."

He had fallen asleep in his clothes, reading about *le milieu*. Joseph crossed the room and picked the book up.

"I like this story. It made me blush. Do you know why we're here, Christopher?"

"No."

"But you do know who we are. You've been doing some research, you scamp, sending letters." Joseph looked away from Kruse and smirked at his brother. In French he said, quickly, "Look, you both have scars."

Lucien looked down.

"Do you have plans today, by chance?" Joseph stood up off the chair and buttoned his jacket. "We were hoping to show you around our hometown this morning."

"I had booked off some time to throw up."

"A side effect of the electricity. You're coming either way, Christopher. My hope is you'll come willingly and happily, as we mean you no harm. On the contrary. We're friends and allies, as you'll see."

"Marseille?"

Lucien walked over and pulled him off the bed and onto the floor, by his bound hands. Kruse landed on his elbows, a fresh riot of pain. Now Lucien pulled him up to his feet the same way. The bedroom tilted and spun. He slammed into the wall and threw up on the floor beside the bed.

"Well, mission accomplished," said Joseph.

EIGHT

Rue de la Cathédrale, Marseille

IN THE BACK SEAT OF A SILVER ALFA ROMEO SEDAN, KRUSE IMAGINED what Tzvi would have done in the apartment. He would have immediately disarmed and disabled Lucien without allowing any other considerations to intervene. He would have used him as a shield long enough to get the knife he had hidden in a Kleenex box under the bed. He would have turned on the light and thrown the knife at Joseph's face before the assassin's eyes adjusted. One shot would be fired, and it would miss. Six seconds, at the most.

Then he would kill one, with maximum cruelty, in front of the other. Finally he would torture the second man into explaining everything. Maybe he would let him live, to spread a message among his masters.

Or maybe not.

"What do you do for a living, Christopher?"

"Nothing, at the moment."

"A man of leisure."

"Something like that."

"Did you have a métier before you won the lottery?"

"I taught school."

"What subject?"

If Evelyn had wanted him to be anything, it was a scholar: they could have dreamy arguments about beauty at the dinner table. "Literature."

"Oh how lucky for us, Lucien. An intellectual like Madame. I never received a detailed report, from our Slavic friends in Paris. How did you evade them?"

"I ran."

"A professor and an athlete, Lucien. Your sort of fellow."

Lucien did not look away from the road. The noseless man's posture was unnaturally stiff and every breath was an announcement. He was, Kruse supposed, the only man in France to follow the speed limit. They passed through a toll station and Joseph turned and watched Kruse equably, benevolently. None of the three men in the car said a word to the toll agent, who did not even look down. Despite all his years of training and, on security jobs, several encounters with what Tzvi called the enemy, Kruse had never met genuine assassins.

Signs began to appear for Marseille.

"What was your specialty?"

"My specialty?"

"In literature, I mean. Doesn't one always specialize?"

"Shakespeare. Keats. Plato."

"Plato is literature?"

"I taught optional courses in philosophy."

"Having been educated here in France, my exposure to Shakespeare and Keats has been limited. But Plato I like. What do you think of Plato, Lucien? *Platon?*"

Again, Lucien did not respond.

"He prefers novels, Lucien. Strange and dirty ones. My brother is something of an *avant-gardiste*. Do you read French, Christopher?"

"Well enough."

Joseph nodded cordially, and faced the road again. Exits to Marseille were approaching. "You're not nervous."

"Should I be?"

"Yes, Christopher. I'm afraid so. I'm nervous myself, to be honest. It has been an unusual *quinze jours*. Since our father died, it's rare I get involved in any actual work. But this is special. You're special."

Lucien navigated slowly through the bland suburban bits Kruse remembered from their drive in from the airport, the part of France that annoys the romantic looking for *la France profonde*. They entered an in-between area, old stone across the street from post-war brutalism. The allies would have bombed here. They entered a hilly bit in the centre, close enough to the sea to sense the water somewhere on the other side of a roof. There was a plaza. It was still dark and the fountain was alive with pretty but mournful yellow floodlights. Two weeks ago, with Evelyn and Lily—to be a tourist again—he would have taken a photo of this spot.

Lucien parked in a tiny garage, and the brothers led Kruse down a thin, cobbled street, Rue de la Cathédrale. He had not seen the cathedral. Somewhere the sun was rising over old Marseille. A man approached in the distance and Lucien took a few steps ahead in his hard black shoes. The man stopped when he saw Lucien, turned around, and walked away. In the dimness, Kruse could see efforts had been made to reconstruct the lost nose. It was half the size of what it ought to have been, a difference of a couple of square centimetres. His brown eyes were bright, almost lovely.

Neither of them had wanted to accompany Kruse to the bathroom, after he threw up. He said he had other business to do. There was a box of blades in the drawer that held his razor. When neither of them were directly behind him, he worked on the rope.

Kruse knew what was coming, as they led him deeper into the medieval quarter. As a teenager he had attended Tzvi's three-week summer survival camps and then, when he turned twenty-one, he began to lead them. There is a colour and a smell to it, Tzvi's specialty. You are walking down a long corridor followed by men with guns, the inquisitors, the brownshirts, and you know that eventually the lights will go out and when they do, in the cold and the damp, you are going to die. It will gallop from the darkness and take you before you can pray. Tzvi had conceived of the summer camps as a profit-making venture but also as a public service; Kruse's first year, when he lied to his parents about the camp being devoted to outdoor education, he was the only non-Jew.

They stopped at a blue door. Kruse noted the number and the flower boxes across the corridor, a wall covered in scaffolding twenty metres farther along, the motorcycles and scooters. The staircase was wooden and crooked, and smelled wet. It led to another door on the second floor. Joseph opened it and turned on the light.

Lucien shoved Kruse inside an open studio. Its walls had been freshly painted white. In the apartment, a faint odour of vinegar filled the room. The ceiling and tall panelled windows at the end of the room were exquisitely moulded. Joseph fussed with a thermostat in the kitchen, which had Nordic cabinetry and a new dining table with six steel chairs. Kruse had done some work in Oslo and Stockholm; the apartment in Marseille looked like an import from the cool north.

Around the corner there was a muffled whine, like that of a well-trained dog keen to see its master. Joseph's fine leather shoes clacked on the wood floor. Kruse had made progress on the rope.

"Do you know why we're here, Christopher?"

"Fire up the bong, open a bag of Cheezies, watch *A Clockwork Orange*."

Joseph turned to his noseless brother, who stared indifferently at the sink. "He's an odd duck, no?"

He was through the first part of the knot. He tucked the rope around, so nothing would hang. "What happened to his nose?"

"Hey. Hey, enough with that, professor. You haven't answered my question. We're here so you can . . ."

"Lead a couple of gangsters to my wife."

"I don't like the word 'gangster.' Otherwise, you've reduced things like a good balsamic—bravo."

"But why, Monsieur Mariani? Why go to all this trouble to find my wife?"

Lucien opened a cupboard door and pulled down a stainless steel medical tray. Joseph waved Kruse over, as though he were leading a tour of his sculpted gardens.

The kitchen led to a room he had not anticipated, a salon that expanded left and right into a T. On the left there was no dog but a naked man bound to a rectangular wooden apparatus that had been built into the corner of the room. His head was bowed before him and his long, curly hair fell into his face.

"What is this?"

"Good question, Christopher. Excuse me, Frédéric. Freddy: What is this?"

The man slowly lifted his head. His hands had been tied to a thick horizontal beam above. At first the man appeared unharmed, merely uncomfortable and sleepy. The damage was below. Both of his feet had been clamped into a metal contraption with heavy antique springs and a tightening lever. The machine belonged in a museum but it worked: his feet and ankles had been mashed into a white and purple pulp of skin, blood, and bone.

If he had not been tied to the ceiling, he could not have remained upright. White fabric had been stuffed into his mouth; a long line of drool hung from bits that had escaped from behind the duct tape. A thick, transparent plastic sheet had been stapled to the walls around him, the ceiling above, and the floor below. Blood pooled below both mangled feet, black and congealed. His penis was a snail teased out of its shell and into the awful light. Two wooden chairs sat before the

man and the chamber. It reminded Kruse of the theatre series he and
Evelyn had subscribed to the first year they dated. She had wanted him
to understand modern artistic motivation, the perversity of it, what she
was up against in the academy.

The naked man's eyes, when he looked up, were at once dead and
ferocious. On the night Lily was killed, when Evelyn had shouted hope-
lessly and ungrammatically at the gendarmes who had arrived to take
Jean-François away, her eyes had held the same look. All she could tell
the gendarmes in proper French was, "*Il l'a tué, il l'a tué.*" He killed her.

"Let him go."

"Oh, Christopher."

"This is disgusting and I have no idea what it has to do with me. Let
him go, now, cover him up."

Joseph's eyes widened but it was too late to duck. From behind,
Lucien slapped Kruse in the right ear. The dull pain in his head, from
the electric shock, blew away. He was accustomed to being hit, but he
had always been prepared; Tzvi felt it was more important to take a
strike with dignity than to deliver one with precision.

Kruse went down on one knee and remained so until he could hear
again, and prepared for the next blow. It did not come.

"I do apologize." Joseph spoke quietly and evenly. He helped Kruse
into one of the chairs and sat in the other.

He knew their weight, their weapons and potential weaknesses, their
access to communications equipment, and he could deduce from the
slap and from Lucien's overall air of confidence that he was skilled, if
not an expert, in close combat. There was one escape route: the way he
had come in.

Though he did not understand the language they spoke between
themselves—Corsican, evidently—Kruse could tell Joseph was now
asking his brother to bring something. He did not speak again until it
arrived: a bottle of pastis, a pitcher of water, some ice, and two long,
skinny glasses. "Will you join me?"

Kruse shook his head.

The cathedral bell clanged once and echoed in the apartment. It revived the naked man somewhat, and he struggled in the only way he could, by twisting his torso. Each torque obviously brought great pain to his mangled feet, and his eyes watered with it. Through the white fabric in his mouth, the naked man cried out and wept.

"Will you turn on some music?" Joseph called out. He asked what Kruse preferred, what genre. "We have everything."

"Who is he?"

"How about one of these new bands from Seattle everyone is talking about?" He clapped and growled an approximation of the lyrics to the song that had lived on the radio and on passing car stereos for the last six or eight months. Again he looked at Frédéric and closed his eyes for a moment. "Old friend."

Frédéric shook his head, said something behind the tape.

"How long have you been a professor, Christopher?"

Kruse was incapable of answering, so Joseph called out to Lucien again, this time in Corsican. A violin and piano concerto began to play, at first quietly. It was not in any of the music appreciation courses and it wasn't in Evelyn's collection, so Kruse didn't recognize it. It was pretty and old. If he had to guess: Vivaldi.

"Louder," said Joseph. "Please."

"Who is he?"

"We're in a bit of a spot, Lucien and I, our enterprise. It's our own fault, a spot of rotten luck, and it involves you, I'm afraid. Your wife. I want you to know, sincerely, what you see before you is not my preference. Lucien, well, he has research interests." Joseph poured an ounce of pastis in each glass and filled them with water. He held one of the glasses before Kruse, and the smell of licorice was both nauseating and delicious.

No.

Joseph shrugged and took a long drink himself. "We're generally a careful operation. My father was a conservative man but we lost him. We took a risk, Christopher, and acted carelessly. The young man before you was part of that carelessness. It was not his fault, not entirely. Some of it was just awful timing, like the death of your daughter. Other bits: careless talk outside our small circle, which we cannot afford. I've known him, this man before you, since I was a teenager. We were working together, the night your poor daughter died. I'm desperately sorry about that, and for this." Joseph lifted his glass in salute to Frédéric. "He knows how sorry I am, about all of this, and how sentimental. *Santé, mon ami.*"

"How could you do this?"

"You're a literary man." Joseph was nearly finished the glass of pastis and water. "Enter my heart."

Small white speakers were attached to the ceiling in the four corners of the room. The music rose slowly.

"If I can convince you to tell us where she is, what you know about where Evelyn might be, so much of this—all of it—will go away."

"What do you want with her?"

Joseph pointed at him. "I mean this sincerely: the less you know about that, the better. All that concerns you, Christopher, is that we most desperately need to talk to your beautiful, frustrating wife."

"*Putain.*" Lucien's first word, delivered like a man suffering the worst cold of his life: whore.

"Easy, brother." Joseph closed his eyes, in meditation. Kruse was nearly through the second layer of rope and tasted what he would do to the beast in the kitchen. *Putain.* Say it again.

"You asked about his nose. Well, when we were young, just out of school, Lucien was the most handsome man in Marseille. A good student, an athlete, a public speaker. Next to him, well, what could a boy like me do?"

The prisoner, Frédéric, fixed his gaze on Kruse and settled it there. His eyes were red and sore, with what looked like wet tea bags below them. He had been here many hours, and sleep had not come.

"Everyone thought he was a . . . how do you say this in English? A cocksman."

Joseph took a deep breath and finished his drink. His mastery had faded.

"But they were wrong. He wasn't like that at all."

Lucien re-entered the salon with a folded wooden card table. He calmly set it up half a metre before the naked man and wiped it with a damp cloth. Then he walked into the kitchen, and returned with the stainless steel medical tray. Knives and other implements, all of them silver and clean, slid and screeched and chinked against one another. He tsked and rearranged them. Lucien opened a closet Kruse had not noticed, and pulled down a set of new white coveralls, the sort men wear to remove asbestos from old office towers, and matching booties that recalled Lily's down-filled slippers from Mountain Equipment Co-op.

Joseph picked up his slender glass, refilled it, and stood. "I hope you don't mind but . . . I'll have to wait in the next room for this part."

"You'll wait here, Joseph." Lucien's accent was French yet also some-how German, and intensely nasal.

"I can't."

"Sit down."

"Lucien, please."

The noseless man looked at Kruse and back to Joseph. "Sit."

Joseph did as he was told. "He's the oldest, Lucien. He wanted to be a doctor. He didn't even care that he was the most handsome man in Marseille. He volunteered at an animal shelter when he was a teenager. Can you believe it?"

"I don't care about you and I don't care about Lucien and I don't care about this awful . . . thing you're doing. Just tell me why you're hunt-ing my wife."

The naked man hooted in triumph and spit out a wad of fabric he had been working on. His top lip sneaked up from the tape.

"Help me," he said, in French. "They'll do this to her."

"Why?" Kruse stood up.

Lucien picked the cotton off the floor.

"She saw us. Tell Evelyn . . ." the man managed, with emphasis on the final syllable: *Eveline.*

Calmly, in time with the violin music, Lucien balled up the cotton and shoved it back into the naked man's mouth. He plugged his nose and the man stopped trying to speak, desperate to suck enough air in around the fabric. From the pocket of his coveralls Lucien produced a half-roll of duct tape, and it squelched as he wound it twice around the prisoner's mouth. Overpowered, Frédéric went limp. His chest heaved as he sobbed.

A door opened behind them and new wind rushed into the apartment.

Kruse turned to see who had entered but no one was there. The door, the actual door, had not opened at all: neither Lucien nor Joseph had noticed. But something had opened: a seeming door.

Lucien selected an industrial-size vegetable peeler, which belonged in the kitchen of a well-compensated chef.

"Wait." Kruse cut through another bit of rope.

With his left hand, Lucien grasped the prisoner's neck. He screamed but they could not hear. Lucien placed the peeler against the naked man's collarbone and apologized and said, "I love you, Frédéric," and in a sure motion pulled straight down. The skin came away like the outer layer of an eggplant.

Joseph twitched but said nothing. His right leg was crossed over the left. He gulped his pastis. A coil of skin and blood gathered on the sheet of transparent plastic. The prisoner hummed something. When the second glass was empty, Joseph refilled it. He placed a hand in his hair, which was thinning on top.

"His nose—our father did it."

"Why?"

"Shut up, Joseph."

"A tiny betrayal, the smallest thing. Lucien complained of our father to one of his associates. He had made a few mistakes, our father, errors in strategy. It's a changing business and Papa wasn't changing quickly enough, for Lucien's taste. Lucien told this man, his name isn't important, that he wasn't sure if our father was the man he once was. How old was Papa then? In his mid-fifties, I suppose. It got back to him, this conversation, and he had Lucien picked up. Papa brought him here, to this very room."

"Shut up. Now."

"It's not so different from poor Frédéric's error. He spoke to one of our associates about the night your Lily died and the politician and his wife. It's a delicate situation. You see—"

Lucien turned and pointed the peeler at his brother. "Stop."

Joseph lifted both hands.

As he peeled the man's skin away in even strips, Lucien spoke. His voice aroused sympathy, or would have. That sad man, whose nose does not work. That sad man from Marseille who was once handsome, whose cruel father ruined him.

"They were ingenious punishers, the Romans who built your town, Professor Kruse. If you betrayed Emperor Tiberius, for example, he would have your urethra tied shut. Then you would sit down with him, like you and Joseph are doing now, civilized—or is this mock-civilized, Professor? What would your John Keats say?—and you would drink wine. A lot of wine. The emperor would drink with you, if you were close. You were usually close. Brothers. Best friends. Father and son. We read about lions tearing prisoners apart, and gang rapes in the coliseum, but that was really for entertainment. Imagine you're drunk and you have to piss more than ever in your life. But you can't. Pressure builds, you see."

Lucien worked like an unhurried cook making, for the thousandth time, his signature dish. The associate, Frédéric, the old friend, ceased to ratchet his body away from the peeler and the knives, as Lucien approached with them. Frédéric closed his eyes and, Kruse hoped, he prayed.

"The ancient Persians liked to throw men into the ashes. What they would do, the princes, for the most special betrayers, is lower them tenderly into a room with five downy centimetres of ash on the floor."

Kruse had forgotten he had told them he was a professor. He knew nothing of Keats but "Beauty is truth, truth beauty," and another bit Evelyn had on a poster in her office: "I am certain of nothing but the holiness of the heart's affections, and the truth of imagination."

Joseph had begun to sway, just faintly, in his chair.

"Do you see why?"

"Why what?"

"Why ash, Professor?"

A week before his daughter's death Kruse had taken her into the small cheese shop on Rue Raspail, a dark street just off Place Montfort where the water drains during a rainstorm. They entered through the beaded door. He was not French, so he did not need an encyclopedic knowledge of unpasteurized cheeses and their appellations to qualify as a gentleman. The *fromagère* asked Lily what she might like. Something simple and mild, like comté? Kids love comté, the yellow cheddar of France. Lily looked at the world of cheeses in the display case and pointed to one covered in a thin layer of reddish-brown ash, a cendré, from Burgundy.

Cendré. Cinderella. Cendrillon.

Lucien removed the duct tape and the white fabric from the mouth of his friend and associate, and pulled his bottom lip away from his face. He sliced through it and then worked on the other. He cut off the man's eyelids.

It was sixty francs, the little round of cendré, and it tasted like sour milk tossed in sand. The horse stable smelled for three days. Neither Kruse nor Evelyn could eat more than a sliver, but by the third night Lily had finished it.

"You really liked the cendré." Evelyn had not been shy about her own feelings for the cheese.

"No," said Lily. "I hated it."

Lucien stepped back, as though he wanted perspective on the paint he had splashed on a canvas. He unzipped his coveralls, pulled off his bloody booties and his gloves, and left them on the plastic. Now he appreciated it, like a painting in the Louvre.

"The prisoner would stand, Professor, as long as he could. But eventually, without food and water, he would grow weary and collapse. He would breathe in the ash. First a little and then a lot."

Kruse had been comforted by the idea that the man had died of shock and loss of blood. Now the blood beast jolted and hacked. His dripping chest heaved. He spoke, or tried to speak, without a tongue.

"Kill him. Please."

"Here is what I find fascinating, Professor Kruse." Lucien pulled a handkerchief from his pocket and touched his snuffling little nose. "Societies that developed in perfect isolation from one another, oceans and forests and great mountain ranges apart, had often devised the same ways to make a man suffer, to humiliate him in front of his community and—really the only justification for torture your Keats would support—to deter others from following his example. Lubricated stakes of wood, for example, rammed into a man's anus in the middle of a public square. This is universal. Skinning, of course."

The mutilated body before them, shivering in the cool of the apartment, had begun to smell.

"Kill him."

Joseph sighed and turned back to the remains of the prisoner. He poured the last of the pastis into his glass and did not bother topping it with water. The smell of licorice, from the bottle, was merciful now.

Lucien turned on the faucet in the kitchen and washed his hands. "Where is your wife?"

"I don't know."

"You have received no correspondence?"

"None."

"Our men who searched your little house—Russians, former Soviets, very troubled—they found nothing. I am inclined, and you are fortunate in this, to believe you. We've been watching and waiting, just as you have been. If Madame does contact you, and you don't contact us immediately, with what you have learned, then . . . then I will get creative with you too, Professor Kruse."

"Why Evelyn?"

"We want what you want: to find her and keep her safe."

"The world," said Joseph, "is complex."

"Professor, what did she tell you?" Lucien allowed his hands to drip into the sink. "On the night your daughter died? She saw two men drinking with Monsieur de Musset."

Kruse shook his head. Two men, one with long hair. The tips of Frédéric's long hair were sticky with blood.

"She went out alone some hours later. Up the hill, yes? Did she come back, even briefly? Tell you what she had seen? Did she send you a note?"

"No. What did she see?"

Lucien removed his hands from the sink and turned off the faucet with his elbow. He dried his hands as a doctor would. "What did you tell the gendarme?"

"Which one?"

"Huard."

"I told him what I've told you."

"You don't know where she is. This is the truth?"

"Yes."

"How did you know to look for us?"

"In Paris . . ."

"The hotelier. Yes. Listen to me, Monsieur Kruse. We want to help your wife, help you. She needs professional guidance and protection."

"What did she see?" He spoke to keep them speaking. Kruse sliced through the last of the rope around his wrists. The tray of instruments was only a metre away. There was a scalpel in there and something smaller. If you know how to use a knife, you want it to be small. If it is an extension of your hand, the enemy will not easily take it from you.

The prisoner gurgled and grunted before them. Bells rang in the square. It was eight or nine or ten.

"This woman in Paris, the one from *Le Monde*, she spoke to Evelyn."

"Yes."

"And what did Evelyn tell her?"

"That the story in her newspaper had been full of lies. She was innocent."

"Hardly innocent, Monsieur Kruse. I do worry for their safety, Madame Laferrière and her daughter. What is her name? Anouk. A tidy one-bedroom apartment on the sixth floor on Rue Santeuil. I worry, you see, because the larger this becomes, the more difficult it will be to contain. My brother and I, at the moment we are in the containment business. Do you understand?"

Kruse did not understand how this man, how men like him, slept at night. This is what had always confounded his parents, when they were exposed to old stories of ruined Mennonites or the Holocaust or shootings in Toronto. How did it work? How did the human heart allow such abomination?

"What will you do now, Monsieur Kruse?"

"Look for my wife."

"And if you find her?"

"Take her home and start again." It was not too late. They could have another baby, another girl on Foxbar Road. "That's all I want."

"We will help you."

With Lucien, it would take four to eight seconds. Joseph, gently weaving, two seconds or three.

Lucien returned from the kitchen. Now he had the Glock. He helped Joseph up out of his chair and together they stood before Kruse, looking not at him but at the prisoner. It would be as simple as his mother's favourite waltz: take the scalpel from the tray and cut Lucien's wrist and throat. One-two-three. Violin music continued to play from the little speakers. Order. Beauty. Courage. To the gun, to the interrogation of Joseph, to the end of them both. For the rest of his life he would consider his hesitations in Vaison-la-Romaine and in Marseille as he fell asleep at night. One-two-three. He feared the gun but knew he need not fear the gun; by the time Lucien raised his arm, his wrist would be cut and his throat would be cut.

"I wanted to be a surgeon, when I was a young man." Lucien said this in English, in a more posh tone than his French, as though he were pretending. Or perhaps now he was not pretending. "When I was being educated in London."

Kruse watched him, to see which it was.

"My brother is going to give you a phone number, Professor Kruse."

Joseph returned to his chair. His eyes were covered in a film of moisture. His hands trembled. "My personal number, Christopher. Call any time." He reached into his jacket pocket and pulled from it a small white card. "If you find Evelyn or she finds you, later today or tomorrow or five years from now, you will call me. And if you don't, well, maybe we won't be such good friends anymore, sharing a jolly drink like this."

"The note in the library?"

"I am an amateur calligraphist." Joseph reached toward Kruse with the card. He dropped it on Kruse's lap. "Can Lucien fix you something else? There's a bottle of rosé. Likely some . . . cheese in the fridge. You can cut your own bonds, I trust."

"Don't hurt her."

"What?"

"If you find Evelyn, don't hurt her."

Joseph looked at his brother and back at Kruse. There was something, a secret or a confession. He said nothing.

"If you hurt her, Monsieur Mariani . . ."

"Joseph, please."

"I'll kill you."

Joseph watched Kruse for some time, weaving gently, as his noseless but vain brother prepared himself for departure in front of a full-length mirror in the WC.

"I'll kill you, Joseph. I'll kill you all."

The Mariani brothers walked out of the apartment together, Lucien helping his brother down the stairs. It took some time. Kruse crossed to the window and looked down, watched them walk up the street in the morning sun. They scared some white birds, which flew up in front of them and perched on a nearby roof.

He breathed quickly, the skinless man, like a small child who has finished a long and unexpected run. Kruse chose the scalpel and sliced the exposed carotid artery of the skinless man in one motion. A quick burst of his blood splashed on Kruse's jacket, and then the rest of it pumped and flowed down the mutilated body, down the mess of leg, and onto the floor.

It was the smell of a butcher's shop. Kruse walked down and out, to the opposite end of Rue de la Cathédrale. There it was, the great grey candy-cane church and the port. He felt the way he had felt after Lily was killed: it was obscene and ridiculous that all these people could keep walking, on their way to work or to a café, these teenagers with guidebooks and cameras, taxi drivers, lovers, dog walkers, fishermen. That a river could keep flowing. It was warm enough up the street, in Place de Lenche, away from the wind, that men and women in suits and dresses and sunglasses sat on the terraces of the square under green parasols in the dawn light, talking about the weather and moving their espresso cups about their tables.

Such a fine season here. Everyone said so.

Kruse climbed a set of stairs, randomly, past yellow buildings and around soft corners, on his way nowhere. He checked his wallet, to see what Joseph had taken, and it appeared he had taken nothing. Everything was as it had been. To sit at a terrace, to be a regular man for an hour, a husband, a father in a shirt someone who loved him had bought for his birthday, talking about the weather. He walked up the skinny maze of a road, past the garbage and graffiti. Children wept and a man shouted from an open window. Then the street opened up and there was another fountain. It was always a relief from some vague torment, seeing a fountain. He had said it in English: I'll kill you both. I'll kill you all. Kruse excused himself and sneaked in among the children dipping their fingers. He splashed water on his face and they backed away, laughed at him. He removed his blood-splattered jacket and dropped it in a garbage can. Two hobos sat under a plane tree, not yet clipped for the winter, sharing a bottle for breakfast. One of them struggled to his feet and pulled Kruse's jacket out of the garbage, wiped it off, put it on, and returned to his wine.

• • •

He took a taxi from the train station in Orange to the gendarmerie in Vaison-la-Romaine. The driver was an unusually fat man from Nyons, where the olive oil is the best in the world. "This is a secret the Italians do not want revealed to the world: the microclimate in Nyons, Monsieur, is a kind of sorcery." If you are an olive tree, that is. If you are a fat man in a taxi, without air conditioning, it is a different sort of thing. The driver played tour guide, explaining each village as they passed it in the sunshine. "A tip, Monsieur: if you want a spectacular wine, make it a Gigondas. Half the price of Châteauneuf-du-Pape and just as good. Better for my taste, Monsieur. And *regardez*: the Dentelles de Montmirail." A mountain of lace.

The rocky tip looked, to Kruse, like an upside-down waterfall. This

was not the sort of beauty Evelyn had prescribed. It would not transform him from a man of violence into a man of culture, this mountain
peak or that perched village, any more than strolling through the October leaves of a Southern Ontario forest would fix him. He was nostalgic
for old anxieties about saving his marriage, about being the sort of man
Evelyn could be proud of, the right sort of dad, everything that had
devilled him. From the taxi, with the smell of skin and blood in his
nose and in his mouth, he longed for the simplicity of a divorce ultimatum, the image of another man fucking his wife, co-parenting, tension
and awkwardness and too much champagne at his daughter's wedding.

Lieutenant Huard was twenty minutes from the end of his workday,
eight to four, when Kruse arrived at the gendarmerie. He sat in his
cracked leather chair, tidying his desk, as Kruse spoke. Then he shook
his head. Impossible.

"Why, Monsieur Kruse, would this man with no nose kill Pascale
and Jean-François?"

"Lucien Mariani."

"So you say."

"You're the investigator."

"I've been removed from this file."

"Why?"

"Don't play-act for me, Monsieur Kruse. I know what you are now. I
looked you up. You're in the system. You're some sort of, what, agent?
Of something?"

"You asked if I thought people were looking for my wife. Yes, people are
looking for my wife. Their names are Joseph and Lucien Mariani. They
confessed to hiring Russian thugs to break into my house and toss everything on the floor, the same men who attacked me in Paris. They know
about the photocopy I sent you yesterday. How could they know that?"

"They couldn't know that. There's no way . . ."

"But they did, Monsieur. And they just skinned a man, their childhood friend, in an apartment in Marseille."

Huard tilted his head, as though he were eavesdropping on another conversation. He lifted his hand, for Kruse to stop. Then he said, a bit dreamily, "Who skinned a man? Your Russian thugs?"

"Lucien Mariani."

Huard reacted to the word "Mariani" as though it were the sting of a small but determined bug. He refused to say the word himself. "But these men have hundreds of employees, family members. Why would they hire Russians? Did they tell you why they're looking for Madame Kruse?"

"They said they want to protect her."

"From what?"

"They weren't telling the truth, Monsieur Huard."

"This man they . . . skinned?"

"Yes."

"Again: Why?"

"He was with them, I suppose, the night they killed Jean-François and Pascale. He said something he should not have said, to someone. They're in the containment business."

"What does that mean?"

"Aren't you going to write any of this down?" Kruse opened his shirt and displayed the burn marks on his chest, from the electric baton.

"I'm done for the day. And as I told you, this is not my file. I'm investigating a shipment of illegally imported truffles."

"Let me take you to the apartment in Marseille. You'll see for yourself."

"Perhaps you didn't understand, Monsieur Kruse. Come back tomorrow morning. My commander—"

Kruse slammed the door behind him. "Did you order an autopsy of Jean-François and Pascale?"

"They were murdered by your wife."

"Did you?"

Huard's breathing had sped up and his neck was pink. He looked over Kruse's shoulder and spoke softly. "I requested one, yes."

"And?"

He slammed his palms on his desk and stood up. "Get out of my office."

"No."

Two other gendarmes, Madame Boutet and a slightly cross-eyed man in his twenties, in a uniform, knocked on the door and entered. Madame Boutet nodded at Kruse and addressed Huard. "Everything all right?"

"Have this man removed."

Kruse stood up. "That's all right, Monsieur Huard. I'm terribly sorry to have bothered you. I'll tell Madame my story, and—"

"What story?"

"All right, *fils de salope*. We'll go."

Madame Boutet looked at Kruse. "Go where?"

"Nowhere!" said Huard. "Disneyland."

She half-smiled and closed the door. Lieutenant Huard stared at Kruse and picked up his telephone receiver. "Where in Marseille, god-damn you?"

• • •

Men and women sat in Place de Lenche, in shorts and T-shirts and sweatsuits, and shouted at each other under cheap branded awnings. It was cool yet no one wore a scarf in Marseille. Adults dressed and drank like teenagers. This city and Paris had very little in common.

On skinny Rue de la Cathédrale, men slumped on white plastic chairs outside apartment doors. The play-by-play of a soccer match— l'Olympique de Marseille against tonight's enemy—burst from fat little television sets and radios. There was no menace in the way the men watched them as they passed but they did watch, and when Kruse turned around to see if they were still watching, they were still watching.

A large, black-and-grey-bearded policeman was waiting for them at number twelve, and Huard shook his hand. He didn't introduce Kruse, and the bearded Marseillais didn't inquire. Instead he pulled deeply on his cigarette, tossed it on the ground, and pressed a button on the intercom. The street had seemed longer in the early morning, when his hands were bound and Joseph was talking. It was just a narrow corridor between Place de Lenche and the cathedral, whose towers were visible in the greying sky. How had he missed them?

Kruse asked Huard why so many people watched them, and the gendarme turned around, looked about him. Then he cupped his hands around his mouth. "Watch us! Please!"

A voice came through the intercom and the cop said, "Police." The door sang and he shoved it open. Huard followed the Marseillais and Kruse followed him.

"Up the stairs, you said?"

Kruse was not keen to see the body again, or to smell it. "Yes."

There were three doors. Kruse pointed to the white one and the big policeman knocked. He identified himself, gruffly, as Marseille police and knocked again. He tried the door handle. "Did you lock it when you left, Monsieur Kruse?"

"No."

The Marseillais turned to them and spoke sincerely, formally. "I have reason to believe, gentlemen, that someone is in danger inside."

Huard pulled his gun. "Noted and agreed."

Despite their air of confidence, both of them looked around—up the stairs and down—to see if anyone in the building was peeking out their doors. The bearded man kicked twice, next to the door handle, but lifting his leg that high was not easy. Despite his girth, there wasn't much power behind his kicks. He stepped aside for Huard to do it and Huard pointed his gun.

"No, no, no. This is my paperwork, not yours." The Marseillais looked at Kruse, from his feet to his eyes. "All right, my American friend."

One kick and the door opened with a slam. The scent of a swimming pool passed into the hall as the door swung open. The Wallace Emerson Centre, Lily in a life jacket, *kick your legs, kick your legs.* The bearded policeman led the way, his gun drawn, identifying himself to anyone who might be inside. Huard pushed Kruse into the apartment and walked backwards, scanning the stairwell. Everything in the kitchen had been shined. The smell was biting now, and painful, as though someone had dumped several bottles of chlorine on the floor. The Marseillais walked into the T and turned left, right. Then he walked to the window, open to the street, and looked out. "Does anyone need a cigarette?"

"It was here, in this corner." Kruse stood where the prisoner had been. There was no trace of him or the contraption, not even a speck of blood between the floorboards.

"I had this fantasy," said the Marseillais. "Joseph and Lucien Mariani would be in here, covered in blood, alone and unarmed, with the dead body of one of their associates. I'd be mysteriously fired for misconduct but also elected mayor."

Huard checked the shower room where Lucien had preened. The cupboards were empty in the kitchen, but for four skinny pastis glasses. The fridge was clean inside and out.

"When my wife finally rejects me I might just move in here. It's a hell of a location." The bearded man looked out the window again. "Are you sure you didn't dream all of this, Monsieur?"

Without any rumbles or even changes in pressure, it began to rain. Outside, some people laughed and jogged. Their soles clapped the cobblestones. "Your forensic team, I'm sure, could find something."

"When Yves—our Lieutenant Huard—phoned me, I laughed, you know. There are hundreds of men working for Joseph and Lucien Mariani, directly and indirectly. Why, if any of this were true, would the Mariani brothers be personally involved? Maybe we should get a drink."

Huard sat at the kitchen table and stared at the wall. The rain intensified and the smell of it was pleasant, on the other side of the bleach. Kruse went down on one knee, to inspect the meeting place between floor and wall. "There's nothing you can do?"

The Marseillais finally lit his cigarette. "I was after Paul Mariani for twenty years, Monsieur Kruse. Any time I came close, he would throw some kid at me. The kid would confess to everything and serve two or three years and come out of prison harder. Soon he'd be a boss. These men don't make mistakes. And when they do, honestly, someone very powerful in Paris will make a phone call and something will be arranged to suit everyone."

"They did make a mistake. That's why they're chasing my wife."

"Why didn't they skin you too?"

"I don't know anything. And I could help them, lead them to her."

Huard tapped on the table and spoke with the soft voice he had used in his office. A voice of defeat. "Go home, Monsieur Kruse."

"You're driving."

"Back to America."

"When I find her I'll go back. When I figure out what happened Halloween night. When I find . . ."

"I will admit these men are vicious," said the Marseillais. "I do believe you saw something up here. But you can't stop them. All of the police forces in the world, working together like the Monteverdi Choir, could not stop them. As long as we want drugs and whores, Monsieur Kruse, gangsters will live and thrive."

"And the Front National? They hired or they're working with mobsters to find and exterminate my wife. Why? If she murdered Jean-François and Pascale, why wouldn't they simply allow you, you two, to find her and throw her in some horror show of a prison? It's proof, all of this, that she's innocent. If not proof, it will lead to proof."

The Marseillais looked at Huard.

"There was an accident and your darling daughter died." The lieutenant spoke so quietly now it was difficult to hear him. "The man driving the car was no Mariani. In fact, he's dead. This is, really, better justice than either of us could manufacture for you. You are still alive, Monsieur Kruse. You're young."

"We can't help you," said the Marseillais. "We're not even permitted."

"They're going to kill my wife."

"You know what I think happened?"

"What, Monsieur Huard?"

The lieutenant didn't answer for some time. It was as though he were studying the tabletop. "I think you failed her, your daughter. Lily."

Kruse looked down to the street again, the rain falling and hopping on the cobblestones.

"You should have been with her. You should have been carrying your little girl, Monsieur Kruse, or holding her hand, standing close to her. Close enough to lift her away. How old was she? Four? Not even four?"

Kruse pushed a loose nail into windowsill. It stopped halfway so he pressed harder.

"You didn't protect your daughter and now she is gone. This is the only truth."

He pushed the nail until his right thumb burst and bled. For the first time all day, his chest was not burning. He shivered, though it was not cold enough for that.

"This idea, that gangsters or the Front National want to find and murder your wife . . ."

"Don't forget the Jews and the Freemasons." The bearded Marseillais finished his cigarette and tossed it out the window. "They also hate little girls and like to chase innocent American women all over France. Who wants a drink?"

"Drive me home."

"This is what I'm telling you. Vaison-la-Romaine is not your home,

Monsieur Kruse. You can either live in regret or you can live. Believe me . . ."

Kruse walked out of the apartment and ignored Lieutenant Huard, who called down the stairs and out to the street. He called him "Christophe." The rain had stopped. It was cooler now but men sat out on lopsided Rue de la Cathédrale anyway, with blankets on their laps, to drink together and listen to the soccer match. The game was in Paris.

At the train station Kruse bought a ticket home. Then he apologized to the woman behind the counter and gave her another four hundred francs. If the game was in Paris he would go all the way.

NINE

Allée des Vergers, Roissy-en-France

KRUSE HAD PAID THE MONTHLY BILL FOR MATT GIBENUS, ANONY-
mously, at the long-term care facility in Vaughan, Ontario. Once every few weeks he would drive out and volunteer to be a buddy—as one of Matt's old friends. He was the only old friend who visited, which charmed the nurses. Each time, Kruse had to reintroduce himself to the grown-up Zen toddler. Unlike other brain-injured residents in the facility, Matt had become a simple and contented man. Kruse would push the wheelchair through the indoor courtyard garden or read passages from what had become Matt's favourite book: *Stuart Little.*

The airplane to Marseille had been due to leave at midnight, so their last day in Toronto was a full day. Officially Evelyn hated packing but she didn't trust anyone else to do it. She was anxious and irritable and could not abide the sounds of dollhouse, hide-and-seek, and hands-and-knees tag, a painful game for daddies on hardwood floors. It was a rainy day so they could not play in the yard. The natural choice would have been to go to the studio, but they had already said goodbye

to Tzvi. So Kruse put Lily in her booster seat, picked up a couple of
au revoir McDonald's hamburgers, and drove out to Vaughan. Lily,
too, liked the sound of an E.B. White story about a polite and well-
dressed mouse. The rain was monsoon-strength in the suburbs, so they
sat together, the three of them, in the too-bright common room of the
facility. The off-white tile floors had just been washed. All the world
smells like the swimming pool, when it is clean. Matt, uncharacteristi-
cally, lacked the patience for a reading. A television had been bracketed
to the corner, and a few of the other patients sat drowsily watching it;
the final moments of *The Price Is Right* was on.

Lily watched Bob Barker.

Matt watched Lily. He pointed. "What's wrong with that girl's face?"

This happened rarely, as the scar became less noticeable with every
surgery, every passing month. She looked to Kruse.

"Nothing's wrong with her face, Matt. Her face is perfect. She's perfect."

Matt turned to Kruse and held his gaze—the wise one.

"We're moving to France. We came to say goodbye."

"Have a nice day," Matt said, slowly and carefully, but what Kruse
heard was *You should have killed me.*

He arrived in Paris before dawn and walked across the river to Jardin
des Plantes. It had rained before he arrived. The gardens smelled of
wet soil and decomposing leaves. Evergreens and holly glistened and
dripped in the spotlights. Winter was preparing itself. He found a dry
bench next to the natural history museum and lay there for an hour,
waiting for sunrise and watching for watchers. Lily woke at six thirty
in the morning no matter what time she went to bed, seven o'clock or
midnight. In his calculations of guilt, he went back to this at least once
a day: if they had left Villedieu on time Halloween night, for her sake,
she would be waking up for school at this hour. If he was not at the
bakery he would make breakfast for her, oatmeal or cereal or, if there
was enough time, pancakes. Maybe, if Evelyn was still asleep, he would

turn on the television so she could watch a few cartoons. Evelyn did not approve of cartoons. They were either violent, like *The Bugs Bunny Show*, or vapid. On nights she did go to bed late, Lily would wake up the next morning helplessly emotional. It would start with giggling fits and end with weeping or temper tantrums. And it was never her fault.

At seven o'clock Kruse hopped the fence and took the long route to the unlovely building on Rue Santeuil. He stopped at a bakery and bought a paper bag full of warm pain au chocolat. No one had followed him, not from Gare de Lyon to the gardens and not from the gardens to her building. He pressed her button and pressed it again, and two minutes later he pressed it again.

"Yes?" Sleepy and frightened. "Hello?"

He identified himself and she said nothing in response. After a long while the door buzzed open.

"Apartment 631, Monsieur Kruse."

The unpainted concrete stairwell smelled of cooked vegetables. At her door he knocked quietly and heard nothing in response. Anouk was evidently not like Lily. Kruse did not like opening the door himself, as it exposed him, but he did it and she stood in the middle of a dim rectangular room with her hands behind her back. She wore jeans and a long white T-shirt with a rendering of Johnny Hallyday, the French Elvis, on a motorcycle—her bed shirt. Her eyes were dark from sleep and her thick black hair was wound up. Her expression carried none of what he had left her with, a bit drunk, after their evening in the Café Delmas. Her feet were planted with care. She breathed quickly.

"Can I come in, Madame Laferrière?" He put the paper bag down next to the door and spoke just above a whisper.

"Why?"

"Let me come in and I'll tell you."

"Close the door then."

He stepped in and closed the door behind him, and then she showed the knife—a large butcher knife.

"I'm not afraid to use this, if you . . ."

"Yes, you are, Madame." He lifted his hands. "I came because some men—"

"What men? Those Russians?"

"No. Well, yes, they're part of the same group. What's happened?"

Her voice quivered and the knife quivered with it. "They've been following me. Us. They waited for me outside the office and asked about you. They wanted to know what you had told me. Then, the next day, they were at Anouk's school. Just standing there and staring at us, at my daughter, just smoking and saying nothing. But I knew what they were saying. These are pitiless men, men without hearts. There is normal life, yes, the way most of us live, and then there is this. This is the advantage men like them have over the rest of us. They feel nothing. It was the same in Bordeaux."

The little girl, in mismatched flannel pyjamas—red with pandas on the bottom, white with floating pink *Je t'aimes* on the top—padded out of the dark bedroom. With eyes still tiny with sleep, adjusting to the light, she looked at her mother and looked at Kruse.

It had been controversial in their house, but Kruse had always paid special attention to first times with Lily. Her mind was tuned to obsession. If her first time in a home or on a bicycle or with a babysitter was difficult or spooky, Lily would lie in the darkness of her bedroom and brood on it, populate the memory with demons.

He knew nothing of Annette's relationship with her daughter, or the girl's personality, but he was not inclined to underestimate a four-year-old. The girl read the fear, the agitation, the crisis on her mother's face: first the Russians and now this man. Anouk, in that instant, received it. Her own breathing changed. She opened her mouth and furrowed her brow, first in confusion. Her mother's face, the big knife pointed and shaking at the stranger with the long scars on his cheek, their cozy home invaded at dawn. Annette did not move. She looked at her daughter and for a long moment said nothing. Available lies floated through the room: the man was a knife sharpener, the man had a loose thread on his jacket that needed cutting, the man wanted to slice a peach and some cheese for breakfast.

"Maman?"

Kruse knelt on the floor. "You must be Anouk."

The girl looked at him, at her mother, at Kruse again. He spoke with an accent. He smelled of outside, of the wet autumn garden, of weather and sleeplessness. Who had cut his face?

"Maman?"

"My name is Christophe. I help people." Without looking away from Anouk, he reached up for the knife. "I make breakfast for my friends. What would you like for breakfast?"

Annette hesitated and then handed over the knife.

"Can I chop up some onions for you?" Kruse pretended to chop. "Do you like onions for breakfast?"

Anouk looked up at her mother.

"Oh, I know. Maybe some garlic? I can chop up some garlic and cauliflower, if that is what you would like for breakfast. Cauliflower and garlic soup?"

"No, Monsieur."

"Beefsteak. Little girls love beefsteak for breakfast. Let me start cooking."

"No!"

Kruse reached up and slid the knife onto the counter. "Maybe you and I could go out together, onto the street, and catch a pigeon. I really love roasted pigeons for breakfast, with mustard. Don't you?"

Annette opened her arms to Anouk and whispered to her daughter, "*Dégoûtant, non?*"

"Disgusting, Monsieur!"

"Shh, Anouk. Our neighbours are sleeping."

"Anouk, I have one last idea. I hope you will like this one."

"Is it gross?"

"Yes. It is probably gross. It's pain au chocolat, just out of the oven. I can just throw it out the window, because it's disgusting. No problem. Let me just get the bag and throw it right out the window."

"No, no, no." Anouk wriggled and her mother released her. Kruse picked up the bag and held it low so Anouk could peek inside and smell. She looked up at him and smiled, then said to her mother, "Can I?"

"We usually have an egg and some yogurt for breakfast, Monsieur Kruse. But maybe, just this once."

"Just this once, Maman."

"Wash your hands, darling."

Anouk sprinted into the bathroom. The spirit of the girl remained in the small room: a sliver of a kitchen leading into a tidy salon with a couch, a chair, and a television. An IKEA bookshelf. They shared one bedroom, dark now with a closed shutter. With the light of the salon he could see the corner of an unmade bed and a box of toys. Annette smiled and then it faded.

"What are you doing here, Monsieur Kruse?"

The girl ran back into the room and stood before Kruse. "I'm ready."

At the kitchen counter, a bar stool with a back on it had been fitted with a booster seat. Kruse helped the girl up. She was heavier and more muscular than Lily had been. Her hair smelled of sleep. He held the bag open so she could choose one, sprinkled with icing sugar. Annette walked around to the other side of the island and lifted three small plates down. "Anouk, Monsieur Kruse and I are going to speak to each other for a few minutes in private. You eat your breakfast quietly, all right?"

"All right, Maman."

Annette led him to the other end of the little apartment and turned on the television, the news. "We'll whisper."

Kruse told her of his encounter with the Russians and of his morning in Marseille with Joseph and Lucien. He left out the skinning. "They didn't mention your name to be kind."

"It doesn't make sense. It's like the president of the republic sweeping shit from the sidewalks."

"The president might, if his mistress had put it there and he didn't want anyone to find out."

"What did they want to know, these Marianis? What you had told me?"

"Not really."

"So?"

"They wanted to threaten me, Madame."

"I don't understand."

"They wanted me to know Lucien Mariani will do anything, abominable things. My daughter is dead, my wife is lost, my only friends murdered. So they mentioned you."

Annette slipped a hand into her thick hair and some of it escaped from the elastic. She stood up and huffed and laughed sarcastically. "I never should have taken that call. I should know my place. I never should have spoken to her and I never should have pursued it. That goddamn hotelier, he never should have given you my card. And then you and I, in the café on a rainy night." Her voice jumped from a whisper to a shout. "If they touch her, come anywhere near her, it's your fault. You and your wife. You never should have . . ."

"Touch who, Maman?" Anouk had climbed down from her booster seat. There was an oval of icing sugar around her lips, flecked with melted chocolate.

"No one. Touch no one. Eat your breakfast."

"But I'm done."

Annette walked across the room, pulled another pain au chocolat out of the bag, and plopped it on her daughter's plate. Anouk looked up at Kruse. He winked.

"Milk?"

"I'll do it." Kruse jogged across the room to interrupt Annette and opened the fridge, which was full of cheeses and condiments that remained extravagant to him, and found the milk. In France, you didn't have to put milk in the fridge until the bottle was open. The glasses were in the cupboard next to the fridge and he filled an orange one halfway, a pleasure and an agony at once: half filling a glass of milk for a little girl.

"Monsieur?"

He had lingered, dreamily. "Yes." He slid the glass over the counter. "Excuse me."

"*Merci, Monsieur.*"

"*Je vous en prie, Mademoiselle.*"

Annette was back in front of the television. There was not enough room to pace, so she walked slowly in a repeatable semicircle. All news, in France, was political news. An affair, a scandal, a humiliating error. The Socialist government of François Mitterrand was not going out with dignity.

"Sit down, Madame Laferrière."

She looked up at him. "No."

"Then just listen. You're going to pack a bag for you and for Anouk, clothes and toiletries, maybe some books. Then you're going to come downstairs, where I'll be waiting for you in front of the building, in a car."

"You have a car?"

"Yes."

"And where are we going?"

"A hotel."

"Why?"

"Because it's safe."

"Our apartment isn't safe?"

"Not anymore, no. If they think I have any feelings for you and your daughter—"

"You have feelings for us?"

His face went hot. "Or if they think you have the story."

"What story?"

"I don't know yet. The Mariani family and the Front National, there is some relationship. Why are they cleaning shit from the sidewalk, instead of one of their minions? This is strange and significant, as you say. There is a reason, and it's an important enough reason to . . ."

"You've ruined my life. You've put my child in danger."

"And you can't go back to work. You'll have to phone, take a holiday."

"I can't just take a holiday."

"Just until I figure this out."

"You're going to figure this out? You're going to, what, dismantle the Mariani crime family? Dissolve the Front National? Why not also cure cancer and AIDS, end the war in Bosnia, feed the starving children of East Africa?"

"Pack a bag."

She stepped forward and shoved him, with tears in her eyes. She wound up to slap him and he allowed it.

"Be downstairs in ten minutes, Madame Laferrière. Please." He took a pain au chocolat from the bag and pulled a coat hanger down from the recessed closet at the door.

"*Au revoir, Monsieur Kruse! Merci encore!*"

• • •

It was not the best time of day to steal a car. The sun was up and kids were everywhere, little ones on their way to school with their parents, and university students with backpacks and pimples, mussed hair, walking quietly up Rue Santeuil to the Sorbonne. Kruse struggled to slow his heart rate, to rid his mind of it—of them. His left cheek throbbed from the slap. He cried for just a moment and laughed it away. Three blocks away from Annette's apartment he found a small pay parking lot and circled it, looking for the blandest, most forgettable car. He chose a beige and boxy Fiat, a Regata, tucked in behind a white microvan.

The door was easy enough, no alarm. Cars he had used for practice in Toronto had been Fords and Chevrolets, but a car was a car. He braced himself against the passenger door, kicked the steering column four times until the bottom panel cracked and fell away, pulled the wires down and stripped them with his fingernails. Tzvi would have beaten him by twenty seconds.

He pulled out of the lot, turned left and right, and moved slowly up Rue Santeuil. No one watched him until someone did, a man across the street in a long beige raincoat. The little girl's voice had been a pretty song: *Au revoir, Monsieur Kruse.* He imagined Lucien or the Russians capturing her, leading them to her, and his hands went cold. For a moment he watched the elevator, then the man across the street, then the elevator. The man wasn't a thug. He had an air of confidence about him, of contemplation: I know who you are and I know what you are doing.

Ten minutes had passed and several people had come down the elevator, but there was no sign of Annette and Anouk. It occurred to him that someone could be up there already, this man's partner, his team. They had followed him so slyly he had not seen or felt them. Kruse opened the door and walked across the street. At first the man didn't notice and then he did, and backed away so quickly Kruse thought he would fall.

"Who are you?"

Kruse took a handful of his jacket. The man turned to run. "Please. Help!" He fell to the ground and covered his head with his hands.

A small crowd had gathered.

"If you want money, take it," the man said, his voice muffled by the concrete of the Sorbonne sidewalk. He reached back into the pocket of his jacket, removed his wallet, and tossed it blindly into a puddle. "Take everything. Just don't hurt me."

Kruse turned. Annette and Anouk were in front of the building. A black suitcase sat before them. He fetched the wallet and helped the man up and spoke loudly, for the crowd. "I was robbed yesterday. I thought you were the robber."

There were tears in the man's eyes. He could barely speak.

"I am sorry, Monsieur."

"Yes," said the man, in a daze.

"I'm American. I don't mean to be rough."

The crowd dispersed and the man staggered a little, as though he were drunk. A scented woman with fresh lipstick crossed the street and broke into a run in her high heels, passed Kruse as he walked to the Fiat.

"Doors are open!" he called out, to Annette.

He turned around. The woman in heels grasped one of the man's arms as though he would fall off an embankment otherwise, and he stuttered and flailed his available arm as he recounted the story. Annette and Anouk were strapped in and they were around the corner, in the Fiat, before anyone could get his licence plate number. Annette stared at him. "What was that?"

"Nothing."

"I ate three pains au chocolat, Monsieur. Three!"

Kruse remembered he had left his own bread on top of the Fiat, as he broke into it. Annette pointed to the broken gearbox. "What happened?"

He shook his head.

"Where are we going?"

Kruse had been foolish in the apartment.

"What? You're not going to talk anymore?"

This was his first time driving in the core of a big city, in morning traffic, since May. Since Lily died and Evelyn left, his life in Toronto had become a detached and unbelievable thing, the life another man continued to lead. His memories and old rituals had become as foreign as the contents of Annette's fridge. At its most miserable, driving in Toronto was never like this. Twice he made physical contact with other

vehicles as they eased into half-lanes too small for two, a strong disin-
centive for spending 300,000 francs on a new German automobile. It
didn't matter how he reached the ring road, the Périphérique, as long
as he reached it. To simplify his route, and to escape notice, he had
chosen a hotel near Charles de Gaulle Airport, in the town of Roissy.
The French will cut you off and bump you from behind. No one will
ever let you in. But no one seems angry.

Annette and Anouk discussed Euro Disney, which had opened in an
eastern suburb of Paris shortly before Kruse and his family had arrived.
It had been an inescapable story, even for a girl Anouk's age, and since
she had only been in the suburbs of Paris once or twice before, the
autoroute signified the road to Disneyland. He tried not to listen but
he listened.

"We could go."

"Monsieur Kruse is taking us to a hotel. You will love living in a
hotel, flea."

"But Disneyland is more fun. It is for kids."

"We cannot go to Disneyland."

"Why not?"

"Because that is not where we are going."

"If we are going somewhere, Maman, why not there?"

"It is too far."

"This also is far. We have been in the car a long time. Monsieur
Kruse: Can we go to Disneyland?"

With every word, it would become more difficult. He would not
look at her in the mirror. He looked at her in the mirror. She wore a red
dress and shiny blue shoes with buckles, and her hair was in a ponytail.
On her lap, a wool jacket with white and black squares. Anouk was
dressed for dinner.

"Monsieur Kruse?"

"The Monsieur is concentrating on the road, Anouk. He cannot
speak to you now."

"Bus drivers can talk and drive at the same time. Monsieur Kruse? Why not Disneyland? Monsieur?"

The answer: I am forcing you to stay in your hotel room and it would drive you insane to stay in a hotel seven hundred metres from Disneyland. Kruse pretended not to hear the girl. They passed the Euro Disney sign, with its enormous arrow. Anouk shouted and pointed. All he wanted was to take that exit and follow the signs and buy them a three-day family pass and stay in some themed hotel, to forget all of this, to forget Evelyn because she was ashamed of him and didn't love him and he didn't know her, the murderer he married, not anymore if he ever did. There was one last Mickey and Minnie, the biggest sign of all. "*Ici ici,*" she begged. He stayed in the middle lane until it was gone. And Anouk quietly wept. Her mother crawled over the gearbox and into the back seat and held on to her.

Roissy-en-France, the actual town, was overwhelmed by the airport. He pulled into the parking lot of the Mercure, slightly better than the Fiat Regata of hotels. The cloud cover was like potato water over the charmless town but the lobby was clean and modern. A man in a red suit jacket greeted him, and Kruse asked to see the manager. The man replied haughtily. His "*Bien sûr, Monsieur,*" was best translated as "I am not good enough for you? You are not good enough for me."

A woman in a tight business suit, the same age as her desk clerk, walked out of a windowless inner office. They might have been married, the way a husband and wife come to look like each other: thin but soft, too many cigarettes, dry hair in a humid town.

"Madame, I do apologize for this intrusion."

"I am at your service."

"Perhaps you can tell by my accent: I am American."

"Very good, Monsieur."

"That may be good but this is not. Someone broke into my hotel room in Paris."

"Horrible. I am sorry."

"My wife and daughter are in a car a friend has loaned us. Our flight leaves in a week and we would like a room, a family room."

"Of course."

"But Madame I have no passport, at the moment, and no credit card. They are being sent to the American consulate."

"I see."

"Can we find a solution?"

"There is always a solution, Monsieur. If you can pay for the room in advance, and leave us a deposit of three thousand francs for incidentals, we can certainly find a way around the rules."

"Marvellous. Thank you."

"Your name, Monsieur?"

"Matt Gibenus. Mathieu, if you prefer."

• • •

The suite was enormous compared to anything in central Paris under five thousand francs a night: two rooms separated by a door. One room had two double beds and the other a sofa. The bathroom had an actual bathtub. Annette opened the curtains. The salon overlooked a small park and what appeared to be the old town hall. Anouk had recovered from the Disneyland tragedy, energized, as Lily always was, by the thrill of a hotel room. She climbed on one of the beds, with a white comforter, and bounced. "It's so fancy, Maman. Look! A trampoline."

"No bouncing." Annette spoke the way she had spoken in the newsroom, when her boss ordered her back to the desk. There was no fuel in it, no power. She looked out the window. "Be good, darling."

He might have assured Annette or encouraged her, touched her arm. Instead he looked into the bedroom, watched Anouk perform somersaults on the bed. Don't roll off. It's a long way to the floor.

"Annette."

"Yes?"

"You're registered as Carole Gibenus."

"Ridiculous."

"You stay in the room. Order from in here, whatever you like. When the food comes and they knock, ask them to leave it in the hall. They will. Wait three minutes before you open the door."

She turned to face him.

"Don't open the door without looking through the peephole. If you want the chambermaid to clean the room, you stay inside with Anouk while she does it. You remember the photograph I sent you?"

"What photograph?"

"Of Lucien and Joseph."

"I received no photograph."

"Jesus. And don't call the newsroom from here."

"When did you send this photograph? It might have been held up in the mailroom."

"Don't use the phone at all."

She whispered a cuss word and laughed. "Prison."

Anouk walked into the mini salon and sat up on the sofa. "I love it here!"

Her mother did not look away from Kruse. "You're not staying with us?"

"No."

"Not even today?"

He pulled one of the knives he had taken from the Russian and gave it to her, blocking Anouk's view. "When you open the door, to get your food—"

"Enough, Monsieur Kruse."

On his way out of the room he willed himself to look straight ahead, not back at her and not back at Anouk, not another word.

TEN

Place Saint-Corentin, Quimper

KRUSE ABANDONED THE FIAT AT THE RER STATION AND TOOK THE
train into Paris. At three hotels he used the same story about a robbery,
but the first two were unable to accept him without a passport number. At the third hotel, in Evelyn's arrondissement, he invented one.
The hotel was tucked between two African consulates—Ghana and
Burkina Faso. There was no television, no radio. It smelled of mould
and many years' worth of cigarettes, the armpits of the singing Polish
chambermaid who cleaned the adjacent room when he checked in. He
stood in the room for a few minutes when he first arrived. A baby cried
on the floor above and he thought, for an instant, that it was his. The
radiator in his suite didn't work. Roofs out his window were covered in
sheets of tin, silver and grey and various shades of rust.

First he walked, just looking for her—playing games. Where would
she choose to be now, right now, in light rain? He went through her
notated guidebook and paid the entrance fee at the Louvre and the
Musée d'Orsay, looked for no art, no sculpture, only her. He stopped

at a bank to check his accounts and take out as much as they would give him *en argent liquide*. Half his savings were gone and the other half would keep him going for another five months. In the Salle Ovale of the Richelieu, the reference librarian remembered him and led him to a desk of privilege reserved for a special cadre of academics.

"Did you find your noseless man, Monsieur?"

"I did."

She leaned so close to him, as she spoke, their faces nearly touched. "What can we help you with today?"

"No messages for me?"

"Not this time."

"I'm looking for information on the Front National."

She pushed herself up from the desk and her mouth transformed from flirtation to formality. "I see."

"The history. How it launched. The current leadership."

It seemed the librarian wanted to comment but it was not her place. There was not one perfect book on the Front National, but Kruse did find three comprehensive magazine articles with the names and addresses he was looking for. From behind her desk the librarian stared at him as though he had sprouted crab legs.

In Canada Evelyn distrusted and despised the Reform Party for its populism, its regionalism, its anti-intellectualism, its evangelicals, and a quality she called "strategic bumpkinism." She was no fan of official multiculturalism but she never spoke a word against immigration. All Kruse could figure out, after spending a few hours with the history and philosophy of the Front National, was that she saw an opportunity to build the Party of Evelyn out of an angry mess that happened to control fifteen percent of the popular vote.

The metro strike had ended, so he didn't have to steal a car or endure a taxi. Line 10 terminated at the Saint-Cloud bridge, in an altogether different suburb than Roissy: it was rich and magnificent, with a riot of Mercedes and BMWs. He exited the station and walked across the bridge toward a fusion of new glass office buildings and, on the right, a more typical Parisian neighbourhood. A miserable wind howled along the water, whipping him with light rain. It reminded him of walking to school in Toronto, the life Lily might have led. On the other side he retreated under a pedestrian passageway, free of graffiti, and along a concrete median planted with now-leafless aspen trees. This was close to Paris but not Paris: it was built entirely for cars.

He reached his destination, Rue Vauguyon, and climbed to a rectangular building that seemed to float over the city and the river below like a yacht. A massive and new French flag waved on a clean white pole on the roof, but the building itself had a neglected quality, especially on a grey day, that also reminded him of home. He arrived at the door and for a moment wished he had stayed with Annette and Anouk, that he had taken them to Disneyland. He wanted to find his wife, but ever since he had read the article in *Le Monde*, perhaps even before that in some hidden chamber of his heart, he found her a mystery, a wild thing, a destroyer. Her secret life shrieked up from the river, terrifying and arousing. She had married the wrong man. To round a corner, inside this ugly building lit with dead fluorescent light, and find her entangled with a modern Chateaubriand. Their sex life these last years was dry and forced. The people she admired were almost exclusively well-spoken, pale men who had grown up wealthy. Her mentors and collaborators and partners in universities around the world were soft, sensual men. Lily was a reason to remain faithful, the ultimate reason, but when he walked across a bridge in France in the rain he remembered what Lily's birth, her deformity, her scar, had meant to Evelyn: both love and defeat. To cry out and to win, to live a more adventurous life. He did not know her.

A long corridor led to a receptionist, a woman in her late twenties or early thirties wearing braces. She watched him approach and smiled; they exchanged *bonjours*.

"Welcome to the new headquarters of the Front National."

Once, this formality seemed strange. "Thank you. It's a pleasure to be here."

"A pleasure, yes. How can I help you, Monsieur?"

"My name is Matthew Gibenus and I'm on the board of the British National Party."

"Excellent."

"I was in Paris on some business and I hoped to drop in on Antoine Fortier. We're old collaborators, you see."

The woman closed her eyes for a moment and shook her head. "Oh I am dreadfully sorry, Monsieur Gibenus. He is in Quimper."

"Quimper?"

"It's a city in Brittany, not far from the coast. He's meeting with some of our candidates."

"How far away is it?"

"You can fly quickly, of course. Monsieur Fortier took the train. It's a five- or six-hour drive, by car."

"Rotten luck. But you know, on my way back to the UK I do have the option of taking a ferry from the north coast of Brittany. Where is he staying, if I go that route?"

The woman stopped smiling for a moment and met his eyes long enough to blink a couple of times. Kruse did not look away. She nodded and opened a folder. "Hotel Ys."

"Ys?"

"They speak some Breton out there, contrary to Monsieur Fortier's wishes."

"French is not good enough for them?"

"Evidently, Monsieur. Perhaps 'Ys' is in Breton."

"Thank you. If I get the chance, Madame, I'll look up Monsieur Fortier—Antoine—in Quimper."

"By the way, Monsieur. Do you have a card?"

"No, Madame. I am only a volunteer in the British National Party. I do it because I believe in it, not because it earns me any money or business."

"Very admirable." She stood up to shake his hand. "Until next time, good luck to you and to your cause."

On his way down the hall, he removed the coat hanger he had folded into the inside pocket of his rain jacket. The cloud over Paris had crashed on the suburb. There were no Fiat Regatas or any other middling cars in the neighbourhood, so he settled on a boxy black BMW. He started it without breaking the gearbox. That distorted Nirvana song started playing, the soundtrack for all the kids' ripped jeans and uncombed hair. No matter how many times he had heard the song, Kruse had no idea what the singer was singing. His ear for English was failing. He stopped at a hardware store on the westernmost edge of Versailles, bought a universal screwdriver, and traded licence plates with an Audi from Belgium.

● ● ●

The city of Ys is under Douarnenez Bay on the northwest coast of France. King Gradlon once ruled the great city; his subjects were a race of ambitious, contented people. Decadence found Ys as it finds all people of piety and sophistication. King Gradlon's grown-up daughter, Dahut, was not what he had hoped despite her perfect childhood. At the centre of aristocratic orgies she bedded the bravest, most handsome men of Ys and, in the morning, killed them. There was not a man worthy of her.

Until there was.

A knight arrived in Ys, dressed in red, and seduced Dahut. In the morning she did not run a blade across his neck. Instead, Dahut fell to her knees in love.

The king was delighted. Long had he fretted for his daughter and knew if only she could settle into a glorious marriage, as once he had done, her abominations would end. King Gradlon organized a ball in the knight's honour.

A storm came in off the Atlantic, normal enough here on the western tip of the known world, *le finistère*. The people of Ys had built a most impressive dike to keep the angry waters away. There was only one key to the dike and King Gradlon carried it on a necklace.

In the middle of the storm the red knight asked Dahut to take the key from her father. In her love for the knight, and aroused by the suggestion, Dahut stole into her father's chamber, fragrant with wine, and took the key from the chain around his neck. The red knight snatched the key away and, despite Dahut's tearful warnings, unlocked the gate. In that moment Dahut knew the devil had captured her heart.

King Gradlon awoke just as the Atlantic rose over the city of Ys. In his sorrow he mounted his magical horse, Morvarc'h, and swept his daughter up with him. A spirit appeared to King Gradlon as he fled the mountain of water and the final screams of his beloved subjects. The spirit, Saint Guénolé, convinced the king to sacrifice his daughter to secure his own safety; if he did, one day the waters would recede and Ys would again become the greatest city in the world. King Gradlon pushed his daughter from the horse and into the water. The red knight transformed her into a mermaid. He punished her with eternal life, and still she lives in the Douarnenez Bay, overturning boats full of men in her frustration and loneliness and fury.

In Quimper the king arrived, alone and ruined, the last resident of Ys, and proclaimed himself a servant of God. Kruse parked the BMW in an underground lot near the river and read the tale on a plaque in the central plaza, Place Saint-Corentin. The city's cathedral was, like most cathedrals, a dark and cool cavern of intimidating beauty. He wandered about the entrance and dipped his fingers in the water. A woman had done it before him and had touched her forehead. He touched his forehead.

Back outside, the sun was preparing to set over the valley, and the people of Quimper, the Bretons, sat on the heated terraces eating early dinners and drinking wine and beer. It was cooler than Paris and after some time in a city of ten million the air tasted like iceberg lettuce. Some kids rode down the stairs with skateboards, botching their tricks. A carousel, with a Jules Verne theme, spun in the corner of the plaza. The city beyond was oriented around the confluence of three rivers. One of them, the Odet, criss-crossed with a series of pedestrian bridges, had guided his way from the parking lot. He had seen giant green fish flashing in the late-day sun. The old town, a village to the west of the plaza, was a series of leaning half-timbered houses atop what was now a series of middle-class chain stores and crêpe restaurants.

The tourist information office was closed but a kiosk of pamphlets, protected from the rain with a Plexiglas lid, had been well stocked. Hotel Ys was up the cobblestone hill. He walked and then he ran. A few metres from the lobby of the five-storey hotel, close enough to see the lamps lit in the lobby, he felt and then heard the footsteps behind him on the shadowed street too narrow for cars. The hotel door opened and a young man stepped out in a dark grey suit.

No exits.

"Much better," Kruse whispered, in Russian. He turned. The one he had kicked in Jardin des Plantes wore navy or black. He could not tell in the failing light. Business attire didn't detract from the brawler's ugliness. "How did you know?"

Neither responded. The brawler opened his suit jacket wide enough to display a small gun. He pointed to the door of the Hotel Ys. The cozy lobby was designed with a nautical theme, a net on the wall and black-and-white photographs. Joseph Mariani stood up from the couch and buttoned his suit jacket.

"It makes sense now."

"Good evening, Christopher."

Bile and rust formed in the back of his throat. There was no one behind the counter. "The trap seemed a bit sophisticated for the Russians."

"Shh. They're right behind you and they have guns. Let's go upstairs."

It was three flights, long enough. The secretary at Le Paquebot, the National Front headquarters, had phoned Antoine Fortier to tell him about Monsieur Gibenus, the British fellow-traveller. Tzvi had warned him: he could never be a spook. The criss-cross scar on his left cheek was too easy to describe and his eyes were too blue to forget.

"So you're working for them."

"For whom, Christopher?"

"The political party."

Joseph sighed demonstrably, and halted at the top of the stairs. He held up one finger, to catch his breath. Then: "What lung capacity."

The Russians huffed behind him.

"A professor! I should have known it when you said Plato. No one studies Plato as literature. It's dead boring, theatre without drama, pedantic. You lied with such an air of authority. Keep walking. It's just at the end of the hall."

"Where is Antoine Fortier?"

"Around here somewhere, I imagine." Joseph opened the door. "After you."

"No."

"They're not as bad as my brother, the Russians, but they're bad. Obedient, lacking in sympathy. Soviet prisons were no fun at all."

"You couldn't find French thugs?"

Joseph leaned against the door jamb. "You and your wife both? It's a curious irony: immigrants to France turn anti-immigrant, join an extreme-right political party."

The brawler kicked him into the room. It was a corner suite, as large as the rooms he had rented for Annette and Anouk. There was another net on the wall in the narrow salon, leading into the bedroom. Joseph switched back to English. "One thing I can't grasp, intellectually, and perhaps I'll speak to Evelyn about it: How can you be anti-immigrant, therefore anti-competition, yet also support a meritocracy? It's either one or the other, no? I hire Russian goons because French goons, my brother excepted, aren't goony enough for a mission like this. They're gossips. Exhibit one: Frédéric. My Frédéric! If I could hire Frenchmen, I would. You must understand that, the business you're in."

"What business is that?"

"Come on."

"I protect people."

"Yes, the protection business. We have that in common, Christopher."

"You're in the fear business."

"Chicken or egg, yes, yes, yes. Either way, this is what my family has done for several generations, and it truly is the reason I wanted to see you here in Quimper, without Lucien. I do apologize for my lack of professionalism the other day, in Marseille. One can't drink reality away."

The Russians had settled, one at a window and the other at the door. No one was posted behind him in the bedroom. Joseph sat on the sofa and crossed his legs. The ugly man he had kicked and disarmed in the garden held a pistol at his side, a Beretta 92—a police gun. He breathed eagerly and changed his weight from one foot to the other.

"We can work together, Christopher, instead of competing. I don't want to follow you around, threaten you, read your mind. We both want the same thing."

"No, we don't."

There were two clean file folders on the coffee table in front of Joseph. The table's chips and scratches had been sanded and varnished. The wallpaper was white with baby blue stripes, above white wainscotting. A dark wooden floor. Where the headquarters of the Front National had been ignored this place was loved, adored. One file folder had a yellow sticker with the initials "C.K.," the other, "E.M.K." Joseph opened Evelyn's and went through her history, from her family's wealth to her athletic years, university, her father's death, marriage to the co-owner of a martial arts school and security firm, a job at York, and the birth of a superficially disabled daughter.

"What, in her file, suggests murderess, Christopher?"

"Nothing."

"So let's brainstorm. I love this word. For me, a latecomer to your wonderful language, it still conjures an image: thunder and lightning. Perhaps we can figure it out together."

"There's nothing to figure out, Joseph."

"All right." He clapped his hands. "What can we take, from what you know and what I know, to help us find her?"

The windows in the suite were small but simple to unlatch and open.

"Let's say you're correct, Christopher. She didn't murder Jean-François and Pascale. Why would she run and hide instead of going to the police, what any normal woman would do? If we were to help her, as a team, where would we look? Apart from the hotel on Champ de Mars? Perhaps you learned something from Madame Laferrière."

"Where did you learn to speak English?"

"Boarding school in England and the United States. Stop changing the subject."

"Madame Laferrière did say something I'd like to share."

"Brainstorm!"

"Why would you and your brother, the heads of a large organization, involve yourselves in this?"

Joseph opened the second folder, with "C.K." on the front.

"If I can answer that, Joseph, I can also figure out why you're paying Russian mercenaries instead of using members of your own syndicate."

"I must say, when I first read your dossier I felt a bit faint. We were so careless with you in Marseille. You could have taken us at any time."

"Tell me what this is all about and I'll let you go."

Joseph grinned without a hint of malevolence. "Christopher, believe me, knowing is awful. It's the reason our dear, clever Evelyn is living in some dank hole, under a pseudonym. But I assure you: a beautiful woman with a strong American accent can't remain invisible forever." Joseph looked down at the dossier again, turned the page. "I have an offer for you. This is why I flew here to meet you, when I learned you were coming."

"I'm not interested."

"It's a complex offer. Behind door number one: a trip home. I will supply you with a first-class airplane ticket and a fair sum of money to just . . . tell us what you know about Evelyn and go. This is, if I were you, an attractive offer. You have a successful business in Toronto. You're still young. And when we find Evelyn, if she co-operates and agrees to our terms, she will be close behind you: innocent, pardoned by the state if not the media.

"Door number two: you continue to sneak about with a third-rate journalist and a truculent old gendarme. To my great regret, we eliminate you from the game. You and everyone you touch."

"That isn't much of a choice."

"It isn't, is it?"

Kruse extended his hand for a shake and Joseph stood up from the couch. The Russian's gun remained at his side. Joseph began to speak about relief. The moment he touched Joseph's soft hand Kruse went for the Russian with the gun. He was out in two blows. His younger partner stepped forward and Kruse blinded him with a finger jab, knocked him out.

"Jesus Christ." Joseph looked at his watch. "Spectacular."

Kruse picked up the gun. "Let's go."

"Where, Christopher?"

The gendarmerie. Kruse would explain about the Russians, this gangster chasing his innocent wife. The Mariani family's relationship, still confusing to him, with the Front National. They were the detectives. They could ask Antoine Fortier, staying right here in the Hotel Ys, and solve it. Joseph opened the door and stepped out into the hallway.

"I'm not angry with you, Christopher. But I'll have to come after you again. This has to be clean, for everyone's sake."

The stairs down to the lobby formed a corkscrew until the second floor, which in France is called the first floor. Joseph leaned on the railing as he walked. Then he stopped. Someone was coming, a family of five. Six. A grandmother first, in an orange muumuu, climbed hand-over-hand.

"*Oh là là*," said Joseph. "*Vacances en famille.*"

"No," said Kruse, but it was already too late.

Joseph grabbed the portly woman, the grandmother, by the face and neck and yanked her down three stairs with him. She wailed and tumbled on a forty-year-old man and woman, and a pre-adolescent boy and girl, who shouted and knelt by her and tried to pull her muumuu back down. The boy laughed and his mother smacked him. There was no room to jump over the family, and Joseph had already strolled whistling out of the hotel, so Kruse helped lift the grandmother to her feet. He pretended not to speak French when the parents asked him what he had seen.

"A madman," he said in English.

The grandmother was bruised and humiliated but not seriously hurt. They helped her to the third floor and into her room at the opposite end of the hall from the Russians.

• • •

Two gendarmes arrived to investigate Joseph's stairway assault on the grandmother. While the manager escorted the police to the third floor, Kruse went behind the desk to read the ledger. Antoine Fortier was on the fifth floor. Two sets of keys to his room were in a marked cubbyhole at his knees.

It was a corner suite with a view of Place Saint-Corentin: the spinning Jules Verne carousel and the cathedral lit up white and yellow for the evening. A trailer had arrived to sell snacks and candy. The chambermaid had been through and had tidied up Fortier's papers.

They were policy briefings and a communications strategy, stacks of pamphlets about the Front National and its squinting Mr. Magoo of a leader, financial statements. Kruse sat in a blue wing chair and read through it all by lamplight. Every time he heard footsteps in the hall he turned the light off. The communications strategy had several lines to repeat about Jean-François de Musset—he was a patriot, a republican, a man of intelligence and action, a true Frenchman—but nothing about Evelyn.

When there was no more to read, Kruse opened Fortier's small black suitcase to see if there was anything he had missed. And there was. The previous day's *Figaro* and a glossy German magazine populated with photos of naked girls, little girls, some of them in sex acts with grown men. At first he didn't understand what he was looking at. Then he did, and dropped the magazine as though he were touching a cut of rotten flesh.

Kruse had not eaten since breakfast—an apple on his way to the Front National in Saint-Cloud, and he was beginning to feel it. Tzvi had taught him ways to stabilize himself, at least mentally, when his blood sugar was low—to trick his body into seeing every activity as crucial. In the hotel room he moved from furious to dreamy and forgetful. Hunger did something to the way time seemed to pass. Lily was with him in the room, reading an Astérix book on the bed. She didn't read, not really. She looked at pictures and told a story to herself and, if he was listening, to him.

"Where is Mommy?"

"I don't know yet."

"Why aren't you looking for her?"

"I am looking, sweetheart. That's why I'm here."

"What if something bad happens?"

"I won't let anything happen."

"You promise?"

"I promise."

"What does she look like, again?"

"You don't remember? It's only been two weeks."

But he could hardly remember: the hair, yes, and the eyes. Her legs in a dress. Putting Evelyn together and feeling her, the warmth of her, an embrace in the kitchen. It was so rare to see her parents hugging and kissing, and so pleasing, Lily would climb down from her chair and run across the hardwood in her socks and hop up, and he would lift her and the three of them would embrace together. There was a song from the Saturday morning cartoons, *Schoolhouse Rock!* "Three is a magic number." They would whisper-sing it together because the windows were open and Evelyn had come from an Anglican family and Anglicans did not sing in public.

A beautiful woman with a strong American accent can't remain invisible forever. Every hour that passed when he did not hear she had been caught by the police or murdered in some alley of a city he had not heard of, a city like Quimper, was the end of one fairy tale and the beginning of another. If he were Evelyn, where would he go? No borders, no hotels—at least not under her own name—no credit card. Through the looking glass.

There were hard steps in the hallway, an unathletic man in leather-soled shoes. Kruse turned out the light. A key in the lock, and with a whisper of assurance the door opened and a silhouette of a man in a suit walked in: short and heavy, though not fat, with a moustache and glasses. A girl stumbled in with him, half-drunk. He closed the door behind them, tossed a plastic bag onto the bed, and turned on the light.

"Monsieur Fortier."

"My God." He dropped his keys from one hand and his briefcase from the other. "Who the hell are you?"

The girl, a teenager, looked away.

Kruse stood and walked across the room. Fortier backed up, into the space between the bed and the tall white table with the white lamp. Kruse put his hand on the door handle and said, to the girl, "You can go."

She looked at Fortier. "But . . ."

"Pay her. Pay her what you were going to pay her."

"Wait a minute here. This isn't at all what you're thinking."

"Pay the girl."

Fortier pulled out his wallet and selected some bills. The girl took them from him and counted.

"Is that what he promised?"

She shook her head no.

Fortier cussed. "Do you have any idea who I am?"

"Pay her."

He did and the girl, in dirty jeans and a tight, weathered motorcycle jacket, turned to go.

"Wait. How old are you?"

The girl turned to Fortier and said, "Eighteen."

"I work for Interpol. Now that I've seen you, I'll find you. I'll know. How old?"

"Fourteen."

"Where do you live?"

"Here. All over."

"Your family?"

"Douarnenez."

"Can you go back?"

Fortier laughed. "You're going to save the day, Monsieur? Change the world? Congratulations. Three times, congratulations."

The girl turned and Kruse called out after her to go home and back to school. He locked the door behind her and leaned against the rough wallpaper. The president of the Front National picked up the phone but Kruse had cut the line. Fortier sat and slouched on the bed. "You're a real hero. She's going to shoot up every franc."

"No one will rape her tonight."

"She propositioned me, Monsieur. How was I to know she was fourteen?"

The plastic bag on the bed, stamped with a hardware store logo, was nearly empty: a new role of duct tape and some rope. "You had some repairs to do?"

Fortier sighed. He reminded Kruse of a penguin.

"I'm looking for my wife."

"I asked you before, Monsieur. Do you know who I am? I have friends in the Gendarmerie nationale."

"Tell me about them. Where are these friends? In Vaison-la-Romaine, by chance?"

"Ah." Fortier pointed at him. "I see."

"You see what?"

"This is about de Musset."

"It's about the woman who is alleged to have murdered him and his wife."

"The American."

"Canadian."

"One or the other, yes. Madame Evelyn. You are, what, her husband? One of her men? One of Jean-François's sexual competitors?"

It was like a drug, not having eaten. He watched himself watching Fortier. "Husband."

"Well, congratulations to you, Monsieur. She sounds like quite the creature. Now, I hope you'll excuse me. I'm going downstairs to alert the hotelier about the intruder in my room, and I'm sure he'll phone the police."

Kruse put his hands on the man, shoved him back onto the bed.

"I will have you arrested."

"I was there that night, in Villedieu, when your man killed my daughter. Ever since then I've been trying to figure it out. My wife, the Marianis, your man Jean-François, Pascale."

"Figure what out?" Fortier pulled a silver cigarette case from an inside pocket and offered one to Kruse. "I listen to you speak and honestly, Monsieur, I have no idea what you're talking about. You're nuts, I suppose." He lit his cigarette. "Here I am, stuck in a room with a madman. Is Kruse a Jewish name, by the way? Such a charming note for my memoirs."

"You hired the Marianis."

"And who are they, my Jewish friend? These Marianis I have hired?"

"Stop it."

"Stop what, Monsieur?"

"Jean-François de Musset, your great hope for the next presidential election, was killed. By my wife, or so you think. So you hire the Marianis in revenge."

For some time, Fortier smoked. Then he moved from the bed to a chair near the window, where Kruse had been sitting. There was an ashtray. "This is extraordinary."

"Is it?"

"First of all, Monsieur, if I were to say anything to your wife it would be thank you. Of course, I could never. It would be beastly. Jean-François was a patriot. A republican."

"A man of intelligence and action."

"Jean-François de Musset was hijacking the FN. He believed in power for the sake of power, not change. He was a coward. If we had wanted to be a centrist party, we would have been a centrist party all along, an ice cream shop with twenty flavours. Gaullists. But I believe this weakness, this spirit of accommodation, is what brought France to the state of insurrection we're in today. We are not all things to all people. Perhaps that is America."

"Insurrection."

"Jean-François did not have permission. It was not his party."

Kruse was dizzy with hunger. He checked his pockets again, for a crumb, anything.

"I realize, Monsieur, that the history of a foreign country does not interest you and your people. But I grew up in Algeria, a city called Oran. My father owned grocery stores. In 1962 General Charles de

Gaulle, the hero of our late friend Jean-François de Musset, surrendered Algeria—my French home—to the Arabs. That summer, the Muslims went through our neighbourhoods and cut our throats: men, women, children. Babies, Monsieur."

"How did you escape?"

"My family had already fled. But our friends were killed, my uncle and aunt, my cousins. All for ice cream shop politics, something for everyone but nothing for France, for the French. This is at the heart of the Front National, why we exist. What did your de Musset try to do?"

Kruse backed against the dresser, held himself up.

"When you see her again, in prison, please give her my best regards. In fact, when our true leader wins the presidency, perhaps she will be pardoned. She is the patriot. A murderer of intelligence and action, in fact."

The lights in the room were not bright but they were too bright. Fortier's skin was the icing on a vanilla birthday cake that no one bothered to eat. He continued to speak but Kruse was no longer listening. He wanted the man to be lying but he was not. Why was Kruse here? Why, with a name like Kruse? Why not Germany? Or Israel, perhaps? Why not stay in his own country, with his own people? When he had dropped the pornographic magazine back in Fortier's bag he had not buried the thing. Now, in the light, it shone up at him. He had come here to find Evelyn and she was more lost than ever.

At home he would open the fridge at moments like this, a fridge full of food, and he would have no idea how to proceed.

"Daddy. What are you doing?"

"I'm hungry."

"What?" said Fortier.

I'm hungry, in English. "Take off your clothes."

"Monsieur?"

"Take off your clothes, Fortier. Now."

"No."

Kruse lifted the aged birthday cake out of his chair, tossed him on the bed. Mattress springs quivered. "Do it or I'll do it for you, and I won't be gentle."

"Please," he said, several times, and spoke of his wife and children—a boy and a girl—now in school. All he wanted was the best for France, for his family, for French families. Kruse misunderstood him. He did not make much money, as president of a political party. It was a sacrifice, a public service. It was true he had a frailty of the heart, but what would a prostitute do, without clients? Steal? Simply die? Was there a society, in the history of the world, without men and whores?

He sat demurely on the edge of the bed in his loose-fitting white briefs and a pair of navy blue socks pulled up halfway to his knees. His belly was soft and his breasts were loose. Kruse imagined him with the girl, what he might have done with the tape and the rope. The girl in the cold morning, with her money and whatever else she carried. Others like her, in every city. Fortier trembled, cried silently.

"Speak to me, Monsieur."

"No."

"This is not fair. It's my private life. In my public life . . ."

"Underwear too."

"Monsieur. I beg forgiveness. I will never do it again and I swear it before God. Whatever you want, money. You want money? I can get some for you. And I will never tell the police."

"Take off your underwear."

Now he wailed. "Help me!"

Kruse put one hand in the man's thinning hair and the other on his face, and squeezed. A roar rose up in him, an old feeling that replaced his hunger, and he looked at Fortier and now the man understood. He rose and removed his underwear and looked up at the ceiling and prayed in his blue socks. The cock that drove him to the magazine and to heroin girls was hardly there at all, hidden by grey-black hair and by the shadow of his stomach. Someone loved him and trusted him, that wife and those kids. Kruse pulled the duct tape out of the bag and Fortier continued to pray. The Lord's Prayer, in French.

He wrapped the duct tape around Fortier's head, covering his mouth but not his nose. "Yes, God has all kinds of time for you." The man didn't struggle as Kruse taped his hands together, behind his back. He bent Fortier over the bed and stood behind him for a while, shuffling unnecessarily, to let him think. Fortier bashed his forehead again and again on the mattress, and called out of his nose. It was a tall four-poster bed with a solid wood headboard. The art, above the bed, was of a storm coming into the bay. He shoved Fortier up on the bed and taped his thin legs together. By the time he was finished, half the roll of tape was gone. Kruse used the rope to tie him to the bed and opened the magazine in front of him. He had not felt so dirty in years, so he used Fortier's room to shower and took one of his clean shirts. He wrote a note about the fourteen-year-old girl from Douarnenez and about the magazine, how he had found Fortier, and propped the door open with one of his shoes.

There was a beige phone kiosk in Place Saint-Corentin, made of a plastic that did not seem to exist on the other side of the ocean. It was close enough to the bistro, Le Finistère, to the smell of spiced meat and hot cheese, that he nearly called out in longing. The number for the police was on a faded sticker behind the phone box. He explained to the woman who answered the phone about the pedophile and rapist waiting in the Hotel Ys: a patriot, a republican, a man of intelligence and action.

ELEVEN

Rue Falguière, Paris

ROISSY WAS EMPTY. HE DROVE AROUND UNTIL HE WAS SURE NO ONE had followed him, and he parked two hotels away on the strip. It was a cool and still night. His shoes on the pavement broke the silence and inspired a dog, standing alone in the middle of the plaza, to bark. Kruse nodded at the desk clerk when she said hello and he took the stairs. For five minutes he listened at the door for any sound or movement. He prepared for a fight and opened the door into darkness, warmth, nothing. At the threshold of the bedroom he heard them first, their breathing, and when his eyes adjusted to the pale sliver of parking-lot light sneaking into the room, he saw them, both of them in one bed, on their right sides, like two sizes of the same woman.

In the closet he found a pillow and a blanket for especially cold nights and lay on the sofa. Earlier at Le Finistère he had been too hungry to eat; the egg of the croque madame seemed as ridiculous as a naked man's moustache. Now he was too tired to sleep: unless Antoine Fortier was the greatest actor of his generation he had not hired the Marianis.

He would never sleep again. This is what he had become. He would seek Evelyn until either he found her or there was nothing left of him but dust, chalk, the outline of a phantom that a sick woman might see in a lonely rest stop in eastern Brittany. In the dream she was whispering to him, Evelyn and then Lily. *Play with me.* He could feel her breath on his face.

"Play with me."

Close up, Anouk had tiny freckles atop her nose. The whites of her eyes were pure and perfect, less than a hand's length from his own, which were so tired they felt glued. He wanted to hide her from men and Mercedes forever. He thought of Fortier in his room, with his vile magazine, a professional destroyer.

"Play with me."

If he started playing with her, how would he stop? "Where is your mom?"

"Sleeping."

He closed the door to the bedroom and folded the blanket and stuffed it back into the closet, with his pillow. Together they sat on the couch. "What would you like to play? It has to be a quiet game."

"You are a horse and I am the rider."

"Only if you can be a quiet rider. You can't say 'giddy-up.'"

"What is 'giddy-up'?"

"It's a thing we say in English."

She prepared her mouth: "giddy-up."

And without another word he assumed the familiar position and she climbed on his back and he walked on his hands and knees. Twice he tried to gallop but there was only a thin layer of carpet over the concrete floor. It hurt too much. It was time for another game, so he taught her an impromptu French translation of Simon Says and then, veering into too noisy, tag. In France you are not it. You are the wolf.

At the end of the game of wolf, Anouk climbed back onto the couch and announced she now had the hunger of a wolf. It was the first time since Halloween night that Kruse had allowed himself to be anything more than cursed; now, coming out of an hour with Anouk, he felt he had betrayed his daughter.

"We'll wait until your mom wakes up."

"But I'm hungry now."

"What does she eat, usually?"

"Coffee."

"What else?"

"Tartine."

"And what do you eat?"

"Pain au chocolat, as you know. Every day I have it, with orange juice."

"That doesn't sound true."

"With you it is true. Every day with you it is true."

There was a notebook open on the coffee table, in front of the television. In it was written:

> le Front national
> le milieu corse
> les de Mussets (aristocratie)
> Villedieu???
> la Gendarmerie nationale

A few minutes after he called down for room service, Annette stepped out of the bedroom, rubbing her eyes. "I dreamt that a man came into the hotel room last night."

"Madame, I did hear the sirens before she was hit."

"Good morning, Monsieur Kruse."

"Why, do you think? Before she was hit?"

"There may have been a heart attack in one of the seniors' homes. The south is lousy with them."

"Who is the anonymous source?"

"People have affairs. It's normal. My husband—"

"I want to find out who told the reporters. The Front National, at least the senior leadership, they know nothing."

"What do you mean?"

"I met with Antoine Fortier."

"And?"

"A real charmer. But he didn't hire the Marianis."

"He could have been lying."

"I don't think so, Madame."

Anouk watched them, back and forth, as they spoke. French children, this one included, were trained not to interrupt when adults were talking. By now, in a conversation like this, Lily would have interjected three times already. What is "anonymous"? Who was hit? How can someone attack a heart?

"You slept in my hotel room. You've endangered my life and my child's life, and you've probably ruined my career. Call me Annette."

Kruse had not kept any of the articles about Evelyn from November 1. "What's the reporter's name?"

"Monsieur Kruse."

"Christophe."

"He won't tell you anything. If the anonymous source is truly an anonymous source, a reporter would rather die than tell."

"What's his name?"

"You do not seem the type to argue."

"Not at the moment."

"Nicholas Durrant."

Kruse went to the desk and pulled out a piece of hotel stationery. "I need you to draw me a map of the newsroom."

"Why?"

"Please, Annette."

She stared at him long enough to blink a couple of times. Her eyes

remained small and strained with sleep or lack of it, and her body radi-
ated heat from the bed. Her legs were bare and the Johnny Hallyday
shirt was the length of a miniskirt. Soon she would be cold. In this light
her skin was sprinkled with cinnamon. He had trouble focusing. As she
drew, bent over the table, Kruse went to the bathroom and returned
with a thin white robe for her. Anouk watched her mother work.

"This is appalling, Christophe."

"The same anonymous source in seven newspapers? That's appalling." He offered her the robe and she looked up, caught him staring.
"I'm sorry."

Again she looked at him a moment too long, a meeting place of curiosity and spite, something else he couldn't read. On the other side of
her, Anouk was handling the small plastic coffee maker.

"I ordered breakfast for you two."

She looked away from him and finished the map.

Durrant's name was in a bubble above his cubicle. She had marked
her own desk, which he remembered, and the boardroom where they
had talked. It was simple and thorough, with a clear route from the
elevator into the middle of the room. The silence lasted long enough
for Anouk to ask about the coffee maker. She wanted to make coffee
for everyone.

"I have to go, so don't make enough for me."

"Why, Monsieur?"

"But I'll be back."

"When, *alors*?"

"Soon. Remember, Anouk, if someone knocks . . ."

She froze and whispered, "Be very still. Don't move and don't speak."

"Correct."

Annette's arms were crossed over her chest. The robe had a hood and
she had slid it over her appealing mess of morning hair. A white nun.
Kruse was close enough to the door to hear the industrial hum of the
hallway, to feel it in the concrete through the soles of his shoes.

"If no one wants coffee I will make some for myself. Maman: How do you make coffee?"

She spoke to the girl without looking away from him. "Put the carafe down, Anouk."

"One last name, Annette, if you know it."

"You want me to betray my colleagues and my principles even further."

"'Want' isn't the right word."

• • •

In Toronto, when he used this trick, his accomplices were sometimes Sikh and sometimes Somali. In Paris that afternoon the secret to invisibility was Polish. He waited on Rue Falguière for the woman and the man, mother and son. It was just after four thirty and the son's ritual was just as Annette had described: a cigarette on the bench in front of the newspaper building. His slouch was as formidable as his bald spot, surrounded by a riot of hair the colour of hay. Next to him his mother stood and smiled, apparently at nothing, her own version of the family slouch moulded into a stoop.

The dusk sky alternated between bright and dark, as fast-moving clouds revealed and then hid the sun. It was cold enough to see his breath as he watched. Kruse crossed the street and introduced himself as a representative of the janitorial union. The woman, white-haired and so inviting a personality he worried for her sanity, took one of his hands in both of hers as he spoke. His mission, he said, was to observe them for a little while this afternoon and evening, as they worked. He wanted to be sure the people at *Le Monde* were treating them well. They were not to focus on him. His investigation, of their work and of the workplace, was holistic.

"Everyone is nice." The woman had, at best, two operable teeth. Still, her smile was lovely. As always, when he encountered Europeans of her generation, he wondered where she and her family had stood during the war: with the Nazis or against them, as they marched through her village.

Her son raised his eyebrows skeptically. "They are French. They don't see us."

"But Monsieur, no one is cruel."

"That's a better way to put it, Mama."

At five o'clock the receptionist in the lobby put on her jacket. Kruse stalled the mother and son, asking more questions, before he allowed them to walk through the security doors. The receptionist saw a lot of men, every day, but few with scars on their faces. Their cleaning carts were in large closets on each floor. Normally, the humourless son said, they started on the first. It was accounting and other services, and those people always left at four o'clock. On the upper floors, the newsroom and management, they tended to work longer hours.

"Then today let's start on the upper floors. I want to see the way people interact with you."

The son looked at his mother and back to Kruse. "I want to thank you, for taking this interest in us. It is hard to come to France with nothing."

"No, thank you. Thank you, Monsieur. Madame." Kruse pressed the up button on the elevator.

Inside, the white-haired woman looked up and pointed at his cheek. "What happened to you?"

"Car accident, when I was a child. My parents didn't feel strongly about seat belts."

"I thought it might be a fight." The son, perhaps twenty-five, tended to focus on a spot ten centimetres in front of his shoes.

Observing human interaction on the sixth floor would be a challenge. It was an afternoon paper, so they were far from any deadlines. If reporters worked longer hours than others in the building they were not doing it at their desks. Four people were scattered through the newsroom. Two of them were on the phone. One man read with his glasses on his head and a woman in a thick fishing sweater and scarf was preparing to leave. Durrant's cubicle and the others around it were empty.

The son apologized to Kruse. "Normally there are more of them. It is Sunday. Perhaps tomorrow is a holiday."

"Perhaps." Kruse pretended to be disappointed. "People or not, on a floor like this, what are some of the challenges you face?"

"Journalists are dirty and disorganized. We think well of them, these writers, but when you see how they work you understand, Monsieur, they are no better than jackals."

Kruse pretended to write all of this down. "Their papers?"

"Yes, their papers. Their books and files."

"When they conduct interviews, they take notes in . . ."

The young man walked across the corridor and picked up a thin flip notebook with a spiral top. "These things are everywhere because the reporters save them. If someone reads a story and sues the newspaper, the notebooks are important in court."

His cart was filled with rags and cleaning fluids, and stocked with garbage bags. Kruse pretended to inspect the cart, to read the list of ingredients on a transparent plastic bottle filled with something pink and bubbly. "Now, go about your work as you normally would as I complete my inspection. I will be writing a report for *Le Monde* and for the union."

"Make sure you write something about the notebooks."

Durrant's desk was an utter disaster, covered in letters opened and unopened, faxes and old editions of *Le Monde* and other newspapers. His notebooks were stacked haphazardly on the floor. Unlike the one the janitor had showed him, none of Durrant's were dated. Kruse just started reading one after another until he found a name he recognized in the sixth: his own. The handwriting was as messy as the desk, but there was a kind of organization about the notes Durrant took.

Evelyn Kruse / May Kruse: tourist but partisan (staff?) of Front
  National??
Arrived May, 1992 (photocopy of visa)
Husband Christopher.
Daughter Lily (died October 31, hours before the murders)
The murdered: Jean-François and Pascale de Musset, in their
  home
Old royal connections—de Musset (irrelevant?), star after Vaison-
  la-Romaine flood
(see flood stories + video France 2). Bouillon de Culture.
See Front National: interview whom?
Check out Philippe Laflamme (transcribe phone message).

Kruse read the entire notebook and a few that surrounded it. He found
information about the Front National, even quotations from an interview with Antoine Fortier: patriot, republican, man of intelligence and
action, true Frenchman.

The actual quotations that had appeared in Durrant's story, identical
or near-identical to the quotations from the anonymous source that
had appeared in the other stories, were not in any of the notebooks
in the pile on the floor. One of the men, who had been on the phone
when he entered the newsroom, stood up from his cubicle halfway
across the newsroom and watched him. Kruse slipped two of the notebooks inside his shirt.

Night had fallen outside. It was cool in the newsroom and quiet. A
radio or stereo somewhere in the fluorescent barn of a room played
one of Evelyn's favourites, by Debussy, a prelude to an afternoon. It
was a slow and dreamy song, the sort of thing she had adored when
she was pregnant. On the day they took possession of the house on
Foxbar Road, which had seemed massive to them—larger than both of
their childhood homes put together—she played a cassette of Debussy
on a ghetto blaster in the living room. There was so much to do. The

movers would be at the apartment soon and not all of the boxes were packed. But this impossible music, echoing from long ago but not so long, in a room of dark wood and stained glass, a chandelier, spoke fantasy to them. They were in love and a baby was coming and they were young. They were in love until Lily arrived, when they merely began to love one another on Foxbar Road, which was different. The difference had never been clear to him, though it had been to Evelyn. Move to France and fall back in love.

Across the newsroom the reporter who had been on the phone spoke to the white-haired woman and then her son, the janitors from Poland. The reporter shook his head and walked over, his right hand balled into a fist. Kruse stood up. He had been to France but not to the country Evelyn had described, not to the South of France, inside a composition by Claude Debussy, where the windows are always open and it always smells of lavender and no one grows old and you are in love and the tomatoes are always ripe. Figs fall from the tree as you pass under it, on your way home from École Jules Ferry, past the cathedral. Your daughter is warm on your shoulders and singing. A bottle has been opened. You will eat outside.

The reporter did not introduce himself. "You stole a notebook."

"Two notebooks, actually."

"Put them back on the desk and leave this place, before I call the police."

Kruse did not have what he wanted, but he did not think he would find it. The reporter was in his fifties, bald and wild-eyed, in a white shirt with visible stains under the armpits, the buttons undone nearly to his belly. On the other side of him, the young Polish janitor looked on hopefully.

"I tricked them."

"Well, they're in big trouble, thanks to you."

Kruse took a step toward the reporter. "No, they aren't."

"What are you? Some American thug?"

"I know who you are, Monsieur, and I know where to find you. This is not the janitors' fault. I tricked them, as I said. I lied to them. I said I was a union representative."

"What? You showed them a card?"

"Yes."

"What have you taken?"

"Evidence."

"I'm phoning the police."

"Go ahead, please. My name is Christophe Kruse. You can tell them she is innocent and I will soon have the proof."

"Who is innocent?"

"Remember what I said, about the janitors. Not a word. Or I'll come for you."

The mother continued to empty garbage bins, but the son stood in the middle of the newsroom watching. The hope had departed from his face. Kruse lifted his hand to wave, as he stepped around the reporter. Impersonating a janitor, a janitorial manager, a union representative, he had only been caught once before—in the head office of a clothing importer that was about to be taken over by a foreign multinational.

"Kruse?" The reporter smelled sour and peppery, like leftover food that hasn't been refrigerated.

"You should go home, Monsieur."

"Oh, that's right: Kruse. The murder in Vaison."

Two men entered the newsroom from the elevator, both in uniform.

"I called security."

Kruse put his hand on the reporter's shoulder. Close up, his smell was excruciating. "If the guards search me and find the notebooks, I'll have to hurt them. Do you want that?"

"Son of a whore. You can't intimidate me."

This is what Evelyn despised about his work, the truth he could not undo. Some men he knew were overwhelmed by sexual desire. They sneaked out to lap dance clubs and eventually the escort agencies and whorehouses on nearly every block in downtown Toronto. Aging men with money who did not take care of their bodies and draped them over girls on afternoons they said they were golfing. Sometimes Kruse followed them and made their weakness his strength. His own weakness was this: his hands were hot with a different sort of desire.

Kruse walked toward the guards, into their arms, and called, "I'm sorry," across the newsroom to the Polish man. He said again, "I'm so sorry. It was the only way."

"But you've ruined me," he said.

Behind him, the reporter said, "Don't worry, Jan."

The security guards, a black man and a white man with mock confidence in their eyes, were not armed. They were not accustomed to this. If they were anything like their counterparts in Canada, they were poorly paid and barely trained. Kruse knew a fighter by his eyes and feet.

"I would prefer to take the stairs."

The guards looked at one another. "It's not what you prefer," said the white man. "Do you want this to be easy, Monsieur, or do you want it to be difficult?"

"The stairs are fine," said the black man.

Kruse waited for the reporter to mention the notebooks. He half-turned to face him. The reporter looked at Kruse and nodded and walked away, leaving him with the security guards, who would do whatever he asked. In the lobby, when the white man asked for his name, he said "Clint Eastwood" and the man wrote it down.

There was a record store at the train station. He had an hour to wait so he flipped through the selections under *D* in the classical music section and found it: "Prelude to the Afternoon of a Faun."

TWELVE

Rue Trogue-Pompée, Vaison-la-Romaine

THE GENDARMERIE IN VAISON-LA-ROMAINE OPENED AT NINE. THERE was a buzzer and a handwritten sign about after-hours police protection—for emergencies ONLY. A young man in uniform, with an agonizing crop of acne on his cheeks and forehead, unlocked the door a few minutes after eight and waited until he was behind the desk and in his chair before permitting Kruse to speak to him.

"Yes, Monsieur. How can I help you?"

"I would like to speak with Lieutenant Huard."

"He is no longer with the force. Sous-lieutenant Boutet has taken over his work."

The young gendarme picked up the phone and Kruse looked at the fading posters on the wall, imploring Vaisonnais to lock their vehicles at night and to stop drinking and driving. The young man's voice went from unselfconsciously loud to quiet. Then he turned away from Kruse and whispered, before hanging up the phone.

Kruse put his hand on the door.

"Stop," said the gendarme, his voice cracking.

The clouds had remained in the north, and the sidewalks of Cours de Taulignan were thick with men and women in sunglasses, with insurance brokers and hair stylists and bureaucrats and butcher's assistants strolling to work ten minutes late. It was a Monday and the Vaisonnais moved like they were being dragged. Kruse weaved through them and then slipped between two cars, sprinted down the road. No one followed, at least not at first, so he jumped the fence in the post office parking lot into the Roman ruins and ducked into a corner of crumbling stone and cedars.

He watched the horse stable, waiting for a team of police to arrive with a warrant, batons drawn, as they had the morning after she was killed. It was just over two weeks ago—fifteen days—but it felt like either ten minutes or ten years.

They could arrest him for taking the notebooks at *Le Monde*. His encounter with Antoine Fortier was surely harassment by someone's definition, and he had stolen several cars. No one came, not for more than half an hour, and then when someone in uniform did arrive, it was the postwoman in her shorts, T-shirt, and satchel, half-jogging up the street as she slipped envelopes through door slots and into mailboxes. She delivered something at the horse stable. Eventually the estate of Jean-François and Pascale de Musset would ask him— them—to leave.

The Russian who had been driving the car in Paris, down Villa de l'Astrolabe, stood up from the doorway of the closed jewellery shop, and walked down to the horse stable. He wore jeans and a black hooded sweatshirt with the words "Too Cool for Skool," in English, whimsically screened on the front. He had not noticed, in Quimper, that the Russian's steps were crooked, from a slight limp. He may have been anywhere from thirty to fifty-five, but prison had aged him, physically and otherwise. His skin was as grey as a smoked cigarette. At the horse stable he looked around, determined that he was alone, and opened the mailbox. He pulled out whatever was in there and half-walked, half-jogged, down the path toward the cathedral. Lily's path to school.

Kruse sneaked across two Roman streets and through a patch of grass, parallel to the Russian. The ruins were a level below the modern street. Kruse jumped and gripped the black fence. His palms slapped the iron bar and alerted the Russian, who ran toward the cathedral.

Kruse was up and over the iron fence, sprinting down the path. It ended at a generous pitch of grass in front of the church. On the left was École Jules Ferry. He could hear her say it as he ran, her first rolled *R*s, *Ferry*. The Russian was not a runner. His destination, it seemed, was a municipal parking lot on the other side of the church lawn. The leaves of early November had been raked away. Kruse might have called after him but instead he jumped the slow, miserable Russian next to a small fountain. One warm afternoon, shortly after Lily had started school, Kruse had splashed water from this fountain on his face. Ten minutes later a woman arrived with a black Labrador retriever and washed the dog in the fountain. Kruse asked if this was the place to wash your dog and learned it was, yes, the best by far. It was not for people. He hadn't used it, had he?

The Russian slammed into the short stone wall of the fountain with the right side of his torso, his ribs exposed. Kruse had trapped the man's arms as he fell. It was not audible, the ribs cracking, but Kruse felt it as they toppled together. There was no fight: the Russian gasped and flailed, and threw the letters into the fountain in frustration. Kruse fished them out and waited as the Russian rolled to his front, his hands and knees, and tried to breathe. There was a knife in the front pouch of his hoodie. Kruse confiscated it.

"I am sorry. I didn't mean for that to happen, not exactly."

The Russian's breathing was poor.

"You should get it checked." Kruse felt the right side of him. "I punctured a lung that way."

The Russian tried to stand.

"The hospital's the way you came, past the jewellery store. I can help you."

"Fuck you," he said, in English.

One of the letters was from the consulate, another from Evelyn's mother, Agnes. There was a postcard with a photograph of Mont Saint-Michel on the front, its wet letters—her letters—fading.

A magic number
Two years before her birth
An October day for you
In three years I will be

"How many days have you been here, stealing my mail? You have more mail somewhere? In your car, maybe, your hotel room?"

A couple walked up the path to the cathedral, arm in arm. Kruse nodded to them. Now the Russian was mumbling, his face in the soil. It would smell of horse chestnuts, wet and dry at once. When they played *cache-cache* on these grounds, Lily had insisted he put his face against something to count. She did not trust him with mere hands over his face, as that was the method of her own cheating. He had smelled plane trees here, and this grass.

The Russian rolled onto his side and extended a hand for help. After reading and hearing Evelyn in the card, he bent the man's arm and cranked it. "Do you have other postcards, anything, from her?"

"Stop."

Not *arretez* but "stop," in English. Lieutenant Boutet stood at the place where the path to the cathedral split. She walked across the grass. Kruse cranked the Russian's arm and he called out.

"Release him." She pulled her gun.

"Arrest this man." Kruse stood up and kicked the Russian over. "He's been stealing my mail. His partners have attacked me. I'm sure he's already wanted by the gendarmerie."

"Of the two of you, only one is wanted. Let's go, Monsieur Kruse. You lead the way, back to the station. Let's not advertise anything here: just keep walking at a regular pace, hands at your side."

"This man works for the Mariani crime family."

"Not now, Monsieur Kruse."

"I'm not going."

Lieutenant Boutet pointed the gun with both hands and aimed. She blew an errant lock of hair from her eyes. "Then I'll shoot you."

Kruse followed her directions, back toward Lily's limestone path. She walked four paces behind him.

"What have I done wrong, Madame Boutet?" Her breaths were quick, as though she had been running. "You've been promoted to lieutenant. Congratulations."

"Stop. Stop talking."

His Moroccan neighbours were gathered at the place where the pedestrian path transitioned into Rue Trogue-Pompée. Boulders marked the separation. The men stopped speaking. Kruse left the fenceline and walked around them.

"Wait wait wait." Boutet scrambled to keep her gun on him.

He doubled back and ducked, using his neighbours as a shield. He apologized to them and jumped the fence. Lieutenant Boutet's voice cracked as she screamed for him to stop. "One warning," she stuttered, as he broke into a sprint. "Final warning!" He was midway through the uneven remains of the Roman mansion, near the small grove of cypresses, when he heard the first shot. The bullet crashed into the soft stone in front of him.

The Moroccan men shouted after him, "*Allez!*"

There were two police cars in the post office parking lot and a gendarme in uniform posted at the tabac and bus station. He looped back to the churchyard and hopped one stone fence and another. Two more shots echoed through the village, not behind him but everywhere. He did not stop running until he was past the graveyard, in the rusty detritus of a mechanical shop on the west side of the village. He sat between three truck carcasses and went over the number again, her code, longing for a mobile telephone. He longed even more powerfully for the Russian mail thief, for an afternoon with him in a soundproof room.

Three is a magic number. Lily was born at the end of the month, this month, in 1988. Two years before: 1986. His own birthday had just passed, October 27. In three years Evelyn will be thirty-eight.

03 86 27 38

If he could figure it out, they could figure it out. Maybe not the magic number, as they would not have played *Schoolhouse Rock!* in the prisons of Siberia. If the Russian had picked up other postcards with easier codes, he wouldn't be stealing mail in Vaison. Was three still a magic number? Two didn't feel remotely magic. Clouds had moved over the village and, with them, a new wind and light rain. No one was in the mechanical shop, but through the window he could see a modern coffee maker and a television set, an open newspaper and bread crumbs. He smashed the window and opened the door. The phone was old-fashioned. Two police cars passed on the departmental highway, and two more. Gunshots and fugitives were uncommon in the retirement communities of the world. He stared at the phone, beige and chipped. He could calm his heart, his muscles, his stomach before a fight. Not now. It was the instant after the Mercedes hit Lily. It was a soft-armed, grey-haired woman from the foreign affairs department at the door to tell him his parents had died in some valley of the Paraguay River.

He dialed the number twice and both times the robot operator asked him for a code. He entered the Paris area code and a half-deaf woman answered. She had never heard of any Evelyn or Agnes. The northwest area code didn't work either: the picture of Mont Saint-Michel on the postcard was not an obvious clue. The phone book in the mechanical shop was only for Vaison-la-Romaine and the vicinity, no help at all.

Yves Huard was in the Villedieu section of the phone book.

"Where are you?" said the lieutenant.

"Vaison."

"You're all over the scanners. There are probably forty gendarmes by now, from all over."

"Madame Boutet shot at me."

"We nearly always miss."

"Why did they fire you?"

"They're charging you for the de Musset murders. Amandine, Madame Boutet, is working with a detective from Paris."

"But she knows . . ."

"What does she know? They've made a lieutenant of her. Monsieur Kruse, we don't get requests and interference from Paris. I've been doing this since I was nineteen: not once before. Your story about the man they skinned in Marseille . . ."

"It was true."

"When I investigated I was presented with an early retirement package, an honourable but non-negotiable discharge. Something strange and miserable has happened here."

"I need you to look up a name for me."

"It's ruined your life and now it's ruining mine."

"He's involved in this but I don't know how. He might be Front National."

"Whatever's happening here, Monsieur Kruse, it's too big for the Front National. They can't tell the Gendarmerie nationale who to promote and who to fire, who to arrest. It's something else. I can't even speculate. The Socialists? It makes no sense."

"Do you believe me now, about my wife?"

"No. And yes."

"We'll figure it out together."

"They won't take you into custody for long. They'll find a way to get rid of you. Suicide, I guess. Before it didn't matter but, whatever you've done, it matters now. My professional advice, Monsieur Kruse, is to get the hell out of here. Just hide far away, some old village in the

Auvergne everyone has forgotten. Make up a new name for yourself, say you're British. The villagers will hate you but they won't report you as a fugitive."

"I had this Russian. He's working for the Marianis. I can speak the language. If we could get him to talk he could lead us to them. We'll find out why. But Madame Boutet—"

"You don't understand: I can't go after anyone. And if this Russian started talking to the police, it'd be the same. There would be an accident. He would trip and fall down several flights of stairs or choke on a bone."

"It sounds like . . ."

The lieutenant grunted as he stood up or sat down. "Don't take a train or a bus. The drivers and security personnel get the bulletins. Steal another car."

"How did you know?"

"We had some reports. A Fiat, right? It's what I would do if I were you. Though I wouldn't have nicked a Fiat. The Italians can't make a car worth shit. It doesn't matter what you take, but when you abandon it don't burn anything or piss on the upholstery. The owner gets the car back and the file is closed. No one even looks. Wait a while, Monsieur Kruse."

"Christophe, if you like."

"All right then, call me Yves. It means 'yew.' Yew tree. I know what Christophe means. Wait for some of the cops to go home for the day."

"Will you help me, Yves?"

"You're a fugitive."

"Yes."

"I'm a gendarme, Christophe, even if they don't want me to be a gendarme."

"Who are you working for? Who do you protect?"

"Let me think about it."

"Yves: the name is Philippe Laflamme."

• • •

The non-traditional stagette party, with white wine and kicking ass, was a line of self-defence business dreamed up by Tzvi shortly after his student became his partner. Kruse had officially despised the idea: it was dangerous and messy and no one ever learned a thing. One night in early August 1983, seven women arrived for their stagette package. All but one of them wore matching aerobics outfits, black leotards under something that resembled a one-piece bathing suit in yellow and hot pink. The odd one was Evelyn May, who wore a collared T-shirt buttoned to the top and a pair of her roommate's grey nursing pants. She had been invited too late to buy into the special outfits. A "pity invite," she called it.

She was athletic in a natural and rangy manner, almost apologetic about it next to her graceless art history colleagues. None of them knew that in her teens and early twenties she had been a biathlete in the winter and a cyclist in the summer. Her achievements in both sports had brought her so close to the Olympics that in later years she could not watch television during the games. Now it was a secret, this incongruous thing she had done when she was a kid. Kruse met her in the studio four years after her competitive days had ended, but there were photographs of her in a silver unitard stitched with old-fashioned logos, a rifle strapped to her back, her unknowable eyes behind a pair of sunglasses that had once seemed fashionable. He kept these photos during his search for her and afterwards. Afterwards he sneaked long looks at them at night, over a glass of something coarse and ashen, when everyone else in Paris was asleep.

There was a speech he made, at the start of these boozy one-night courses. The women, who had already had a drink or two before arriving and now sipped cheap Australian Sauvignon Blanc from clear plastic picnic glasses, interrupted to comment on his musculature. Evelyn, who sat on the mats with royal posture, shushed them. When he needed a model, for demonstrations, Kruse used her. She was strong and fast and sober, with bright-green eyes and a crooked smile she doled out so sparingly it was a grand achievement every time he drew one out of her. At the end of the class he asked the poor blonde graduate student out for dinner. One of her friends heard and broadcast it through the room. When Evelyn answered, she answered for everyone.

They were married four and a half years later in March, the off-season, one of the cheapest months of the year for a wedding. MagaSecure was not a martial arts school anymore: no more white wine stagettes. And Evelyn was no longer a graduate student. Their oddly matched friends, hers from the university and his from various dojos, studios, gun ranges, and security firms, and Tzvi's bald comrades from Mossad, had collected cash at the reception so they wouldn't return to the triteness—Evelyn's word, during her thank-you speech—of their apartment on the most blissful night of their lives.

Kruse had paid their landlord eighty dollars to light the path of tea candles he had hidden under red paper bags leading from the door to their bed. He had bought two dozen purple roses—her colour—and had tossed the petals on their bleached white duvet in the shape of a heart. The plan was to open the door and run in first to turn on the music—her favourite album at the time was a collection of cello adagios. He had just married a woman who knew what an adagio was.

Triteness hurt.

"Let's go home," he whispered between songs, under the disco ball in the Regatta Room.

"They collected money, Chris. Let's have an adventure." Something by The Cure started up. She had been drinking champagne since picture time on the lakefront and had slurred her way through "adventure." The bridesmaids hopped over; she pushed him away and twirled into them and danced for him.

Tea candles burning out: a bad omen. Even worse, the apartment burning down, and with it all they had accumulated: records and cassettes, books, clothes, furniture, and weapons. He had read a book about the modern marriage, precarious and doomed, in preparation for the ceremony. As close as we can be to her, we can never really know her heart, her secret life, the thoughts she entertains as she falls asleep at night. Her eyes were thin and dark in the dance-floor light of the ballroom. She danced with abracadabra arms, as though she were putting a hex on him. Two was the magic number.

Kruse walked into the hallway and called the landlord, who wanted another twenty dollars to blow the candles out, and they sealed themselves in the fourteenth-floor junior suite at the Westin Harbour Castle. She went in for a shower. Lights flickered out over the lake and at the airport beyond. They hosted three weddings per weekend at the Westin, fifty-two weeks a year, each of them perfectly unforgettable. A bellman brought a yellow bottle of champagne to the room in a bucket of fresh ice, and Kruse opened it, stared at it, poured it into two flutes, and handed one to her through the back of the shower curtain.

"I'm sobering up in here. You aren't helping."

He didn't want to drink alone, or drink at all. All day and all night he had politely declined, sipping club soda. But the demands of the occasion, now that they were alone, threatened to undo him.

For three and a half years they had lived together in a spacious but cheap apartment off St. Clair Avenue, close to MagaSecure. In the early days they couldn't fall asleep without making love. Then it was once or twice a week, when they could arrange their schedules. Evelyn's hours had become erratic, which offered them a fine excuse for allowing the days to pass. She was too tired, had a stomach ache, felt flustered, was obsessed; they'd have sex tomorrow—tomorrow for sure. By the time Kruse proposed to her, on a weekend cross-country skiing trip to upstate New York, they were doing it twice or three times a month. She said yes to his marriage proposal and, starting the following Monday, enforced Victorian Englishness. For six months before the wedding they would not sleep in the same bed or even look at each other naked. Kissing was all right, as long as it did not progress beyond lip-on-lip.

They had lost something: youth, yearning, mystery. Evelyn wanted it back.

On their wedding night, Kruse finished the glass of champagne, Veuve Clicquot, and poured another. It made him sneeze. What was an adagio anyway? Evelyn called out from the shower that the "till death do us part" bit had freaked her out a little. It didn't have to be in there at all. Why couldn't everyone just calm down for five to seven minutes? They were a couple of kids, pretty much, who had decided to throw an expensive party of a March evening and recite a couple of uncommon sentences in front of their friends. That's it. "Billie Jean," the best dance song ever written, played twice. Had he noticed?

"'Billie Jean' times two was a call I had to make," she shouted.

It had been a windy day and the branches had not yet sprouted leaves. All but pockets of the snow had melted and most everything remained brown. Winter wasn't the problem in Canada. Spring was the problem. He took off his shirt. The window was a mirror when he wanted it to be one. He did and he didn't. Once, as a kid, he had discovered a turtle on Toronto Island; his father had taken him there, some church business.

The disc jockey had tried to argue against Evelyn's wish: playing "Billie Jean" twice could ruin his reputation. It would seem careless. He was the son of a client, a Sikh man who called himself Mister Music, and Kruse's only real contribution to the wedding plan.

She walked out of the shower in a white Westin robe. Her hair was not wet. "So I said to him: 'Your reputation? You live in Mississauga!' And he didn't find me at all charming. Was that wrong?"

Thirty wasn't old. Why did all of this make her feel so old?

She had not brushed her teeth in the bathroom. Her breath, hummus and champagne, was curiously delicious. After the wildness of the reception, thanks to Evelyn's collection of smashed academics—

Kruse's eerie friends had long departed—the smallness and cleaning-fluid quiet of the room ambushed them. Who was this woman, really? The unexpected tension, the near vertigo of the occasion, inspired him to turn on the television. He helped her out of the bathrobe.

So it was that Lily was conceived on their wedding night in March 1988 by the flat blue-and-white flashes of *Murder, She Wrote*.

• • •

He drove just to drive on small departmental roads an hour and a half north and east, through Nyons and into the low, rocky hills of the Drôme. Evergreens and cypresses and cedars played against the clear blue of the autumn sky. In Ontario, on a day like today, it would be raining or snowing. The elevation past Nyons was too high for grape-vines, but there were olive groves and fruit orchards. Houses built along the thin highway carried an exhausted look about them, as though the owners had finally given up patching the mortar. Weeds grew up through the cracks on the narrow, unforgiving shoulders, a nightmare for cyclists but they didn't seem to care. Every few kilometres he would pass one or two or twelve of them in neon outfits plastered with logos. Were they pretend-sponsored? Evelyn would know. Now and then a palm tree would show up on the side of the road, in some yard of hope. His car was a new Citroën BX Prestige with Spanish licence plates. He had waited four hours at the mechanical shop, until midway through the siesta, and then he had crept back into the centre of town. There were two gendarmes in front of the cathedral and more at the entrances and exits of the ruins. The rest were on their lunch breaks. He hid in the children's park and watched the owners of the Citroën, a white-haired couple in out-of-season Lacoste pastels, park the car and get into a small van for a guided tour of the wine route.

Saint-Nazaire-le-Désert is a tiny village with a small church, a bistro, and a plaza with a simple fountain. If Villedieu had not been close to a population centre, and so popular with a certain kind of tourist, it would look like this: a simple farm town with twisting roads to confound the mistral. The trees had been lovingly clipped but many of the stone buildings were falling apart. Blue had been drained from the shutters, red from the terracotta. An unneutered hound loped across the main street. In the plaza some old men played *pétanque*. A mini-market with white awnings had been set up to sell fruit, vegetables, and dried sausage across from a *boulangerie-épicerie*. The telephone booth looked as though it had been scrubbed clean earlier that morning. He had escaped the cloud and it was not only sunny now but warm. Villagers wandered with their baskets to the market, nodding at him as they passed. They wore short-sleeved shirts and held on to summer tans.

In the square he leaned on the high, rusted fender of a tractor and stared at the telephone booth. He had stopped at a gas station outside Nyons and had copied the national area codes out of a more complete phone book.

"Are you all right?" A man in a brown hat stained nearly black leaned over a cane. His plump wife stood nearby with a basket of zucchini and garlic, and a bottle of wine, in a floral dress and new shoes.

"Yes, Monsieur, Madame, thank you for your concern."

"Do you need a glass of water, young man?"

"I have to make a phone call. Then I will fetch a glass of water."

"You are not from here."

"No."

"Where are you from?"

"Toronto."

The man shook his head.

"Canada."

"Ah, our little cousins. Welcome, Monsieur. And I do hope you feel better. You look like . . ." Before he could finish, the gentleman's wife apologized for him and pulled him away. Kruse wanted the frail little man to come back, to talk to him all day.

• • •

His France Télécom card was black and a little bent, warm from being in his pocket. He pushed himself off the tractor, unsure if he could walk, and made his way across the plaza to the telephone. The card went in and the robot woman welcomed him, and the European dial tone that would never sound right hummed in his ear. He tried three more area codes. One rang out, another was for a bakery in Cahors. The last geographic code didn't work at all, as the number was unassigned. Maybe two was the magic number. Before he started over he tried a mobile code. There was a click and static.

Behind the static, in the distance, "Chris?"

Her voice was Lily's voice and the nighttime creaks of the house on Foxbar Road, the subway in the middle of the afternoon when almost no one is on it, the studio in MagaSecure, the smell of her shampoo, the skin on her neck, holding her hand in the soft seats of the O'Keefe Centre while someone from China or Israel plays the viola, the Westin Harbour Castle on their wedding night. He spoke and she did not hear him, as the static washed over the line.

"I hate cellphones." The connection was weak and, in the distance, it sounded as though others were having a conversation. She was underwater. "Are you there?"

"Yes."

"I can hear you now. It's wonderful. Where are you calling from?"

"A little town in the Drôme." All the things he wanted to say to her and they were talking geography. "They came for our mail. It's criminals, Ev."

"I know."

"Hired criminals. Working for . . ."

"That's the part I don't understand. The men at the bar with Jean-François that night. He didn't drink, not really, not like that. Did he?"

"You saw the noseless man."

"At the farmhouse. He killed them. How did you know? Have you seen him?"

Kruse told her about the Marianis, about his suspicions, the Front National, his day and night in Quimper, Annette Laferrière. He didn't say much about Annette Laferrière.

"Can you come?"

"I'm coming. Where?"

"There's a narrow street in Lyon, Rue René Leynaud, one of those places the sun can't get at. The church is called Saint-Polycarpe. It's being renovated so it looks shut up. I'm in here."

"Does anyone know you're there?"

"Only the priest. He believes me."

"Believes what, Evelyn?"

"I didn't kill them. You know I didn't kill them, don't you? I couldn't."

"I believe you."

"You had a funeral for her?"

"Yes."

"And it was beautiful?"

"When it came time to talk, to say something, I just blubbered away."

"Lily knew. I don't know what I . . . part of me just wants them to come and take me. The police, this man without a nose."

"She was happy enough."

"I could have made her happier. I was ashamed of her."

"You weren't."

Evelyn sobbed and spoke. "I thought people would look at her face and think the girl is flawed and the mother is flawed."

"Stop."

"Don't interrupt me! I told the priest too. And I told him I blamed you for that. It was your fault and I had to live with it, to carry it. And the university. When I could have been playing with her like you did, dollies or what the fuck else, anything, just colouring or just sitting and holding her as she watched *Sesame Street*. What are we here for, on this planet?"

"Evelyn."

"Don't interrupt me. We're here to love."

"She loved you."

"And I was ashamed."

"Did you have an affair with Jean-François?"

"I'll tell you everything."

"Did you?"

"Come on, Chris."

"So: yes. Yes?"

"It seems ridiculous now. It makes no sense. Just get in the car and—"

"Why?"

"He said things no one said, about my ideas, and he understood me and I could hear him say words I had given him that made him better. When he won I'd get a job in Paris, doing things I always dreamed I might do."

One of the market stalls, the one selling vegetables, had run out of onions. "*Oignons!*" a man shouted to another, in a white truck.

And a moment later the second man appeared with a wooden tray. "*Oignons!*" he said.

It was charming to the small crowd, the call-and-answer routine, and a few people clapped.

"I never imagined."

"And I love you for that, Chris. You never imagined."

Static came in again like a wave, and if she was speaking now he didn't hear her. His stomach had gone sour, his hands cold. Her voice returned, still under the sea. She finished a sentence: ". . . why I believe. Do you understand? Can you forgive me?"

There were twenty-five credits left on his card, which couldn't be right. It had come with twenty-five credits. He was asking the wrong questions. If he knew what had happened in the farmhouse Halloween night, and if he knew why, he could tell someone.

"You're coming now?"

"Yes."

"Rue René Leynaud, in a neighbourhood called La Croix-Rousse. There's scaffolding in front of the church. You'll find me through the side door. It looks broken but it isn't. Just shove. Kick it if you have to kick it."

"I'm two or three hours south of you."

"No one is watching?"

"I'm alone, Evelyn."

"Her birthday would have been in a week. Less than a week. Our Lily: four years old. Can you believe it? Four."

A woman tripped on a loose stone in front of the onion men and her basket of apples and sausage overturned. Several people helped her back up.

"I'm a different woman now, Chris. I want you to know that."

"We can start over."

"That's what I want, to start over. I'm sorry. I didn't get it before but I get it now."

A blast of heat started in behind his nose and bloomed over his face, and he didn't want her to hear him so he softly hung up the phone. He turned away from the plaza and stared at the small digital display of the phone box until the tears stopped and he could buy a peach for the road.

THIRTEEN

Rue René Leynaud, Lyon

IT WAS A LIE.

He had imagined her in the arms of other men hundreds of times: in her ugly office at York, in their bedroom when he and Lily were at the Canadian National Exhibition or tobogganing, but mostly in downtown hotel rooms. Her official philosophy, what Evelyn taught and what she believed she believed, could never really account for the encroaching thump of middle age and how we surrender to it.

Evelyn was a stranger who called him Chris. He had not seen her in two weeks and he was forgetting her face.

It was a horror. He could not abide it. He thought he could not abide it. He could abide it. It was nothing. There were thousands of places to hide north of Saint-Nazaire-le-Désert, tiny roads plastered with dust that went into the past. Provence was lush but this was something else, more extreme, more familiar, more Canadian. It could snow here, any day now, and cover the brown grasses and thin trees, cover the spruce boughs white. Smoke was visible above chimneys. They could live in an abandoned cabin along some green river, an hour from Grenoble, eat fish and boar and berries and nuts until all this was forgotten.

He entered Lyon from the south, along the glassy Rhône. Thick clouds and a thin mist crouched over the city but there was no wind and it was warm enough that walkers and motorcyclists went without jackets. Concrete apartment buildings, the jollier French versions of brutalism, faced the autoroute and the quay. Aging overpasses and graffiti, low-income towers, and young men driving like psychopaths, Dr. Dre and Nirvana and Pearl Jam thumping in their tiny cars, all the ruin of European romance, escorted him into the medieval city.

The quay was named after Jean Moulin. While Evelyn had read guidebooks to prepare for their year in France and Lily had looked at pictures of Paris, Kruse had read about the war. Jean Moulin was one of the country's top Resistance leaders, betrayed and captured by the Germans. The head of the Gestapo here, Klaus Barbie, the Butcher of Lyon, tortured him until he was just about dead. Then he died.

Before he entered La Croix-Rousse there was an accident. Two ambulances and a police car sneaked through the traffic and he waited in the Spanish Citroën for an opportunity to turn left. He looked around him, thinking about Evelyn's question: "No one is watching?"

No one was watching. In just a few minutes he would see her, and the anticipation came with a purr of nausea. She had said it once before, when she was angry with him and a little drunk on white wine one evening on Foxbar Road, that without Lily they were nothing. Strangers. In front of the Citroën the traffic was now entirely gummed. The woman next to him, driving a small truck, honked her horn and slapped her steering wheel. No one is watching? But a thought shoved his sweeter anxieties away, like a silent blast: *no one is listening?* His calling card, twenty-five credits forever. It was either a mistake or it was not a mistake. The map was open on the passenger seat: four blocks ahead turn left. Take the first right and then . . . in the van the woman honked again and shouted so loudly he could hear her through two windows. "*Mais non!*" Kruse grabbed the map and opened his door and ran past the cars and trucks and scooters and motorcycles. Someone shouted at him to stop. The accident was not serious: a woman and two men argued as a cop tried to calm them and a paramedic smoked a cigarette. They all turned to watch Kruse.

On the other side of the accident the quay opened up and he called out in frustration, a cuss word in English he had not said aloud since Lily was born. Rain started to fall, light and cool. Tzvi would abandon him for his stupidity, his fucking *fuck* stupidity. He turned left at a parking lot entrance and a pedestrian plaza and broke into a sprint, shouting nonsense now. At the end of the plaza he veered right and arrived at an intersection of five narrow routes, the sorts of streets Evelyn had described. Some Lyonnais watched him, backed away as he spun madly. "Saint-Polycarpe!" he said, to all of them. "Saint-Polycarpe!" He looked at his map for a moment, the absurdity of stopping to look at a map.

"Monsieur," said a woman with a shopping bag on wheels. She pointed up at one of the blue signs: Rue Saint-Polycarpe.

The street rose gently to a church with scaffolding and a clock, Evelyn's church. He dropped the map and ran past a group of young men and women, students, who mocked him for it. "Faster," one said, in a silly voice.

"Faster," they said together.

Birds sat hunched on a power line before Saint-Polycarpe, waiting for the rain to stop. One fluffed its feathers. The bird's gesture convinced him the France Télécom card was simply broken. He was a mess, an idiot, a fabulist. He had abandoned the Citroën for nothing. Sleep was what he needed. "A little perspective!"—one of Evelyn's phrases. The two heavy doors were wooden and pasted with a laminated piece of paper apologizing for the construction. Mass on Sunday would start as usual, at 11:00. What passed for a side door was a gate covered in plywood. Someone had written on the plywood, in black marker, that God is dead. The gate was propped open. He didn't have to kick it. Kruse shoved and it creaked for him, and then he was in the cool and the darkness of the place. Water dripped in a smelly puddle. He climbed a set of stairs, his heart audible. There were lights somewhere, enough to see Jesus suffering on his cross, carved arches and pillars and Renaissance balconies. A sign had been hung from two poles in front of the choir, below suffering Jesus: "*REVENEZ À MOI DE TOUT VOTRE COEUR.*" Come back to me with all your heart.

"Evelyn?"

His voice echoed. Water dripped. Beyond that, the sound of feet shuffling over a hard floor. She was in Jean-François's bed, or perhaps in the sunshine of his garden, at the precise moment that Lily broke her last porcelain teacup. She was the shy athlete in his self-defence class, his abracadabra wife. Two is the magic number.

It was much colder in the church than outside, and it smelled faintly of candles and of diesel. Wet stone and something else, something dark and fresh.

"I'm here. Hey, I have the funniest story to tell you."

The churches of his childhood were boxy and unadorned, homely vessels for a beautiful God. Peace was a fetish. There was no mystery or invitation in any of the banners or posters. His father had spent a teenage summer in southern Manitoba, in a city full of Mennonites, where two of the churches were split on whether or not it was a sin to put whitewall tires on a car. Men and women would hide record players in their attics, to play Chopin without being outed as ostentatious fools. Ceilings were not high and decorated, like this one, to make us feel little before God. They were just ceilings, with cheap lighting fixtures, because Jesus—the one true Jesus—would not have approved of anything fancy.

"Evelyn!"

To eat, she would have to leave. He had passed several unappealing African and Middle Eastern food stalls. Perhaps she had become a Frenchwoman: perhaps she was sleeping. The pipes of a giant organ gleamed in the half-light, and a white statue of the virgin and her baby.

He ran up the stairs, to the organ, and looked down into the emptiness of the church and called out to her again. "Please," he said. The vessel for holy water looked empty. Kruse went back down and lit a candle because it was too dark to see into the chapels, and he said a few words for Lily and meant them. He stepped closer to the chapels and prepared himself, said no out loud and no again, no no no.

It looked as though something had been stacked in a few of the chapels, for the renovations. The holiness of a holy place could be turned off, it seemed, and on again.

He fell to his knees in the chapel of St. Francis Xavier.

Evelyn had been tied to a wooden chair, her wrists bound in front of her with her favourite white scarf. He crawled to her, through the warm puddle, and said her name. There was a word for what they had done to her: garrotte. A bruise on the side of her neck, above the fishing line and the deep wound, still leaking, reminded him of a hickey. Marie-France, the turtle *doudou*, was in her pocket, so he took it out and kissed it and stuffed it in his own. He called for help and understood it was stupid. He touched her face with the back of his hand, and like her blood on the floor it wasn't cold, not yet, there was still hope, and he kissed her and told her he forgave her, it didn't matter what had happened, they would go off to Spain. It was his fault. All of it was his fault: their marriage, Lily's death, and now this. He untied her wrists and used the scarf to stop up the flow of the blood on her neck. The left side of his wife, the white silk blouse and skirt, were soaked. They would never get these stains out. She must have been freezing in here. "Shh," he said, though there was no sound outside him and he knew it. He had made an error, between Saint-Nazaire-le-Désert and here, out of the weakness in his heart. Before they had spoken on the phone, before she had said the words, his plan had been to bring her flowers. Red chrysanthemums, he had heard somewhere, these were autumn flowers. An enormous bouquet, utterly useless. They would steal a new Volvo with Italian plates or German and go to some obscure border crossing in the Pyrenees, the flowers in the back seat like a sleeping child. Spaniards were relaxed about this sort of thing. He was so angry with her but he loved her and kissed her again, apologized for getting blood on her perfect face.

He barely heard it over his own voice, the foot behind him in the puddle, a bare foot. He turned and looked at it, at both feet, and up at Lucien who breathed into his swing: a bat but not for baseball.

Of all he had imagined these last weeks, nothing had led him to this. The taste of it, to kill this abomination of a man, and now to be killed. He did not lift his wet hands. It was too late, just long enough to close his eyes and reach with his mind for Lily and for Evelyn in forgiveness somewhere, in the Paris of their imaginations.

PART THREE

FOURTEEN

Montée Saint-Barthélémy, Lyon

DID KRUSE UNDERSTAND THAT A LIFETIME IN A FRENCH PRISON WAS a multitude of horrors? Did he understand what they did to Americans in there? Americans who think they're smart and cool?

"I don't know if he thinks he's cool." The larger of the two men did not raise his voice. He did not address Kruse. "He had a dolly in his pocket, a turtle dolly covered in blood, when they brought him in."

There were no windows in the concrete room, the room he had expected all along. The walls were beige, the paint cracked and mottled. The floor was untreated, with a mouldy hole in the middle and a black stain leading to it. One of the fluorescent bars zapped on and off. It was an abattoir. The smaller of the two police was bald, his head cleanly shaved. He had thin legs but his chest was muscular. He spit when he spoke, like a stage actor.

"So you think you're a big, tough American? How did you get those scars on your face? Tell us about it."

Cops were called *flics* here. He had said nothing so far, not at the church and not at the police station. No one had read him his rights, if he had any rights as a foreigner. No one had charged him with anything.

"The judge will have all of this in your confession, which is the easiest way to go about this, Monsieur Kruse. Your daughter is hit by a car and killed by Jean-François de Musset. That night you and your wife go to their house and kill Monsieur and Madame de Musset, in revenge. Then your wife, who had fallen in love with Jean-François, is so disturbed she runs. But you don't know why she's running until you see the newspapers. You had no idea! A cuckold! She had been sleeping with the prick. So you hunt her down and murder her in a chapel in Saint-Polycarpe."

"No."

The bald detective stood and shouted at him, his heavy shoe clanking on the metal-rimmed hole. Foam and slobber formed on his lips like snow on a curb. A pregnant vein was visible where his hairline had been. A foreigner comes to his city, kills his wife in a seventeenth-century church. This does not happen in Lyon. This is not New York City! Motherfucker, he called Kruse, in English.

Kruse nearly laughed, not at their theory but at the way the flic had said "motherfucker," like in a *Saturday Night Live* sketch making fun of Frenchies. "The Marianis killed Evelyn. They killed the de Mussets too, and you know it."

He sighed, the bald man who had been shouting, and walked to the reflecting window. "I see. The Marianis, the actual Marianis, would risk everything to come personally to Lyon to kill a woman in a church. Why?"

"I don't know, Monsieur."

"He's an assassin." The larger and younger detective pulled out a card and handed it to his small explosion of a partner. One of the men wore the same cologne his father had worn, a drugstore cologne.

The bald one lifted his glasses to read the card. "MagaSecure, based in Toronto, hired by . . . a European client?"

"No."

"Don't tell me this was business. How many others have you killed, here in my country? In Lyon. My city! The city of my ancestors and my children!" The bald detective leaned over the table and spoke softly into Kruse's ear. "In certain cases, special cases, we can make sure you're treated monstrously in prison. Like a pretty girl."

"*Je m'en fous.*"

The policeman lingered over Kruse, as though he were wrestling with the idea of punching him in the face. He took a cigarette from his partner.

Kruse had worked through the concussion on a hospital bed, guarded by three young policemen in uniform. Why three? Kruse had spoken the truth: he didn't care what happened to him now. Lily and Evelyn were gone. There was Tzvi but Tzvi was special—he needed no one and nothing. Kruse only had one thing left to do and he was impatient to do it.

"We have others here, unofficial police," said the larger one, not at all the good cop. He sat with perfect posture, as though he had been too shy to say the ugly words. "Laws about treating murder suspects with decency and respect do not apply to these police. They don't exist, you see."

"I murdered no one."

The bald policeman jumped and landed in a fighting stance. More screaming ensued. Lies, foreign lies, importing American values, the violent sodomy he was in for. It would hollow out his sore head and leave him a withering walnut-shell of a man. They had caught him in the room, with the knife, with a motive.

"With a concussion."

"She fought back, brave woman. Brained you one."

"It was a baseball bat. Lucien Mariani—"

"No one plays baseball in France, my friend."

Kruse had not asked for a lawyer, a translator, or a representative of the Canadian embassy. He would have been as happy in prison as on the streets, an eternal wanderer.

The large man finally stood and stretched. He turned on a tape recorder in the corner of the room and asked Kruse to begin at the beginning. At first the bald one mocked him for inventing a story. What they wanted was the truth, not some fairy tale. Then, slowly, both of them shrank into their hard chairs and stopped pretending to be hangmen. It had not suited them. These were family men, readers of detective novels, playing at being hard.

"We should . . . we must make a phone call." The larger of the two policemen spoke softly when Kruse was finished. "In case there's anything to this . . ."

"A call to whom?"

"*Merde.*"

"It's all lies, I'm sure," said the bald man, with fading conviction. They knew what a lie sounded like. "But it's easy to test them. It's easy to test your filthy stories, Christophe."

A North African policeman in a new uniform, one of his guards from the hospital, escorted him to his cell. It had a small bed and a very clean stainless steel toilet. There were no bars, like in the movies, and no window. His door was another giant hunk of swinging concrete with a slot at the bottom for his trays of food. At dinnertime he received a small paper cup of red wine with his slab of meat, his bread and butter, his cooked beans.

Evelyn would have found that charming, wine in jail.

• • •

They brought him two changes of clothes: a navy blue suit and a typically French casual outfit of jeans, a well-ironed white short-sleeved shirt, and a sweater. Salon shampoo, a box of aftershave and eau de cologne by Christian Dior, a new electric razor, socks, and underwear with the word "Givenchy" stitched on the white waistband were all in a white cotton bag. How sorry they were for his treatment—not just today but since his family's arrival in France. In the basement of a hospital they introduced him to Evelyn's blanched and waxy body, left him alone with it in the refrigerated room. The silent and bowing woman who tended the morgue had unzipped Evelyn's bag too low and he was abandoned to all of her, from her dark eyebrows and little nose down to her knees. He didn't know what to do or say.

Several times they assured him it was the best hotel in Lyon. Maybe not for men of business but certainly for men of taste. This was, he supposed, a compliment. It was a former convent, painted soft yellow like so many of the others in the pastel city, overlooking the river and downtown—the Presqu'île. It didn't feel like a convent, with the arches and statues and tapestries. His own room was drunk with French classicism, la suite Médici: chandeliers, tapestries, gilded everything, and a view over a lush and fussy courtyard. Two men and a woman with walkie-talkies waited in the salon—for his protection, they said—while he showered the prison from his hair and skin, and sat in an ancient burgundy chair with the door closed and the lights out. It wouldn't be difficult to escape now but he wanted to wait and see if he could do it without hurting any of these people. They were not the ones he wanted to hurt. He put on the clothes they gave him, the outfit every middle-class French father wears on a Sunday afternoon in Luxembourg Gardens, with his daughter in one hand and an ice cream cone in the other: new jeans, a polo shirt, and a soft blue sweater. The city of Lyon, from above, was butter and Easter eggs. He could see, from his terrace, the top of the church where the noseless man had cut the life out of her.

They returned the bloodstained turtle *doudou* to him in a plastic Ziploc bag. Kruse opened the bag and smelled Marie-France. It no longer smelled of Lily. At dusk the small party arrived, five bodyguards in suits to replace the others who had put in a full day, and their bosses—a man and a woman. The way they walked and smiled and dressed, the way they watched him, he thought of meetings in Toronto and New York and Washington with senior bureaucrats and executives who hired him and feared him the way they feared a zoo tiger.

The agents introduced themselves, Monsieur Meunier and Madame Lareau, without stating their titles. Evidence of long-ago military training lived in their posture and in the confident but uncomfortable way they stood next to each other after the introduction. They inhabited a space between funeral director and tap dancer. Both wore conservative autumn suits. Monsieur Meunier was balding grandly, shamelessly. He was a man who had gone soft and fleshy, with girlish eyelashes and a careful manner of walking about the small hotel room, his feet pointed out, his pelvis and soft belly in the lead, his fingers knitting something small and invisible. What remained of his hair was a blow-dried black and grey hood of curls. Madame Lareau had been careful not to allow herself to be beautiful on the job. She wore no makeup. Her own deep brown hair had been pulled back so tightly it had an air of self-torture. One of her eyes was different than the other, and he didn't concentrate on what she said because he didn't care and because he was trying to figure them out. Neither agent asked for information about him, what he did back in Canada and what he had been doing here in France. Monsieur Meunier, who was either a homosexual or pretending, spoke of Lyon as though Kruse were here on holiday. Had he experienced dinner on historic Rue Mercière? In a *bouchon*, a classic little *restaurant Lyonnais*? This had been the Roman capital, the financial centre of Western Europe, a silk-weaving city, a publishing city and, today, an eating city.

One of the guards was actually a server in white gloves. When there was a knock on the door he worked with hotel staff to prepare the table and to open the champagne. The door was open as they worked. He thought of going now because none of this mattered, but one last sleep would be useful. The guard in white gloves poured three glasses of champagne and there was another knock on the door: crackers, cheeses and fruit and charcuterie, grape tomatoes. He stood at attention for a moment, waiting for someone to compliment the spread. Finally the woman—Madame Lareau—dismissed the server.

Then all of the guards went out the door. Kruse knew which of them was armed, which had seen combat. The others were frightened.

"To France," said Madame Lareau, and she lifted her glass. One of her eyes was smaller than the other. At the correct angle it was clear, the reconstructive surgery like playdough without dye. There had been an accident or not-an-accident. Her hand trembled, with the champagne in it.

Monsieur Meunier raised his glass and placed his right hand over his heart, stood comically at attention and chuckled. He said, in a mock-serious voice, "To France." His partner glanced at him and his smile faded.

Kruse said nothing and did not drink. The agents prepared small plates of food, passing glances, and sat in two luxurious red and gold chairs made to look old. For a time Kruse didn't sit and then he pulled the wing chair from the bedroom into the small salon of the suite, next to a decorative table. Soft horn music was playing on the clock radio in his dark bedroom, and he wished he could lie down into it instead of speaking to a couple of ruined functionaries.

Madame Lareau chaired the meeting.

"Let's begin, shall we, by stating your crimes."

Her partner took care of this, with both precision and a tone of apology: the murders of Jean-François and Pascale de Musset, several counts of auto theft, a grave assault on Antoine Fortier, the president of the Front National. An undocumented Russian man is in the hospital with fractured ribs and a punctured lung. He had slowly strangled his wife in the chapel of an historic church with fishing line, and he had kept tightening the line until it cut through her carotid artery. For each allegation, Monsieur Meunier produced a black-and-white photograph. He described the recommended penalty for each crime and assured Kruse he would be convicted. The French Republic was certain. He would spend the rest of his life in La Santé. Had he by chance heard of La Santé? Monsieur Meunier described the prison, located in the fourteenth arrondissement of Paris, the way he had described Rue Mercière. Again he provided helpful photographs: this time blurry images of vomit- and feces-strewn concrete floors, suicides, murders, and—saving what he called the best for last—guard-sanctioned gang rape for the most visible enemies of good taste and the republic.

Madame popped a tomato in her mouth and chewed and stared at him. "Do we understand each other, Monsieur Kruse?"

"You have fabricated my guilt."

"Guilt is guilt, Monsieur. Are you sure you wouldn't like a glass of champagne? It's from a lovely small producer south of Reims, a family friend."

Meunier squinted and opened his arms. *Come on, man, it's delicious.*

"No, thank you."

"But wait, Monsieur. Don't despair."

"I'm past despair."

"We do have much prettier photographs to show you."

The first pictures were of a landscape similar to that which surrounded Vaison-la-Romaine, minus the white patches of holiday houses: low mountains and green valleys, vineyards, a river. Meunier handed them over delicately, like religious objects: a soft-yellow two-storey farmhouse in the sunshine, a *bastide*, surrounded by its own small vineyard, with freshly painted blue shutters. Without consulting them, Madame Lareau described the images like a real estate agent crossed with a poet. Interior photos were of a modern kitchen, an old fireplace surrounded by the sort of furniture Evelyn adored: a boxy white couch, old wooden wing chairs, a dining table surrounded by contemporary, perhaps slightly over-designed chairs. Three bedrooms: one, curiously, with a crib.

Madame Lareau placed her glass of champagne on the table and

switched to American-accented English. "The republic, in its munifi-
cence, has chosen to see you as a victim. But all choice and all charity
can be rescinded, Mr. Kruse. Do we understand each other?"

"No."

"You can go to La Santé or you can help us, you see? And this is your
reward."

"Help you do what?"

Monsieur Meunier had saved three exterior shots for the last: a shiny
new tricycle on the gravel driveway, a wooden swing set in the shade of
a gigantic tree, an in-ground swimming pool.

Kruse took the photos. This is what he had imagined for them, from
his bed on Foxbar Road: no cities, only the three of them. A garden,
a small white truck. This was his South of France. "But they're dead,
Madame, Monsieur. My daughter's dead and my wife is dead. None of
this matters."

"What matters to you?"

"I'm going to find them," he said, in English, "and I'm going to kill
them."

The agents looked at each other for a moment; it was as though
an unexpected smell had come in through an open window. "You are
operating, whether you know it or not, at a very high level, Monsieur
Kruse. The situation you've found yourself in is unique. Lucky, even."

"Lucky."

"You could be in prison already. A judge, any judge, would convict
you."

"Lucky."

Monsieur Meunier pointed a triangle of cheese at him. "What did
she see, that night?"

"What night?"

"The night of the murders? Your daughter was killed and, a few
hours later . . ."

"I don't know."

Monsieur Meunier sniffed and sat back, crossed his legs. "It's one of two things. Either he knows nothing or he's lying. He can't help us. He's haughty and dismissive. I say La Santé for him."

"We can help him help us," said Madame Lareau.

"He's too proud."

"I don't think so. He is an artist, deep down."

"An artist, she says." Monsieur Meunier stood up, refilled his glass of champagne again and refilled Madame Lareau's glass. He strolled into the bedroom. "What did they give you to wear, Monsieur Kruse? Just one outfit, that old man outfit? I can help with that, you know. Get you something decent. What are you, a fifty-two?"

Madame Lareau presented Kruse with a business card emblazoned with the French flag and motto: "Corinne Lareau, Sous-directeur, Direction de la Protection et de la Sécurité de la Défense." She continued to speak English.

"Our current president, as you know, is François Mitterrand, leader of the Socialist Party. Once he was popular and now he is not. This is entirely normal in politics, as you also know. But the depth of his unpopularity, at the moment, is rather special—at least in the Fifth Republic. There have been scandals and others will certainly be uncovered. He has been a naughty, if principled, president. My personal view: I like him. Others will not agree. All I want, in the coming years, is fairness. I want democracy to prevail. This is what we fought for, in the war, is it not?"

"What war?"

"Good point. War is different now. I was involved in Libya. My clandestine days." She touched the nearly invisible scar, around her eyes. "Do you know much about politics, Christopher?"

"My wife did."

"Yes, she did. She helped her friend—her boyfriend, yes?—Jean-François de Musset craft a wonderful little narrative. Didn't she? Let me tell you, his interview on *Bouillon de culture* was the talk of Paris. I will put it very simply. Let's say you have one viable political party on the left, the Socialist Party. Yes?"

"Yes."

"And, I don't know, five on the right. Six, even. Still with me?"

Kruse crossed his arms.

"The old establishment, here in France, they are in love with the ghost of Charles de Gaulle. They will do anything to bring him back. Do you see? But where is he? If five parties are fighting with the socialists, even weakened socialists . . ."

"The socialists could win. Yes. What does this have to do with Evelyn?"

"There are many powerful people who want to grasp the coming opportunity, to destroy the Socialist Party and the legacy of President Mitterrand. Historically, you would call these men and women Gaullists, as I have said, republicans . . . businessmen and the ideological allies of businessmen. Even the ones who say they are not Gaullists are Gaullists. Those who feel born to lead, entitled by education and breeding. You have those in America. It's the natural way of things, your late wife would have said. I read one of her publications. She sounded terribly French! Now, these men and a few women have been plotting for some time to stop arguing among themselves, over minutiae, and unite several parties into one. One party. This is an internal matter and ought to be very boring to someone like you. But there is one complication: the Front National."

"Why don't they join the other parties?"

"The Front National is unlike the others. They're populists. Their historical alignment with fascists is distasteful to the men and women who worship, as I have said, the memory of brave generals. The party is growing in the south and in the industrial north. You know this from your wife: the Front National takes an extraordinarily dim view of immigration. Institutional racism is quite normal in Europe but rarely is it written up in a party's vision statement. It is a party of stereotypes and cartoons, angry men, fundamentalists. Then along comes Jean-François de Musset and his chief adviser, Evelyn May Kruse, the segment of *Bouillon de culture*. He says everything our men who live in the sixteenth arrondissement of Paris would like to say only he's a real man, a baker, a man of the provinces and of the people. He is handsome and reasonable and gallant, a romantic."

"So."

"So this is disruptive to our moderate right-wing government-in-waiting. What can they do to get the talking donkeys back on television representing the Front National?"

"The ghost of Charles de Gaulle killed Jean-François and Pascale?"

Madame Lareau did not say yes or no. She did not nod or smile. For some time she stared at him.

"So you work for Mitterrand."

Madame Lareau stood up out of her chair and filled her glass of champagne again. She filled the third glass and handed it to him. "Have a drink."

"Jean-François would have been a convicted drunk driver and, after he hit Lily, a murderer. Why kill him and Pascale?"

"Exactly. Why?"

"Why not just ruin his career? Discredit him. He slept with the wrong woman or stole money or snorted cocaine."

"Yes, Monsieur Kruse. We think alike."

He sipped the champagne. It was wasted on him, if it was an expensive bottle. Madame Lareau stood at the window, looking out over Lyon at night. The lights reflecting off the river, the bridge, and the waterfront. He watched her and she looked back at him, waiting. In the bedroom the television news was on, the explosion sounds between stories at the beginning of the program. It was seven o'clock. The truth arrived with his fourth or fifth sip of champagne and it all went sour with him.

"They got him drunk."

"Somehow, yes."

"Evelyn saw them: two men. Joseph Mariani and a man called Frédéric."

"Frédéric Cardini. He joined the Mariani family business when he was seventeen. He began by hijacking transport trucks at the Spanish border and moved his way up."

"Jean-François didn't drink, not like that."

"They drugged him first. We found it in his system. He would have drank anything."

"I thought you didn't do an autopsy."

"They didn't. They wouldn't. We exhumed his body."

"It was supposed to be a drunk-driving conviction, which would have been enough."

"The call went out, to patrols, before your daughter was killed."

"I was walking down to the car, with Evelyn and Lily. I heard the sirens."

"They were sent to pick him up."

"But who can do that, Madame? Organize a drunk-driving conviction? And why did it have to be Joseph, instead of one of his employees?"

"They wouldn't have trusted anyone else, Monsieur Kruse. It had to be invisible, impossible. Imagine the finesse. Then, when Lily was killed they had to get rid of the politician and his wife. Quickly, quickly. The drugs in his system would have exonerated him. He would have remembered. Then, when it was finished, if someone like Frédéric got drunk with his friends and started talking . . ."

The television went silent and the pudgy agent rounded the corner with a thin brown briefcase. He placed it on the chair Madame Lareau had been sitting in and entered a six-digit combination. Inside there were four thick stacks of francs and a portfolio. Madame Lareau slowly removed a French passport, an identity card, bank cards, and a title deed to the property in the Var—under the regional authority of the office in Brignoles. First she showed him the passport, which contained a photo of him with the name Claude Roulet, born in Lille, a current address in the Var. The identity card was also made out in the name of Claude Roulet, with his photo. The bank cards were Claude's and Claude owned the house and land.

"Who's Claude Roulet?"

"You are," said Monsieur Meunier. "Don't you already feel like Claude Roulet? Of course, your parents split up when you were a youngster and you were sent to live with your British mother in Rhode Island, United States. This explains your accent. But you are a Frenchman. You have always wanted to be a proper Frenchman, no? Retiring quietly at forty to a *bastide* in the country?"

Madame Lareau explained the investigation would be announced publicly in two months' time.

"You'll bring in Joseph and Lucien?"

"Who?"

"The murderers, the—"

"You don't understand, Roulet. This plot was conceived in Paris and Marseille by some of the most powerful men in France. Return the Front National to cartoon status, unite the legitimate right wing, wipe out the Socialists."

Madame Lareau had taken the liberty of printing out the story he was now obliged to tell, in a secret military tribunal in Paris. None of this would ever reach the public. For his trouble, he would stay in five-star hotels like this one. He would be guarded twenty-four hours a day, of course, until it was finished.

"Do you have any questions?"

"What's in this for you, Madame? The Socialists stay in power?"

She acted as though she had not heard him. "I want to leave you with one image."

Madame Lareau reached for the large photo her partner had produced. She slapped it on the table next to him like a poker shark unveiling the final hand of the night. It was Evelyn, cradling Lily on the cobblestones of Villedieu, ten minutes after the end of her life. His life.

"I have never lost a child. I have never lost a spouse. But I would not want my loved ones to die in the service of a conspiracy. Yes, children are killed and we are all terribly sorry for that. But their murderers are punished, in a modern democracy, and their parents are soothed, however imperfectly, by justice. I cannot say you would still be with your wife, but she would certainly be alive. And you, you would be what you came here to be."

"What is that?"

"I don't know. A father?" Madame Lareau tilted her head. "A good man?"

• • •

There were so many guards travelling with Madame Lareau and Monsieur Meunier they had to take three black Citroën XM cars. Kruse was in the back seat of the middle vehicle, with Madame Lareau, who carried a small pistol and spoke on a cellular phone. The original plan was to take an executive airplane, but there was so much fog at the airport they switched to cars. She booked him in the Tuileries suite of the Hotel Regina in Paris for twelve nights, under the name Claude Roulet.

Madame Lareau told him about working in Libya to depose Colonel Gaddafi. The general was fighting a war against another lunatic, Hissène Habré, president of Chad. It was like dealing with autistic children, she said, only they had fighter jets and machine guns. Yet somehow, as always, Gaddafi survived. Some people are like that, she said; you see it in politics and war. They live through anything, while others—fine people, often enough—die by the first bullet. Madame herself was injured in an explosion in N'Djamena. The rail of an apartment terrace flew through the air and struck her in the face. She saw it coming and she remembered thinking, "Duck," but the thought was quicker than her reaction, and she woke up in a hospital with a very black, very beautiful woman in a yellow hijab reciting prayers for the dead over her body.

South of Auxerre, not far from Chablis, the three cars stopped in a convoy at a gas and restaurant complex so that various passengers might use the toilet. The plan was to practise his testimony between Auxerre and Paris, so it would seem natural. If it sounded like he was reciting a speech someone had written for him, the judge would throw them all out. He had not read it yet.

An armed guard stood at the side of the car, but he looked away often enough for Kruse to enter the combination and pull a stack of money out of his Claude Roulet briefcase. Monsieur Meunier, who carried the same small pistol as Madame Lareau, accompanied him to the toilet. Monsieur Meunier leaned against the bank of sinks while Kruse addressed himself to the urinal. "Have you heard of Philippe Laflamme?"

"Laflamme. Of course, Monsieur Kruse."

"Who is he?"

Monsieur Meunier looked at himself in the mirror. "You'll meet him in court. No hurry. He's Rally for the Republic."

"What is that?"

"A political party, Monsieur Kruse. It's in your testimony. There are two large political parties that want to be one enormous political party. You'll be speaking of them. The mayor of Paris—Laflamme is one of his . . . what would you call this in English? He holds the pitchfork for the devil."

Monsieur Meunier inspected his left eyebrow in the mirror. A single grey hair was longer than the others. He licked his fingers and yanked at it as Kruse dried his hands. Two of the guards waited outside the door.

Kruse finished.

"You needn't worry about Laflamme. Not after your testimony."

"No?"

"He'll be in prison soon enough. So tell me, honestly, what do you think of the place in the Var?"

"The pictures are pretty."

"We did have options for you, Monsieur Kruse. A central apartment in any city but Paris. For you, with a German name and a French heart I was thinking Strasbourg. But isolation is always best for someone in your situation. The moment I saw the ad I knew it was the one . . . a lovely start to your new life, Monsieur Roulet. I inspected the bastide myself. Wine and a bit of music, some soft lights on the terrace, cicadas, memories. A man of our age, middle age, yes? Entering middle age? What else can you ask for? Love, of course, love. But that may come."

"Thank you."

"*Je vous en prie.*" Monsieur Meunier moved to allow him a turn at the sink. "Your testimony will put you at no small risk. It would be better than prison no matter what, but you've had a rotten bit of luck here in France. A quiet bit of luxury is precisely what you deserve. And perhaps we can work together in the future. The more we read about you and your business in America, your skills and talents, the more appealing it all seems."

"I do apologize."

"For what, my friend?" Monsieur Meunier struggled to grasp at the errant eyebrow hair with his chubby fingertips.

Kruse hit him just hard enough, in the jaw, and dragged him into a toilet stall. An announcement came over the public address system that the restaurant would be closing at two o'clock. It was loud enough to overwhelm the sound of his footsteps. Kruse walked past the guards, drinking espressos, and into the crowd. One of them spotted him and stuttered, shouted, "Monsieur! Stop!" Kruse ran to the end of the white hall and out the automatic doors. There were two gas stations, one on each side of the highway, and both led to thick evergreen forests. Kruse sprinted deeply into the trees, slicing his right arm on a branch, and hopped a fence. The forest opened up into a light industrial suburb, with filling stations for large trucks and a series of warehouses. On the other side, brown farmland, wet from recent rains, and a football pitch with white goalposts at each end. A thin fog rose from the grass.

The guards came out of the forest in a line with Madame Lareau in the middle. She shouted orders to her men in suits, as the trees opened into Burgundy. Then she spoke—screamed—into a cellular phone that it was not her fault.

Kruse removed his shoes and crept from one delivery truck to another in the wraparound parking lot of a wine co-operative. At the back of the warehouse one man in jeans and a hooded sweatshirt with Kermit the Frog on it sat on a wine barrel and smoked a cigarette. The door was propped open. Kruse asked the man, politely, if he might hide from an intelligence agency inside. Before the man answered, Kruse pulled out the stack of money. "You can keep a thousand of it, when they're gone."

"What did you do?"

"They want me to testify against politicians."

"What did the politicians do?"

"There isn't time to discuss it, Monsieur. Yes or no?"

For too long the man stared at Kruse with his mouth open. He had lost one of his front teeth. Kruse didn't want to hit him. Outside the warehouse, Madame Lareau told someone to run and hard shoes clacked on pavement, getting closer. The shop man smelled the stack of francs. "Two thousand."

The warehouse was painted white, the walls and the mopped floor, and crowded with stainless steel bins and bladders. It was warm and humid, heavy with the scents of rot and fermentation. Kruse climbed to a white, rusting catwalk. The bins were open and most of them were full. Only one had a thick layer of must on top. There was nowhere else to go so he lowered himself into it, holding on to the rim.

Voices echoed through the warehouse. The man in the Kermit the Frog hoodie delivered one-word answers—one yes and a disinterested no, twice. Kruse knew the man wouldn't tell the agents the truth, even though it would be to his financial advantage to walk away with all of the money now, though Kruse could not say why. They didn't believe him. Two of the agents, in hard-soled shoes, walked through the warehouse.

"Where is everyone?" one of them said.

Kruse could not hear the answer, something about the end of the *vendange* and a holiday.

"How can you be sure?" someone else said, and he heard footsteps on the iron stairs.

Holding his breath underwater had been part of his training, his least favourite after deliberately ruining the nerve endings in his shins by kicking a hunk of wood wrapped with a yellow rope. Kruse grew up certain he would never have to wait underwater on the Jordanian coast of the Dead Sea, as his mentor had done, and pop up at two in the morning to kill a Palestinian bomber with a guitar string. The footsteps grew nearer and he slid all the way down through the must and into the juice. The cut he had opened on his arm stung in the wine.

He counted to sixty, to one hundred, to one hundred and forty. It had been a long time since he had done this and his body rebelled. His heart beat everywhere inside him. His chest was a balloon ready to pop. In Toronto, after Lily was born, he was often stricken in the night by the conviction that something was going wrong inside him: a tumour, a ruined heart, some disease of the brain invited by too many blows to the head. The thought of dying too young, of not seeing Lily move into school and find her way and thrive, not protecting her, tormented him. He hardly slept during the first week of school, when Lily was shut away from him in École Jules Ferry and some mental defective or even a teacher could say something to her, about her lip. Or in high school, where it would be worse. Where men like Matt Gibenus stomped about waiting for a sign of fragility to pounce.

He floated gently to the top and took a shallow breath, out of the must, and sunk back down to the bottom of the tank. Some of it was in his mouth now and it did not taste right, the decomposing Chardonnay skins, so he spit them out and allowed his body for an instant to accept he was in danger. They might have shot him in the face just now, as his lips broke the surface of the juice. His uncle, his father's brother, had jumped off the Prince Edward Viaduct after his wife had confessed she had fallen in love with a gym teacher. It was in Kruse and he didn't fear it, especially now, but he was not yet finished.

When Tzvi was a soldier he was injured and captured. Some men tortured him in a jail in Beirut. At the height of it, when he was sure he was going to die, something or someone appeared at his side and told him to ease his heart and remain hopeful and focus on returning to these men and killing them, one by one, for all of this pain and indignity. It helped him survive the ordeal and it opened up a new world to him, a world still ungoverned by a God but filled with spirits. This was not a confession he delivered lightly. Kruse was the only one he had ever told, and Tzvi was open to the idea that he was slowly going crazy and this was the incitement of it. But Kruse, who had grown up in a church and with parents who did not know doubt, found it both plausible and comforting. No ghost or angel had come to Lily or Evelyn and nothing came to him now, at the bottom of the barrel of wine.

He could open his mouth and his nose to it and remain down here, fill his lungs with alcohol. This was the moment. Instead he floated again to the surface, his body burning and bursting with the emergency of it, and again he quieted his heart and breathed. This time he remained in the must, blind with it. He prepared to descend again when he heard a whisper.

"Monsieur?"

He remained with his face in the must.

"Monsieur?"

Kruse spit and tried, while treading juice, to manage a whisper himself. "Are they gone?"

"Yes. Where are you, Monsieur?"

The janitor helped him out of the juice and asked him to remain on the lid. He produced a small folded pile: a T-shirt with "La Chablisienne" on the front, a pair of rain pants, and aged canvas shoes. He had a plastic bag for Kruse's wine-drenched outfit, his gift from the agents: Claude Roulet's clothes.

Kruse paid him four thousand francs and promised him another two thousand if the janitor would drive him to Roissy.

"The airport?"

"A hotel near the airport."

"Three thousand, which would bring our total to seven thousand francs."

Kruse took the bills from the janitor and paid him. He washed his face and hair as best he could in the employee washroom, while the janitor drove one of the white Chablisienne trucks around to the back. Kruse stepped in. It rumbled and dieselled. Here in the cab of the truck, as everywhere, Nirvana was playing on the radio. The janitor, who introduced himself as Mehdi, pushed a cassette into the deck and they listened instead to Charles Trenet.

Mehdi had grown up in Tunis. His children went to a good school in Auxerre. If it weren't for his name, he said, no one would know he is Arab. He named his daughter Roxanne and his son Tristan, gifts to them.

"You came to France to be French."

"Of course, Monsieur."

"Christophe, please, Mehdi. You know, you should send a letter to the Front National, telling them about your intentions."

Mehdi slowly rolled down the window, spit on the autoroute, and closed the window back up again. Then he asked Kruse if he had a family.

"Not anymore, no."

"You're alone."

"Yes, Mehdi."

"May God intervene."

FIFTEEN

Allée des Vergers, Roissy-en-France

NORTH OF BURGUNDY THE AFTERNOON WAS DARK AND SOAKED AND wind-rocked, the flags alert, the tips of evergreens swaying along the autoroute, and the bare branches of everything else assailed and miserable. Mehdi stopped at a park in the centre of Roissy that so surprised Kruse with its beauty, he explained about Canadian airports, about how they were never so well loved as this.

"What sort of man would live in a place he does not love?" said Mehdi. "We are not on this earth long enough to make such errors."

Kruse called him a true philosopher and shook his hand. Mehdi blessed him in his princely way and drove off. The park was filled with gracious old trees and a curving sidewalk and clipped bushes. There were a few cars but otherwise Roissy was as deserted as Vaison-la-Romaine during a mistral. It was the middle of the afternoon, a time of neither coming nor going. Kruse had begun to smell, in the cab of the truck, but when he apologized for it Mehdi had told him his nose was no longer tuned to the smell of rotting grapes. We all have our rotting grapes, he said.

A men's clothing store was at the end of the block, with a pleasing hint of liquor and cigar smoke inside. A small, white-haired man squinted at him from behind the counter, where he read a newspaper. He carried a long string of measuring tape around his neck, the last real haberdasher in the world.

The haberdasher, in a brown suit and a large yellow tie, stepped down from the counter. He greeted Kruse and then seemed torn between wanting to help him and kicking him out of the store. Roissy was not a town of vagrants. Perhaps he had never seen a man so dirty, in his store.

"I've had an accident."

"Yes, Monsieur?"

"A wine-related accident, in Burgundy."

"White Burgundy, I would say."

"Chablis, in fact."

The haberdasher crossed his arms. "Nothing you're wearing fits you."

"My clothes are here." Kruse lifted the plastic bag. "All this is borrowed, from the winery."

"When we're done, all of it will go straight in the garbage. Fortunately, it is a slow day. My wife is watching television in the back, the best tailor in la métropole and nothing to do."

The tailor knew his size by sight and pulled two suits down, a navy blue and a brown, and some white shirts. He was more a blue man than a brown. Twenty minutes later, Kruse was waiting for the haberdasher's wife to finish his cuffs. He had come in to buy a pair of jeans, a simple shirt, and shoes that fit. The haberdasher stared at him, as though he were an object of study, and chose a trench coat to go with the suit.

• • •

Kruse walked swiftly through the hotel lobby and pressed the up button on the elevator, to avoid drawing attention to his hair or to his smell. The key was in his wine-drenched bag of clothes, and by the time he fished it out he could have knocked several times. If someone was inside, he wanted to surprise him—or them.

The room had been made up and their clothes were still here, Anouk's books. He had ordered them to remain inside and they were not here, so all he could do was call her number at *Le Monde.* When the secretary answered at the end of the seventh ring he hung up. His hair itched with the rotting grape juice. He was furious with Annette and he would tell her so, that around every corner was a car coming for them or a Russian with a knife. He could not leave without doing it, so he showered the Chardonnay out of his hair and skin and plotted his immediate future: he would walk the streets of Roissy in a navy blue suit and trench coat, with a hotel umbrella, and find them. The suite was empty when he exited the shower. His underwear and socks were with the suit, so he wrapped a towel around himself and walked into the small salon just as the door opened.

Anouk clapped her hands. "*Bonjour*, Monsieur Christophe."

All of his plans to be angry and victimized by circumstance and obsessed by men of cruelty were ruined by her, the way she half-skipped to him and stopped herself a foot or two away. She wore a small red peacoat with tiny drops of water resting on the wool.

"*Bonjour*, Anouk."

Her mother looked at Kruse with new tears of defeat in her eyes and looked away. She emptied a plastic bag: milk, cereal with chocolate inside, a package of individual-sized yogurts, a bottle of Bordeaux, a colouring book, and a package of crayons. "*J'ai le cafard*," she said. This phrase had something to do with depression, melancholy. Kruse didn't chide her for leaving the room. Instead he apologized and carried his new clothes into the steamy bathroom. When he was dressed, he prepared himself and stepped out.

Anouk sat on the edge of the bed, directly in front of the bathroom door. "Have you seen *The Little Mermaid*?"

"No. I haven't."

"It was on TV last night. We watched in the dark."

"What fun."

"And pizza."

"A movie and a pizza. That does sound wonderful."

She whispered, "We can do it again tonight, Monsieur."

"We'll ask your mother."

"*Non, non, et non.* Last night she said only this one time. Tonight would be more than one time."

"It will take some sly manoeuvring."

"What does that mean?"

"I might have said that incorrectly."

"What?"

Anouk sat up straight and rested her hands on her knees. She had removed her wet peacoat and wore a pink dress and white tights. Her mother had brushed the knots out of her hair. Rather than pretend it did not fill him with joy and longing to see her, he sat next to Anouk on the bed and took her hand and together they looked at each other and at nothing, the doorway into the steamy bathroom. He had failed at everything he was charged by nature and by his heart to do. They were gone forever. Yet he allowed himself to feel good and useful, holding a little girl's still-cool hand. He had grown addicted to sitting in quiet rooms with Lily, to seeing her at the end of a day of work, so addicted he found himself creating false reasons to home-school her, to keep her all to himself, his, to protect her as long as he could.

The unnecessary marriage counsellor in Toronto had said something he did not forget. At the moment it had seemed obvious and banal. He had been ignoring the counsellor, the four-syllable nouns poached from psychological experts on *The Oprah Winfrey Show*. He had stared at an unhappy ficus on top of her gunmetal filing cabinet.

"There is nothing more attractive, and more comforting to ourselves and to our partners, than truth." The counsellor had enormous and fragrant hair, teased up and blow-dried and treated with sprays and mousses. She wore a shirt with shoulder pads and several silver bracelets on each arm that clinked like wind chimes as she spoke with her arms. "As Hamlet tells us, 'to thine own self be true.'"

Part of Evelyn's education of her wretched thug were black-and-white film adaptations of Shakespeare's plays. Hamlet didn't say, "To thine own self be true." The windbag Polonius had said it, and clearly Shakespeare was making fun of a certain kind of person: the kind of person who says things like "To thine own self be true." But he had thought about it, in the room with the ficus, and Polonius and the counsellor had been correct. It was good advice, windbaggery or not. Evelyn had wanted him to be a certain kind of man, his own self by her.

He put his arms around Anouk and gently lifted her onto his knee. He kissed her on the top of her head, which smelled of the outdoors and faintly of the herbal shampoo he had just used.

"I will die in France," he said, in English, aloud by accident.

Anouk turned up to him as though he had burped in her hair. "What, Monsieur?"

"It makes me happy, to be with you."

"Me too, Monsieur. Do you have a car that is also a dog?"

"No."

"That is something I think about."

"If I see one, I'll buy it for you."

"I still sit in a car seat."

"Until you're ready, I can drive the car that is also a dog."

"That sounds like a good idea. Will you drive me to Disneyland?"

His favourite moment from any of the old movies Evelyn had made him watch was when sad old King Lear huddled with the daughter he had mistreated, his only true love in the world, Cordelia, and said sweet things that would never be: "We two alone will sing like birds i' the cage."

To lock the doors and all doors ten doors thick and remain here in this hotel room in Roissy with Anouk and her books and some *doudous*. Maybe a tea set could be arranged, their private Disneyland.

"Are you okay, Monsieur Christophe?"

He shifted Anouk back onto the bed and walked into the salon. He leaned on the door jamb and watched Annette, who had opened her bottle and had already finished half a glass. Her hand quivered. She had prepared, it seemed, to say something. She said it flatly and quietly. It was vicious, what Kruse had forced them to do. If they had gone to the police instead of coming here, to the goddamn airport, everything might have turned out beautifully. She might have written a story about it in the newspaper. Instead, Anouk had missed school and she had probably been fired *in absentia* from her degrading job, and now all she could do was go back to foggy Bordeaux and beg someone, a family friend or her philandering ex-husband, to take pity on them. No one can stay in a hotel room this long without going mental, in the same clothes, washing underwear in the sink and eating salty dinners every night.

"We'll go in the morning."

"Where?"

"The newsroom first. I will finalize our bill, downstairs. Then the concierge will find us a taxi and the three of us will go and we will stay safely in the newsroom until the story, your story, is published. Then it will be safe for you."

"And you?"

"That doesn't matter. I have to go south the moment your story goes to press."

"You're wanted for murder."

"I am and I'm not."

"It was on the television news."

Kruse filled up her glass of wine, and filled a glass for himself. "I know what happened now, on the night Lily was killed, what really happened and why."

"Who is Lily?" Anouk had followed him into the salon.

Without a word, Annette stood up and walked Anouk into the bedroom and turned on the television. It was the end of the day, so cartoons were on. "Monsieur Kruse said we could have pizza tonight again and watch a movie," he heard the girl whisper.

When Annette was back in the room with him, the door closed, she pulled a notepad from her bag and pushed the wet hair from her eyes.

He had taken the copy of the story Madame Lareau wanted him to tell in the courtroom in Paris, to ruin the Gaullists. It had not mattered to him whether he told the true story or the false story, until he was in the toilet with Monsieur Meunier, who spoke so movingly of the farmhouse in the Var. Meunier had picked it out especially for Kruse, with a lovely feeling for the cicadas and the nighttime and maybe the smell of lavender and rosemary, grapevines, lemon trees. The old armoire of Provence meets the white countertops of Sweden. A dog? Why not?

But each of the photos had been stamped on the bottom with the date July 5, 1990.

Annette took a sip of her wine and prepared her pen. She looked up at him. "They killed your wife, didn't they?"

"Yes."

"Tell me."

• • •

They finished the Bordeaux and they did order a pizza, the final hotel-room pizza, Annette vowed, of her life. The only cartoon available on the movie channel was *The Little Mermaid*, so Anouk watched it again. Midway through each of the songs, she had learned the tune well enough to sing along. At the end, when the bad sorceress mermaid grew to gigantic proportions and threatened to kill them all, Anouk took his hand and squeezed.

When she had packed for this trip to the hotel, Annette had thrown four storybooks into the bag. Kruse volunteered to read the bedtime book Anouk had chosen, after brushing her teeth and putting on her mismatched flannel panda and Je t'aime pyjamas and trying to pee. The book, *Mimi Cracra*, was a series of tales about a little girl whose curiosity and naughtiness lead her into harmless messes. Anouk laughed at the typically Canadian way he pronounced words like *chien* and *viens*. The tradition in the Annette Laferrière household was to turn out the lights, after the book, and sing a song. Annette invited Kruse to lie beside her, on the double bed adjacent to Anouk's, and sing. She smelled of sandalwood and they were both a little drunk and faintly touching, the skin of her arm on the skin of his arm. Annette's swallow filled the small room.

One of the only songs he knew all the way through, apart from selections from the Mennonite hymnal, was "The Dock of the Bay." Anouk did not know the song, and she particularly liked the whistling part. It did not bother her that it was in English.

"More," she said, "please."

Again he sang the simple song and when he was finished, the room was quiet but for the mother and daughter breathing. He turned and watched Annette by the parking-lot light that sneaked in through the curtains.

He whispered, "Are you awake?"

Annette smiled without opening her eyes. "I'm enjoying this enormously."

It was nonsense, both a lie and drunken treachery, but he imagined living with them in the big farmhouse in the Var. He dozed off, and woke just before midnight in the midst of a bloody dream. The wine had left him with a touch of vertigo. Annette had fallen asleep on her side, her dark hand on his chest. He sneaked off the bed and took off his jacket and found the blanket he had used the last time he had slept here, on the couch. He covered Annette with it and watched Anouk sleep for a while as his heart slowed. He slipped back into bed with her, and put her hand back on his chest.

A scream, a muffled scream. Half in and half out of a dream he sat up, or tried to sit up, and the ugly Russian from Villa de l'Astrolabe and Quimper whispered for him to stay exactly where he was. He grasped a handful of Kruse's hair. At the door another man carried Anouk out of the bedroom, sprawled in his arms like she was sleeping there or worse. Kruse knocked the ugly Russian's hand away and hit him and rushed across the room. He reached the doorway and shouted at the man with Anouk, to stop.

"Don't worry. I'm coming."

There was a hiccup behind him and his left arm caught fire, sprayed blood. Another man, another Russian he had never seen, stepped into the bedroom from the salon and punched him in the face. Like the shot in the arm it was a graze. Kruse kicked this new man in the groin and when the man fell to his knees Kruse kicked him in the face.

The ugly Russian was close. "Stop."

A younger man in silhouette, from the light of the salon, held a hatchet in one hand and a gun in the other.

"We're not supposed to kill you yet." The ugly one spoke quietly and calmly, behind him. "But if we must, we must. It's a dream of mine."

On the other side of the young one, Annette struggled in the salon. They had gagged her. In the two rooms he counted five men, four conscious. Kruse stepped into the salon and the ugly one hit him with the butt of his pistol, opened a cut on his forehead.

It was difficult to see for a moment, with blood in his eyes. The man with Annette opened the door into the hallway and guided her out. She stopped herself at the threshold and reached out for Kruse.

"I'm coming. I'm sorry."

"He's right, Madame, though you might not recognize him when he arrives." The ugly Russian stood close with his gun. Annette disappeared with her captor into the fluorescent hallway.

The one with the hatchet copied his accent—"I'm coming. I'm sorry. I love you."—and laughed.

"Clean up," said the ugly one, and the last man in the salon came into the bedroom to carry the unconscious one like a limp battering ram out of the suite.

Now they were alone, the three of them, in the flat light of a cheap chandelier.

"No sucker punches this time, Monsieur Kruse."

"Where are you taking them?"

"Tie him up." He was so ugly he was handsome.

Blood dripped on the floor from the wound on his arm. His left eye was a mess of gluey blood. "Can I tend to these first?"

The ugly one eased in closer with his new Beretta, pointed it at his chest. "If you give me a good reason, we can hurt you and then kill you and what can they say?"

"They: Joseph and Lucien?"

"Shut up."

"What are you supposed to do?"

"Tie you up. Beat on you awhile, for our pleasure. Take you south."

"Is that where you're taking Annette and Anouk?"

"Who?"

The one with the hatchet laughed again.

"So tie me up, then. Let's get to work."

A first-time lion tamer, the one with the hatchet. Last time Kruse had seen him, in the hotel room in Quimper, he had poked him in the eye and knocked him out. The left side of his jaw had a blob of a bruise about it. He put his pistol and the hatchet on the table.

To ease the lion tamer, Kruse turned around for him and put his hands behind his back. Kruse closed his eyes and waited for the first touch, on his wrists. He turned and slapped the rope out of the lion tamer's hands, stunned him in the nose and wrapped the rope around his neck. The ugly one shot once. His partner the lion tamer screamed and bled from his nose. Kruse used him as a shield and guided him like a mule into the ugly one, who cussed at him and threatened him with death some more, something about murdering and fucking in confused French.

The ugly Russian waved the gun about and took three more shots. The window clicked and then shattered behind them. Kruse stalked and trapped him and turned off the light. Cold blew into the room. He leapt away from the broken window, remaining low in the dark. He took the hatchet from the table, a moronic weapon, and threw the gun into the bedroom. The shot in the arm and the two blows in the head had replaced his faint Bordeaux headache. More shots popped into the drywall and the Russian cussed. A Beretta 92 had a nine-shot magazine. Kruse counted down and prepared himself.

One more bullet.

In the dark Kruse tossed the hatchet against the table and a fire twinkled in the darkness, the last shot. He remained silent for a moment, blood trickling down his face and arm, crouched on the hard floor.

The lion tamer whispered in Russian, "Did you get him?"

"Shut up, Sergei, shut up, shut up."

"Let's turn on the light."

Kruse eased himself closer, and struck with the click of the light. First, the lion tamer. He allowed the boy to swing once, then twice, and hit him where he had hit him before. This time he only went down on one knee, so Kruse had to slam his head into the door.

The ugly one threw the gun and Kruse dodged it and stalked him into the bedroom. He outweighed Kruse by fifty pounds, and he was scarred from prison. There was nothing to pick up. The gun was under the bed and the lamps were screwed down.

"Did you hurt them?"

"Who?"

"The girl and her mother, when I was sleeping."

"Fuck you."

"Where are they taking them? Where south?"

No answer, only heavy breaths, so Kruse eased in. The Russian trapped himself behind the bed, without much room to fight, and when Kruse came for him he pulled a knife. In his flailing, before Kruse could disarm him, the Russian cut the back of his hand. They fought silently and Kruse loved this part and closed his eyes again, did it by feel. The ugly one was sure he could win and then he was sure he could not, and it was like a first kiss. Kruse said things to him, in his calm voice, and with the man's face in the carpet Kruse barred his right arm and cranked it slowly, deliciously, in an unnatural direction and destroyed the muscles and tendons in it, and then he fetched the knife from the top of the bed and asked the ugly Russian another question. The Russian said he fucked his mother and Kruse cut tendons in his left arm and told him to stay quiet or he'd kill him. It didn't matter now. Maybe the Russian knew that and maybe he didn't.

Kruse cut the rope in half and tied up both of them. The ugly one remained conscious and spit at him and said he would have his revenge. Kruse carried the lion tamer into the bathroom and lay him in the tub, on top of his bound hands. Then he dragged the ugly one inside, so they were all together. The pain of lying on his hands, and the brightness of the light, woke up the lion tamer. Kruse put a pillowcase over his head and detached the shower head. He turned on the water and adjusted its temperature to lukewarm, took off his own clothes and sat on the boy's legs. How old was this one? Twenty-five maybe.

"What are you doing? What is he doing?"

"You're going to tell me some things."

"Tell him nothing," said the ugly one, in Russian. "Be strong. Die with honour. Don't humiliate yourself, Sergei."

"What is happening?"

"Sergei, don't tell him anything."

Kruse spoke softly in Russian to Sergei, about what was about to happen. If Sergei did not answer his questions, honestly and clearly, he would drown him and then he would do the same to his partner.

"Don't listen to him, Sergei. He can't kill you. He's a coward."

Kruse sprayed the water in the lion tamer's face, through the pillow-case. He could not move his arms or his legs and he could not scream. All he could do was turn his face away from the water. Kruse followed his face with the water and held him in place, by his hair. He told the lion tamer, as the water collected on his face, that if he struggled too much he would dislocate his own shoulders. It would not help anyway. Only the truth would help. He moved the water away and the lion tamer tried to scream, so Kruse shoved a bar of soap into his mouth, through the wet pillowcase, and hit him in the sore jaw again, twice, and told him if he called out it would only get worse for them both. There was only one way to make it stop, and that was by answering his questions.

"I have experience in this. I know when you are lying."

"Sergei, say nothing."

"Please stop. Please don't kill me."

"Sergei."

Kruse winked at the ugly Russian on the bathroom floor because they both knew Sergei would tell him everything.

"Who the fuck are you?" said the ugly one on the floor, in a philo-sophical tone. "Just some dad?"

"Yes."

SIXTEEN

Route de Vaison, Villedieu

AT THREE O'CLOCK IN THE MORNING THE ALFA ROMEO HE HAD STOLEN
was the only car on the narrow road, and the farmhouses were dark.
His headlights surprised a deer on the border of a vineyard, just as the
D94 rose up out of the valley. The animal looked into the light, petu-
lantly. There were no other cars in the plaza.

Kruse had not planned this. With his heel he loosened the cobblestones on the edge and pulled up five of them, gathered the soil where
she had bled. He worked while the indifferent water of the fountain
trickled and splashed behind him. When he was finished he gathered
the soil into his pockets and for a moment he felt silly, like the devotee
of a new religion, and then he didn't feel silly at all. He replaced the
cobblestones and stomped them back into the earth.

The lieutenant's house was at the bottom of the village, under the
château.

Bats swooped over the vines on each side of the house. In the darkness it smelled of rot: no one had harvested the lettuce in the small

vegetable garden behind, and it had grown too tall and wilted and died. Terracotta roofing fixtures and some cut wood lay in a sun-bleached heap between the concrete shack and the road. At this hour, not even the bakers were awake. No cars passed.

Under the lieutenant's front window lay a burst of lavender that would have been pretty and fragrant in July. Apples fermented under the bare tree, and a blend of clover and native grass had not been cut in weeks. The window shutters were unpainted. Next to the door, peeling blue, was his house number and the words spelled vertically, top to bottom, "*Bienvenue mes amis.*"

He unlatched the shutters at the side of the house, pushed a window open, and climbed in. It was warm and still, heavy with cigar and roasted meat. The small bathroom had been tagged with the lieutenant's aftershave. Water dripped. His snores were loud enough that Kruse did not worry about his footsteps on the concrete floor. Street light filled the kitchen, which opened through sliding glass doors into a small clearing before the vines. The doors were open a crack and the kitchen was a tidy corridor with heavy handcrafted cabinetry that Kruse had always associated, a little sadly, with Ontario farm life.

A police scanner lay in front of the television, turned down low. The lieutenant's wallet was on the unwashed kitchen counter, in between the blender and a pile of drying chicken bones. A freshly cleaned and oiled service pistol—another Beretta 92—was in a shoebox. Kruse sat on a worn chair in the small salon and picked his way through the wallet: money, receipts, identification as a driver and as a lieutenant, a black-and-white photo of a young woman from long ago. Several minutes passed in the dark, with rustling sounds coming from the bedroom. We tell ourselves it is nothing even when we know.

It took ten minutes for the gendarme to convince himself. "Who is it?"

The light came on, in the bedroom. The lieutenant walked into the kitchen as he put on his glasses and stood before the bones and the blender, his chest as hairless as a baby's. The lieutenant wrapped himself in a robe and turned his rocking chair away from the television so he would face Kruse. Huard rocked the chair without sitting in it. "I heard what they did to her."

"They."

"We? I don't know. You must know, by now."

"It was my fault." An enormous hairy insect wiggled with startling speed across the floor. "I led them to her."

"None of it is your fault."

"The morning they skinned that man of theirs in Marseille they looked in my wallet, as I've been looking in yours. I was woozy. They had stunned me with that cattle prod. I couldn't tell what he was doing. He swapped my telephone card for another."

"A France Télécom card?"

"Yes."

"Listening, recording. So someone in the ministry of posts is working with them, someone senior."

"I led them to her."

"A lot of very senior someones."

Huard sat and rocked and stared at Kruse. His bare feet were dirty. Kruse told the lieutenant about Madame Lareau and Monsieur Meunier.

"What did they want you to say?"

"The Front National and the Gaullist coalition were working with the Mariani crime family to divvy up the southern half of the country and wipe out the Socialists, before the next election. They didn't want to split the right-wing vote any longer. Jean-François de Musset wouldn't go along with it, so they killed him and they killed his wife. Evelyn knew about it so they killed her too."

"It sounds plausible. Is it true?"

"I don't like the Front National but they are innocent. That part they invented. The agents had these photographs of a house they were giving me, in the Var. It doesn't exist. They were going to have me speak and then there'd be an accident, no doubt." Kruse pointed at the scanner. "What did you hear, the night Lily was killed? How did you get up the hill so fast?"

"There was a drunk driver, up in Villedieu, on his way to Vaison-la-Romaine. In a white Mercedes. There's only one white Mercedes around here. I was going to Jean-François's party anyway, so I ran up the hill."

"You wanted to find him before anyone else did?"

The lieutenant shrugged. "When I was your age it was nearly blinding. All this moral force. I knew there would be some reward, some spiritual reward." Huard closed his eyes and looked at the ceiling and rocked. Then he opened them again. "What are you doing here?"

"What are you doing with the pistol?"

"When Jean-François and Pascale were killed, I thought: this is it. I'll catch the crazy woman, your wife, and make sure she's punished. If I could leave off doing something right, then I could retire happily. Something like happily. As you can see, here in my kingdom, my life as a gendarme has come to shit. I kept thinking, for years and years now, that just on the other side of this season, this assignment . . ."

"Yves."

"I've never been out of France. I have no heirs, no real friends left. I haven't been with a woman in fourteen years. Now I'm at that age where I live entirely in the past, and with no pride, Monsieur Kruse. Especially now. I don't even have the gendarmerie. And if I were to have it: the Gendarmerie nationale and the Mariani crime family, working together?"

Huard went into his bedroom and walked out ten minutes later in his uniform. It looked both new and old, far more decorative than anything a police officer would wear in Canada, and gleamed darkly in the greasy fluorescent light of the salon. The medals were polished. He pulled a bottle of whisky from his cupboard and took a long drink.

"We have a festival every year, in honour of Georges Brassens. It starts next week with a ceremony. Every year they ask me to be part of it. Not this year. I had the suit pressed anyway. Every day I've been putting it on and holding that pistol, in the chair you're in. We've done away with our religion but it still lives with me, in my heart and in my bones. If I do it myself I'll be damned, I know it. I know it even though, when you think on it hard enough, the Lord was himself a suicide."

Kruse wanted to say the correct thing, as it seemed the time to do it. There was no right thing, nothing the lieutenant hadn't already considered. So he listened.

"The other argument is to forget it, forget all that has governed my life. Everything I vowed to do for this country, since the war, since I was a teenager, has been a farce. My parents were collaborators, you know. I was a teenager, in school. The Americans came through."

"Were they killed? Your parents?"

"Hung, you mean? Shot as traitors? No. It was more like cooked chicken left out to slowly spoil."

"That has nothing to do with you."

"It has everything to do with me."

The close smells of cooking and aftershave mixed with the deli-meat scent of a man who has been sleeping.

"Let's walk outside a moment, Yves."

"In the dark?"

There was a worn path through the vines, half-lit by the moon and the street lights. Huard wore white gloves and rubbed his hands together as they walked.

The lieutenant's shoes were well shined. They were delicate things next to the stone and weeds. A helicopter flew over them, on its way to Avignon or Marseille. "Someone's been hurt, probably in a car accident. The roads around Mont Ventoux are a mess, especially at night. The early morning."

Mont Ventoux was faintly visible in the moonlight, as it was during their first exhausted days in this place.

"Will you do it to me?"

"No."

"You can smell the morning coming, Christophe."

Kruse pulled the envelope out of his pocket. "I wrote this up. Excuse my grammar. It's a summary of what they did to the de Mussets, to Lily, to Evelyn . . ."

"To France."

"I've placed copies in a few places. There's something else, Yves: in Canada I own a large house and a share of a profitable business. I never bothered with a will."

"You can go home to your house and your business and forget. Don't you want . . ."

Kruse continued between the grapes. "I want to turn a corner and see her there, ten metres away."

"Yes."

"And she'll say, 'Daddy,' because we've been away from each other a long time."

"'Daddy.' This is the English way, yes."

"And she'll open her arms and run to me. I'll take a few steps toward her, but only a few. I want to watch her run. It's a beautiful thing, to watch your baby run."

"I can imagine."

"And when she reaches me . . . she's wearing a dress and tights, and her hair is up. I don't know why. I think of her that way. I can hardly bear it, waiting for her. I love her so much I think it will destroy me."

The lieutenant stopped and reached for a vine. He looked away, mercifully.

"When she reaches me I'll hold her close and she'll breathe on my neck, just here. Her breath smells like milk. And I'll whisper questions to her and she'll whisper answers. My clever girl. She was already learning how to read."

"Of course she was."

"Letters anyway, backwards half the time. And her name."

"She was still just little."

"And I'll carry her home and make dinner for her. She'll sit at the table watching me as I do it. Her favourite: spaghetti. Then we'll eat together and I'll give her a bath—with bubbles—and help her into her white pyjamas with butterflies on them, and brush her wet hair straight and read two books to her. Then, with the lights out, I'll tell her a story about us. A perfect adventure, swashbuckling."

Huard pulled a handkerchief from the inside pocket of his uniform, and passed it to him. It had been a few days since the lieutenant had shaved.

"There's a journalist, from *Le Monde*. They took her and her daughter."

Huard looked at his watch. "Marseille?"

"Aix-en-Provence."

"You want to find this journalist and her daughter, release them somehow."

"Yes."

"They know you're coming?"

"Yes."

"Impossible, my friend."

Kruse told the lieutenant what he had done to the Russians, in the hotel room in Roissy. The men in Aix would have been up all night, like him, waiting. "They'll be tired. As tired as me."

The lieutenant took the envelope from him. Back inside the small concrete house Kruse changed the bandages on his arm and forehead. The lieutenant read what Kruse had written. "So it started as mischief," he said, in a whisper, as though he were admitting a secret.

"They wanted to embarrass him and the Front National, make him quit. That's all."

"But they killed a little girl and then they got nervous. They would have tested his blood and discovered the drug. Your wife had seen them." Huard smelled his gun. It had never been shot. "Now, in fact, it's a *coup d'état.*"

Another hairy insect, or the same one, scurried across the floor. It had a hundred tiny legs. Neither of them tried to kill the thing. It would have made a terrible mess.

SEVENTEEN

Place des Martyrs de la Résistance, Aix-en-Provence

HE USED DEPARTMENTAL HIGHWAYS TO AVOID TOLLS AND EYES. IT was a Sunday and the parking lot at the train station in downtown Aix-en-Provence was nearly empty. A bearded man in ragged clothes sniffed at a discarded bag of chips that had blown into the side of the station.

The narrow residential streets south of Place de la Rotonde, a majestic fountain topped by the statues of three women, were pink in the morning light. At the roundabout's quietest entry point there was a carved carousel surrounded by mature trees, a hedge, a white food truck. His shadow was long and thin and alone. Windows above had been open to let in the night air; lucky families with early-rising children had already started their day. In one apartment, at the corner, the night had not yet ended. Arms flailed and young voices sang drunkenly along to "Losing My Religion," a rare modern pop song Evelyn had approved of.

On the grand boulevard of old Aix-en-Provence, the Cours Mirabeau, two young lovers dressed like farmers kissed and clutched at each other's shirts on a bench under one of the clipped plane trees. A man who looked like he had slept in his suit sprayed the generous sidewalk in front of an estate agency. Kruse stopped to read a historical plaque. The black-and-white waiters were preparing the terrace of Les Deux Garçons, even now walking with stiff posture and raised chins. This café, this soft air, this picture-snapping place where Cézanne and his friend Émile Zola took crackers and wine, these trees, this empty cathedral of a city, was precisely, perfectly, why they had crossed the ocean. He sat down and ordered a coffee and a pain au chocolat.

Waiters at Les Deux Garçons were pleased to fire up the espresso machine. It was warmer here than it had been in the Vaucluse. The gilded dog walkers began arriving on the Mirabeau.

Kruse was about to leave when the lieutenant, still in his dress uniform, sat across from him.

"Jesus Christ, Yves."

"Don't blaspheme. Not this morning."

"What are you doing here?"

"I had not prepared a last meal, not once. Maybe that's why I couldn't go through with it. Eternal damnation and a precooked chicken, a bad combination. What are we waiting for, Christophe? Let's go."

Kruse lifted his coffee. He was nearly finished. "Yves, thank you, but—"

"If I were to have a last meal, and know it was my last meal, it would be my grandmother's soupe au pistou. I would start with a glass of champagne and ease into a bottle of Château de Beaucastel, do you know it? And a steak tartare on the side, even though it makes no sense. For dessert, a simple flan and some melon and a glass of very good cognac. Oh and a cigar. And Catherine Deneuve."

"Stop talking about last meals, my friend."

"What would you have?"

Kruse looked down at the table. "Pain au chocolat, coffee."

"Amuse me."

"Maybe I'd have fish of some sort."

Huard sat back in his chair. "Fish of some sort? You are such an American. Why not a hamburger then?"

"A hamburger would do."

"'Fish of some sort,' he says!"

They had not yet turned on the music in the bistro. The waiter arrived with a coffee for Huard and he raised his tiny cup. "To France, *alors*."

"And to your grandmother's soup."

"And to blood, Christophe. If we're honest." The gendarme reached over the table and took Kruse's hand for a moment and squeezed it and released it and looked away.

"Are you sure about this, Yves?"

"Tell me what you want me to do."

Kruse borrowed a slip of paper from the waiter, and drew a map based on what the drowning Russian had said. Huard would stay back with his gun, hidden.

Men and women with baskets and pull carts arrived in morning sweaters, from every direction, for the Sunday market. In the autumn sun it was warm and cool at once. Kruse led the lieutenant past city hall and a fountain. Nearly everyone on the old marble tiles stopped to look at the gendarme in his dress uniform, which had turned a magnificent blue in the sunlight. Kruse led him to the plaza, dedicated to martyrs of the Resistance, bursting with white tents and humming trucks and already, at this hour, hundreds of people. A breath of fish and cheese filled the square. Shoppers jostled them and vendors shouted claims about their sausages and chèvre, plump early tomatoes, *les fraises de Carpentras*, the best in the world. Women hugged, kissed three times, reeked of Shalimar perfume and therefore of Evelyn.

"What if the Russian lied to you? They could have her in London. Brussels."

"He started by lying."

Sun shone harshly off the upper windows of the plaza. He established north and scanned the apartments. A thin boy of nine or ten, hunching and glancing about him as though he had recently been punched, walked out of the shadow of the arcade and made straight for Kruse. His hair was nearly shaved, like a recent victim of lice, and his ears stuck out comically. "Excuse me, Monsieur, do you have the time?"

Kruse looked down at his watch and heard a rustle. The boy ran past Huard and darted between the women with their baskets, slammed into a wheelchair and disappeared behind a tent.

"Hey!" Huard had been eating samples from a fruit vendor. His hands were wet with strawberry. "He took my gun."

Kruse saw his error. "I have a new plan. Go get your car and park in front of the café. When I come out—"

"No." Huard looked up and around the plaza. "Why don't they just shoot us, if they know we're here?"

"The envelope. Who knows how many envelopes I made?"

Huard looked at the address and led Kruse toward it. "One thing I don't understand: the Russians. Why hire foreigners?"

"To protect themselves, the family business. Remember how this started: two or three men. They couldn't tell anyone."

A small municipal vehicle marked the outer ring of the market. Kruse and Huard crouched behind it and looked up at the windows that rounded the top-floor apartment. No visible lights, no movement.

The lieutenant sat on the curb. "They know we're here. Perhaps we knock?"

"Yves, please. Go get the car. Without a gun . . . my will is important. I'm ordering you."

"You can't order anyone. Not in this country." Huard stood up and straightened his shoulders. "First I'll use the toilet and then we'll find our man without a nose." He crossed the narrow street, his chin up and his chest out, and marched through the busy terrace of a bistro. Diners looked up at him and he nodded in benediction.

The heavy grey door was between a bakery and a children's boutique. It was unmarked and controlled by a keypad. Kruse watched. The grey door opened shortly after nine. A man with dark hair falling over his eyes, viciously chewing gum, peeked out and looked around. He wore a suit without a tie. He was Mediterranean, not Russian. At that moment, the lieutenant stepped out of the bistro and looked directly at the young man—who stopped chewing and reached down in a hurry. Kruse sprinted to the door and slammed into it. The man grunted and slumped to the ground, half in and half out of the doorway, a gun in his hand.

Men and women and children on the terrace and on the street behind gasped and shouted. A child screamed. The lieutenant turned to them and announced that this was an operation of the Gendarmerie nationale.

The lieutenant took the gun from the fallen man, who moaned unconsciously. "Fall in behind me."

"Yves, wait."

Kruse dragged the man by his ankles into a long corridor cut out of stone, with a low ceiling, and shut the door behind him. At the end of the corridor, a burst of light. The lieutenant was nearly there, walking freely, each step an echo. It was uncommonly damp in the corridor, like a basement in a river town. Kruse pinched and slapped the young man to revive him but he remained out. A low consistent moan came from his nose. The lieutenant had paused a few paces from the end of the corridor. It was unnecessary now but Kruse crept along the stone wall in a crouch.

"Have you ever done anything like this before?"

"There is little call for storming a fortress in the villages of the Northern Vaucluse."

Up ahead was an atrium, a courtyard covered with a massive skylight. Soil had been set into much of the space, and pots had been organized in swirls. It was an immaculate jungle, its watering system the source of the dampness and of the perfume. "You stay here with the gun. If you see anyone who looks like they're going to shoot me, shoot them first. Or just shoot. Then go out and phone this woman." Kruse handed him the card: "Corinne Lareau, Sous-directeur, Direction de la Protection et de la Sécurité de la Défense."

A busy collection of palms and ferns in terracotta began just past the end of the corridor. The floor was white marble.

"Is this a joke, Christophe? You don't understand why I've come?" He refused the card and began counting down from ten.

"What are you doing?"

He continued to count down. Kruse prepared to knock him out to save him, before he reached one. But at five Huard dropped and rolled onto the spotless marble floor of the courtyard. He ended up off balance in front of a terracotta pot, his breaths rattled and his cheeks purple.

"Yves. Come back."

"Go."

A voice echoed through the courtyard. "We're here to escort you upstairs. Don't shoot."

Kruse sprinted toward a low set of stairs, to draw attention away from the lieutenant. He saw no one until it was too late: the sun flickering off the silencer. His right ear and the back of his head burned. Kruse ran and went down behind a white angel statue tucked into the greenery.

"Christophe!"

"Shh."

"Are you okay? I saw blood."

"Yes, Yves. Quiet now."

Bullets slammed into and ricocheted past the statue; half its white head crumbled away. Slowly and soundlessly he made his way closer to the man with the gun. Kruse was nearly close enough to pounce when a voice echoed through the courtyard.

"I am Lieutenant Yves Huard of the Gendarmerie nationale." Huard stood in the open. "Monsieur: I will give you ten seconds to walk into this courtyard and surrender your firearm. Yes, you can lead us upstairs and, yes, your bravery will be remembered at your trial. One. Two."

The first shot came at three. Huard howled and kneeled and shot his own gun several times. Kruse had a poor view of him, but it looked as though he was smiling through his wails. Huard's gun clicked emptily now. The sniper, in a brown suit, stepped out of his hiding place and aimed.

Kruse took him from behind and dropped him from the riser onto the marble. The courtyard went silent, but for water dribbling somewhere and ambient noise from the market.

Huard was still smiling when Kruse arrived. His voice was small. "I got him."

"You sure did."

Both of the bullets had entered his abdomen.

"Yves, I'm going to take you to the hospital."

"I'll die and haunt you for the rest of your life if you do that."

"The bullets have—"

"I know damn well what the bullets have done."

"Then I'll just take you to the street. Someone will call an ambulance."

"I want to stay right here. With all my heart I do. You go."

"You were very brave, Yves."

"Yes."

"You're a splendid policeman."

"Yes."

"And an honourable man."

"Go on now."

Kruse fetched the sniper's gun and pressed it into Huard's right hand. "If anyone tries to escape . . ."

"*Blammo*," Huard said, as though a gunshot were an English word, and grimaced. "Sit me up."

Kruse propped him against the base of the angel statue. It had one eye, one ear, and half a mouth. One of its shoulders was missing. Huard's pretty blue uniform had turned a dark purple where the blood ran. Kruse borrowed the gendarme's white sash and used it on his own wound. The bullet had chewed the top of his ear and ripped into the back of his head, painfully but superficially.

"Don't think poorly of yourself for this, Christophe. I am dying well."

"Yves." Kruse placed a hand on his cheek. "You're not permitted to die. I'll be right back. We'll go to the hospital together and they'll fix us both."

The lieutenant reached up with his bloody right hand, not for a shake but for a squeeze. Then he leaned back and readied his gun. "Excellent, son. Excellent. Until then!"

There was an inner stairwell, built from the same marble as the floor, and an elevator. Kruse took the stairs. On the first, second, and third levels there were planters filled with clipped herbs and flowers. The soil was black and moist from recent attention.

On the top landing he waited to restore his breathing and heart rate, to do what he had taught his students—what Tzvi had taught him when he was still a teenager. To turn his feelings into something else, something useful. He allowed himself to wonder if some of them on the other side of the door had studied savate, an old pirate art with odd kicks. He had never fought a savateur. This was why he had crossed the goddamn ocean.

Just as he reached for the door it opened on its own, into a hallway. Three men in suits, giants with shaved heads, stood before him. Brothers in this. None of them were Russian.

"Welcome, Monsieur Kruse," said the one in the back, the oldest and most confident of them. "Joseph was expecting you hours ago. Your girlfriend and her daughter are here, and safe. They're all very tired. Oh no: you're really bleeding."

The first man held a gun but it wasn't yet aimed. His free hand was still on the door handle and already he was off balance. He was not a savateur. The man lifted his gun and Kruse ducked it and disarmed him, hurt him with his knee and his elbows. The man was heavy and Kruse fell back with him, tossed him into the stairway.

"We can't shoot him," the older man said to the one between them. He changed his tone and said, "Monsieur Kruse, why are you doing this? If you make us kill you, Lucien will be furious."

The man between them held a knife. He seemed confused by Kruse or by what his boss had said. He lowered himself into a fighting stance and jabbed the knife.

Kruse parried it and tweaked the man's arm at the elbow. He stiffened and Kruse went for his eyes, then his groin, took the knife and, as he went down, punctured his lower back. The boss shouted at him to stop. Kruse was calmer now than he had been at any time since Lily's death, moving correctly from man to man in the hallway. There was a trick Tzvi had taught him, to make the world feel like it is operating in slow motion, the speed of a waltz. It was long ago, when he was still a kid, and he received the advice more literally than Tzvi had meant it. When he was fighting, really fighting, he heard his mother's favourite song: "The Second Waltz" by Shostakovich. Only he, among the dancers, could move faster than the music.

This is how he had planned to feel in the Louvre, in the churches and cathedrals, in the amphitheatres and royal gardens and palaces, on the grand boulevards, in the pretty squares. The boss, who no longer carried a look of confidence, a muscleman with the right kind of salary and the right sort of car, a bully, took a step back.

"*Mais attendez*," said the boss, and turned away in retreat. "Others are coming."

Kruse jumped up and kicked him in the side of his face. His head clonked against the wall. The man crouched, turtled, asked Kruse to give him a moment. Kruse cranked his big arm and stomped it just below the shoulder. As the muscleman lay on the floor, spitting and then praying, Kruse kneeled down to ask questions.

Inside the apartment, they knew he had arrived. How many were there? Too many to defeat without a bomb: six in total. The muscleman was the security director, the best of them. Up here and downstairs, their job was to wound the intruder, to take him inside weak and woozy but alive.

"Did they tell you who I was?"

"A Canadian."

"Did they say why I was coming, Monsieur?"

"The mother and the girl."

"They're inside?"

"You can't get back out, now that you're in. Not you and not the mother and not the girl. More are on their way. Lucien will make you suffer for this."

Kruse bled on the security director, who was now recounting the ways Lucien might bring him to suffer. *If you destroy your tea set in your fury, darling, you'll regret it.*

He walked to the door and listened for a few minutes: nothing. He opened it into the smell of fresh herbs.

No one aimed a gun or a knife at him, or greeted him. The long room, with an antique dining table over an elaborate Persian rug, was populated by portraits instead of people. Bushels of herbs and vegetables, presumably from the market below, lay on the table: preparations for a feast. Several bottles of red wine and baskets of fruit and flowers were on adjacent serving tables.

There were voices on the other side of two French doors. It was dark in the long room, as the windows were blocked. Each of the lighted lamps was dearer than any car he had ever owned, and the tapestries were the sorts he had seen in the Rosedale mansions and Upper West Side apartments of his wealthiest clients.

"The Second Waltz" played in this room and through the doors. It was the sound of what he had become when he was fourteen years old. What Evelyn had not wanted him to be. There was no one here so he reached back for the blood and wet his hands with it, both hands and his arms, and called out for them to come. The voices quieted but the music did not. He opened the doors, to do what he had crossed the ocean to do.

Four men stood waiting in a white anteroom. None of them had a gun, so he moved quickly through them. One of the men sliced his left arm with a small knife and another punched him in the mouth while he was finishing the third man. The cut was deep but no more serious than the wound on his head.

The door at the other end of the anteroom was unlocked. He opened it into fire—a fire in a massive old hearth, dark walls.

Anouk ran across the cold room and he fell to his knees for her. She ran into his red arms. Her face was wet and warm with tears. The door slammed behind him. He apologized as he hugged her, for staining her pyjamas.

"Make it stop, Christophe," she said, into his bloody ear.

"Take the baby away."

Kruse recognized the voice at the first vowel: a man in the throes of the worst cold of his life.

Lucien stood at the back of the room, farthest from the windows, next to Annette. Annette: naked. Her hands were tied above her and her ankles were bound. She turned her body away from him, as demurely as she could manage. The rope squeaked. She was conscious but something had faded from her eyes.

"Take the girl away from him, Joseph." Lucien had arranged his cutting tools on a folding table, just as he had in the small white apartment in Marseille. "This isn't a family reunion."

Joseph sat in near-darkness, his legs crossed. He wore a dark suit, as always, and a tie. He held a drink aloft, despite the hour. One side of his face was lit by the fire burning next to him. Slowly he stood and crossed the room. With a few words in French, sweet words, Joseph leaned down and put a hand on her shoulder. That he would bring her here, touch her. Kruse took Joseph's hand from Anouk, slapped the drink away, and bashed him into the wall, twice.

"Yes." Joseph did not fight back. "Please."

Behind and below him, Anouk cried quietly into her hands.

"I'm taking her out of here."

"Release him or I kill her mother now, Monsieur Kruse." Lucien spoke softly. "Quicker than I would like."

There had been a boy in his neighbourhood, P.J. Banks, who suffered a speech impediment. Kruse was not one of the bullies but he had done nothing to stop them. One hot afternoon, as the boy wept on the railroad tracks before a bunch of them, calling out for mercy, Kruse had nearly been overwhelmed by a desire—it had a smell and a taste—to smash his head in with a rock. It was a thump of shame and fullness at once, a war feeling.

He was hugging her again. Kruse told Anouk he loved her and she whispered in his ear that she loved him.

"I'll protect you."

"Why are they doing this?"

"Because they're scared, Anouk."

"What are they scared of?"

"I don't know yet."

"I'm scared of him."

Lucien clapped his hands. "This is all very touching. Now: Monsieur Kruse. Stand up."

A final kiss on her salty, soft cheek, and he stood.

"Surrender your weapons."

He pulled the knife from his back pocket, tossed it on the rug.

"Joseph, pull yourself together and take the girl away from him. Now. The two of you, sit."

Kruse untucked his shirt. With the bloodless side he wiped the tears and the snot from her face and told her she was going away now, with her mom. Back home.

Joseph laughed.

Lucien walked around his table of silver instruments, his hands folded before him like a professor at the beginning of a lecture. He addressed Anouk. "We're here to bargain, little girl."

"There's no bargain," said Kruse. "They give nothing."

"You've seen how I like to work." Lucien pulled an instrument from his tray and approached Annette with it. "There would, no doubt, be some pleasure in watching her punished. Even for you. It lives in all of us. We can't look away."

"Why should you punish her, Lucien? Punish her for what?"

Annette looked up at her hands and swung, softly.

"No one is innocent."

"My daughter was innocent. Anouk is innocent."

Joseph gave up on Anouk and crossed the room, sat back in his chair. He spoke in English. "Just get on with it, Lucien, you fucking lunatic."

Lucien looked over at his brother, then back at Kruse. "It's you or it's this lovely woman."

Kruse knelt to whisper in Anouk's ear but there was nothing to say.

"Maman!"

The girl squeezed his hand with both of hers now, hung from it.

"Christopher, who did you tell?" Joseph put his palms together.

"Oh shut up," said Lucien.

"It never ends. It's a virus. The maniac will be chopping people up for years."

Lucien spun the tool he had taken, a scalpel. "I thought I'd take her eyelids first, so she doesn't miss a thing."

Anouk screamed. Annette whispered a prayer.

"Cut her down."

"And? And?"

"Take me."

"Oh splendid choice! Joseph, tie his hands."

Joseph sighed and said, "Jesus Christ almighty," and stood up with his rope. "Is the gendarme dead?"

"Of course he's dead," said Lucien.

There were heavy footsteps outside the door, men's voices. The stirred fire had a familiar odour about it: grape wood. The night Lily died had smelled of this. Kruse pulled his daughter's blood and soil out of his pockets and kissed his hands. Joseph tied them behind his back. "It was an accident. You must know that."

Lucien addressed himself to Annette's wrists, almost giddily.

Annette stepped out of her leg binds and ran across the room to Anouk. They hugged and wept, both of them, and then Anouk told her to get dressed. Annette fastened a skirt into place, first, and turned around to put on her bra and step into her panties.

Joseph untied and restarted Kruse's knot. "You heard of flunitraze-pam? A marvellous drug. He was drinking Badoit, making such lovely, sincere eye contact with me. I told him I was in shipping. Then, when the drug kicked in, Monsieur de Musset was happy to drink wine. He was happy to do anything."

"You phoned your contacts in the Gendarmerie nationale."

"I phoned my contact in Paris, who phoned someone else. It was all very innocent, Christopher, I promise. A racist gets a drunk-driving conviction and his political career is over and everyone is happy."

"An innocent man is ruined."

"That depends on your politics and sense of history. My father put the family business on hold to kill Nazis. If he and others like him hadn't, where would we be today?"

"Jean-François was hardly a Nazi."

"I put him in a car and told him his wife needed him. He had a lot of women—am I right?—but he did love his wife, deeply. It would have destroyed his political career but not his baking career. It would have weakened a fascist political party."

"Endeared you to your clients and partners: the government-in-waiting."

"It's an easy choice, for me, between Philippe Pétain and Charles de Gaulle."

"This is different. Jean-François was—"

"All right, all right, all right. Christopher, I mean this: it was the worst night of my life. When I learned the bastard had killed a little girl . . . there will never be another day I don't think of it and tear at myself—metaphorically speaking, not really *tearing*." Joseph stepped away and walked around, faced him. "All right. You're done."

"Hurry up," said Lucien.

"Who knows what you know? The gendarme, but he's dead. Anyone else?"

"No."

Joseph pointed at Annette and Anouk. Both of them were looking out the window now, into the market. Annette held her hand and whispered to her.

"I didn't let the lunatic torture Evelyn. I made him kill her quicker than he wanted. And she *had* cuckolded you. That's no kind of wife. This one over there, now that's a woman. You know what? She didn't even complain. Her hands were up there for . . . what Lucien? Four hours?"

Instead of responding with words, Lucien walked across the room and did a little hop and kicked Kruse in the stomach. Kruse went down on his knees and stood back up, and Lucien slapped him in the face. Then he did it again, with the back of his hand. Blood from the gunshot wound had transferred to the back of Lucien's hand and he wiped it on Kruse's shirt. Then he grasped Kruse's shoulder with his left hand and punched him in the face, twice, the eye and the mouth. The wound on his forehead opened up. After the first kick, Kruse had refused to fall again. Lucien looked in his eyes and Kruse watched him watching. He watched himself, bleeding some more, from his mouth and his forehead, his ear, his right cheekbone. His arm throbbed.

"I'm going to kill you, very slowly, and then I'm going to kill her somewhat less slowly." He spoke English, softly enough that Annette would not hear. "The girl will watch but we won't kill her. We're not barbarians."

Lucien punched Kruse one last time, in the nose. Broken again. He blinked through the blood in his eyes and staggered and more dripped from his chin now.

"Lord," said Joseph. "What a mess."

"You're familiar with the English phrase 'hanging, drawing, and quartering'?" Lucien backed away, like a lecturer. "The word 'drawing,' I had always thought, referred to the drawing out of entrails—which is an important part of what we'll do this morning, together. But it's actually drawing the prisoner to the place of execution, through the streets, as a warning to others, publicity. Did you know that? Like I said when we first met: on an occasion like this, if torture is not a deterrent, what is it? Immoral entertainment. Of course, I have no trouble with singularity of purpose. What does art do, really?"

Lucien stood up on the chair and, with his left hand, fussed with the rope. He knotted it into a noose and continued in French. "We don't have a horse and obviously this space is too small to drag you around. So we'll go straight to the hanging. First I'll cut your clothes off or Joseph will. Unless your girlfriend . . ."

"Girlfriend." Annette cleared her throat and ordered Anouk to continue looking out the window, to look out the window no matter what. Annette picked up the knife Kruse had dropped, the knife he had taken from the agent in the hall, and gently cut off his jacket and his shirt. She looked in his eyes when she wasn't at work. There was pity in her face and disgust, more. She transferred the knife to his empty hand.

"Remove his pants. And come on. Take the knife back. Throw it up here, you scamp."

Annette slowly unfastened his belt, his buttons. She lowered his pants to the ground and went down on one knee and removed them leg by leg. She took off his socks and looked up, took the knife and lobbed it toward Lucien.

He couldn't take any breath in through his nose. "I am sorry, Annette."

There were tears in her eyes. He knew it would be difficult to look at him now, with a hood of blood over his face. "You came for us, even though you knew . . ."

"Enough," said Lucien. "Pull them down."

Annette slid her fingers into the band of his underwear and squeezed him with her soft hands all the way down. Kruse stepped out of them and looked away from her.

"Christopher: this is not what I want." Joseph lifted his glass. "To you!"

"Please, can we go? Just wait in the hall?" Annette put her hand out for Anouk and called her. She ran to it. Her eyes were already sick.

"No," said Lucien.

"Yes," said Joseph. "Wait in the anteroom. Some men have arrived, I think. You don't have to watch this."

"It is like having Wagner himself in the parlour, conducting. You'll never have an opportunity to see anything like this again, Madame Laferrière. Not that you have much time left for banal entertainments. Onward!"

Annette kissed Kruse on the bloody lips. He tried to hide his naked-ness from Anouk, who hugged his leg and said nothing more. Joseph stood up and opened the door to the ruin of the white room, where two guards now stood among the four on the ground. One of the new men appeared wounded.

Yves.

"Watch them for a moment, please, gentlemen." Joseph took a step into the anteroom. "Where is everyone else?"

There was some mumbling. Joseph escorted Annette and Anouk. The mother and daughter looked back at him as Joseph spoke quietly with his employees. Anouk blew three quick kisses.

"All right, brother." Joseph returned and closed the door behind him. "Work your magic."

"Art," said Lucien.

Joseph pushed him along. "Just do the thing."

"Was it surprising to you, Monsieur Kruse, to learn you had been cuckolded? It was Monsieur Laflamme's idea, thinking you might just abandon your wife to us."

"Us?"

"We have legislative elections in the spring, you see, and not long to prepare for the presidential race." He turned to Joseph. "But he's right. It is queer to say 'us.' We."

"A profitable partnership."

"Joseph didn't let me have any fun with Madame Kruse. The police were supposed to hand you over to us. Then you disappeared into . . . what? Our partners were nervous. But I knew you'd come. Didn't I, Joseph? You're a simple creature."

Kruse considered the tray of stainless steel instruments. He had practised this many times, hundreds of times, at the survival camps. But he had not done it in ten years, longer. Fifteen. His arms were long enough, his shoulders flexible enough, or they once were. There was some reason for doing it he had long forgotten: perhaps it was for this very thing. Tzvi had been so moved by the assassinations of Israeli athletes at the Munich Olympics that he had studied hostage-taking, minute by minute, to be sure his own students would be prepared when the bastards came. Surely they would come.

The waltz played again. Kruse closed his eyes, waited for the right moment, made a pact with his knees. "How did you learn to tie a noose, Lucien?"

"Oh, practice."

"It's a fine knot."

"Yes, you see I studied—" Lucien looked up at his fat knot, and Kruse sprang and jumped. In the air he lifted his knees and shoved his feet backwards through his hands. His feet slid across the rope. Another half centimetre and he would have tripped himself, landed on his back. Lucien opened his mouth to speak, to protest, but the bloody soil was already in the air. It sprayed the torturer in the eyes. Lucien tried to swing, tried to fight, but he was too slow. Kruse used his feet first. Then he chose a scalpel from the table, cut him, and kicked him into the wall. Lucien bled and howled and called out for his brother.

Joseph pointed a revolver at him. "Again, very impressive."

Kruse cut the rope from his wrists. "Put the gun down."

"That wouldn't be a fair fight, Christopher."

Lucien was on his hands and knees now, spitting the soil that had landed in his mouth. Blood ran onto the floor from his face and neck. "You won't make it out of here."

Kruse positioned himself behind Lucien, put his right arm around his neck and secured it.

"Joseph!"

The Corsican pointed his gun.

"Shoot him."

His finger was on the trigger. Lucien growled and shoved himself backwards on top of Kruse but he couldn't escape the blood choke. There was enough air for Lucien to speak.

"Don't forget . . . who you are, Joseph."

"Good advice, brother."

Lucien reached up to pull Kruse's arm, to create more space to speak. "Wait, wait. If you're going to do this, make it beautiful. Do something . . ."

Kruse whispered as he tightened the blood choke. Between seven and ten seconds for unconsciousness. Half a minute would do. "I'm going to put you in a nice, clean facility."

"Mercy," he tried to say, and that was it.

Kruse shut off the killer's carotid artery and watched Joseph's face. He released Lucien at the right time and hopped to his feet. He caught the faintest glimpse of his own bloody face and his naked body in the shining tray as he passed. The music continued to play.

"How many did you walk through to get up here: five or six? They're the best we have, you know. And I didn't even hear you come. One last drink, together."

"No."

"Dulls the mind. Slows the reactions."

Kruse bent down and made a small pile of the holy dirt that remained on the floor next to Lucien, who honked and murmured on his back. He collected it up.

"A professor. That I believed you!"

"A dad. A husband."

"Tell yourself whatever you like, Christopher." He aimed for Kruse's face. "I know what you are."

"Do it."

There was a knock on the door. Had Joseph locked it? It would have to be the window.

Joseph caught him looking. "We're too high. There's nothing to climb. If you want out of here, you'll have to walk. And there are men on the other side of that door with guns. You can't walk out, certainly not with your ladies."

Lucien was unusually strong. He was on his hands and knees again, buzzing and drooling. The sound rose like an old engine and grew louder. He fell on his side and crawled toward the tray, knocked it over.

"I suppose I can either shoot you or let you go."

"Those aren't your options, Joseph."

"Enlighten me."

"Put the gun away or die."

Joseph laughed. "You are quite the fellow. Quite the fellow!" He took a drink and lurched toward the window, righted himself, looked out over the market and mumbled to himself; then he crossed the room again, said something in Corsican, and shot his brother in the back of the head. Then he dropped the gun and opened his arms, palms to the roof.

"I have some cousins who would like my job, but they're all fairly dim." Joseph sat back in his chair and picked up his drink, crossed one leg over the other. He loosened his tie.

"Why haven't they come in?"

"The staff knows not to come in here."

"Your Russians . . ."

"Lucien ordered them killed this morning, in case you had spoken to them. No one who works for us, none of our genuine employees, knows a thing about this. Your daughter. If not for your daughter! Sit with me a moment and think about it: your daughter changed France."

"I'm taking them out of here."

"Christopher, I am sorry but the journalist . . ."

"I have five copies of the story hidden in various places. Even if we don't walk out of here, it's going to come out. I've engineered it that way."

"Have you? How clever."

"This is about the people who hired you. Make a deal with Annette. Make the story work for you and your family. Then, whatever new line of business—"

"You were hard on us in your version?"

"Brutal."

Joseph crossed his arms. "Well. Goddamn you."

Kruse reached for the door handle, his arm and hand covered in blood. He looked over at Lucien one last time. Two men in suits stood in the white room, alert. A third joined them and, before the naked man with a handful of soil, painted with blood, they lifted their weapons.

"He's one of us." Joseph cleared his throat and said it again, and the Mediterranean men in suits repeated it to each other and looked away from Kruse, embarrassed. In Corsican, Joseph called out an order and a young man, maybe twenty, draped a white sheet around Kruse and led him into the first lamplit room with the tapestries and the dining room table covered in vegetables and herbs. Joseph followed. "The others had the misfortune of meeting your partner downstairs."

"What do you mean?"

"I mean he shot four of my men. What did you do to the good lieutenant?"

"Do to him?"

"He quit the gendarmerie for you."

"They forced him to retire."

"No, Christopher, they asked him to set a trap and arrest you. Instead, he quit. They promoted his partner, the young woman, Madame Boutet. He didn't tell you?"

Annette and Anouk sat holding hands on a green couch. Drinks in crystal sat before them, on a decorative table. Anouk screamed when she saw him. Later she would tell Kruse she thought he was a ghost, a demon in a white sheet and bloody face. Her mother had told her he was dead. The dragon without a nose had killed the nice foreign man and he was here to haunt France forever.

He kissed them and ran out the door, down the hallway littered with fallen Corsicans and into the atrium. The lieutenant lay sprawled among the greenery, a gun in his hand.

EIGHTEEN

Place de la Porte-Maillot, Paris

THE PALAIS DES CONGRÈS, IN THE SEVENTEENTH ARRONDISSEMENT, looked and smelled and felt like home. It was built with seventies concrete, with a food court and a mall and a tower. On a grey afternoon the concrete conspired with the low cloud to refute every pretty song about Paris.

He had registered as a *Wall Street Journal* reporter, in the city to write a series on the Maastricht Treaty—the new dream for a European Union. Annette had helped with the paperwork. At the desk in front of the conference hall they did not ask for his credentials. His name was on the list and they handed him a lanyard and a ticket for one free glass of wine at the reception. The doors to the hall were closed, but it sounded as though a war or an orgy were going on inside.

"What's happening?"

The elegant black-haired woman at the conference desk pushed out her lips as she searched for the right phrase. "The anticipation of victory?"

There were almost five hundred delegates from two centre-right political parties, Rally for the Republic and Union for French Democracy. The coalition, and the conference, were called Union for France. A cartoonist had drawn exaggerated caricatures of the current president, François Mitterrand, and other Socialist Party ministers on the left side of the hall. On the right, even more ridiculous drawings of the Front National leader.

Kruse had expected an atmosphere of French reserve. The suit he had bought in Roissy had been cut to pieces, so he had bought another at a second-hand shop in the fifth arrondissement. He had prepared and practised questions about the common market, in case he was forced to play journalist. He carried a photograph of Philippe Laflamme into the hall and walked to the front of the room, as close to the podium as he could manage.

The mayor of Paris was speaking calmly and slowly and beautifully of his passion for the soul of France, and for a unified Europe. He spoke of a new alliance in the spring legislative elections and its vow to cut taxes and create jobs and ease the dominion of the labour unions seeking to stomp the talent and the creativity from the hearts of true Frenchmen and Frenchwomen. The lunacy and the hatred of the extreme left and the extreme right was intolerable in a country so great, so curious, so tolerant, so prepared to lead civilized nations, to lead Europe itself into the future. With each new idea and poetic flourish, the crowd before him hooted and shouted. While the mayor did not denounce President Mitterrand, the crowd did and he stepped back from the microphone and listened like a cardinal taking a communal confession.

"*Oui, mes chers compatriotes. Oui.*"

Three times Kruse walked around the rectangular mass of men and women standing and staring at the front of the room. Only a few of them made eye contact with him as he passed. His injuries had nearly healed; all that remained were yellowish bruises. Still, he did not have a political face and he would never learn to walk and stand like a Frenchman. If Philippe Laflamme was in the crowd he was somewhere in the middle, in brown camouflage. He was a difficult man to miss, tall and thin and entirely bald on top, with a ring of orange curls in the back and above his ears. After the speech delegates would move into another hall for *l'heure de l'apéritif* and, eventually, dinner.

On his way to the back of the hall, Kruse walked backwards. The mayor spoke of his close friend Charles Aznavour, who would perform for the delegates during dinner. It was rare in Canada, but from time to time, when he and Tzvi worked for politicians and celebrities, Kruse would feel that buzz of magic from certain men and women. The mayor of Paris had it, and it lived in every word. Three men and two women stood at the back of the stage, next to an enormous French flag, clapping along with everyone else. One of them, in a sombre grey suit, had a short ring of orange hair below his bald head. The moment Kruse spotted him, the mayor leaned forward and said, "*Vive la république et vive la France,*" and stepped away from the podium. The men and women before him behaved like well-dressed teenagers before Madonna.

Some of them moved to the stage, to touch the mayor or at least come closer to him. The rest moved to the doors, to the champagne in the hall. Kruse slammed into several of them, as he made his way toward Philippe Laflamme. He was in his early fifties, a man of confidence, a listener. Nearly as many surrounded him as the mayor, who had walked down from the stage to greet his admirers. Laflamme smiled and shook hands and nodded and peeked over the heads of everyone else—the privilege of the tall. Ten minutes later, the population had shrunk in the conference hall to twenty or thirty. Workers in dark uniforms removed chairs. Two of Laflamme's colleagues carried the French flag down from the stage. Kruse stood in the corner, near the public restrooms, and watched.

Laflamme freed himself of the white-haired men and women who had surrounded him, and spoke to a couple of staff with clipboards. A moment later, they were escorting the mayor of Paris toward the exit. Laflamme didn't follow. He crossed the floor to the restroom. He glanced at Kruse, who stood in shadow, but his eyes did not rest on him. His body stiffened just slightly before he pushed through the door.

A few others had gone in but all but one had left. A small man with an umbrella stood at the mirror, washing his hands and whistling. Kruse stood next to him and washed his own hands until the man departed. Laflamme was at the urinal. Kruse bent down and looked below the cubicles, to be sure they were alone, and locked the restroom door.

"Do you know who I am, Monsieur?"

Laflamme didn't answer. Then he sighed. "I have no idea."

"How much did you pay them to kill Evelyn?"

"You are mistaken. I'm not who you think I am, Monsieur."

"I know you've spoken to Joseph Mariani, about Aix-en-Provence. You know what's happened."

The man did not respond.

"Do your bosses know? Were you hoping it would just go away?"

He finished at the urinal and took a step back, zipped himself up, flushed. Then he turned and sighed again, as though Kruse were a mosquito he could not squash, and approached the sink. He turned on the water without looking at Kruse or even himself in the mirror. There were a few stray orange hairs on the top of his head, and sun spots. He was a smoker. He smelled of cologne and of sour cigarettes at once. His eyes were red with fatigue.

"What do you want?"

"I want you to admit it."

"Admit what, Monsieur?"

Kruse pulled a small tape recorder out of the inside pocket of his jacket.

"What are you planning to do with that? You are a madman. I have no idea who you are or what you are talking about. If you don't allow me to pass and leave this room, I'll phone the police." He finished washing his hands and placed them under the dryer. There was a distinct tremble in his voice. When he turned away from the dryer, his breath in crisis, he fumbled in his pocket and pulled out a large cellular phone. Kruse took it from him and threw it up and over the cubicle doors; it crashed into the toilet.

"I'll shout for help."

"You have one choice."

"No, Monsieur. You have one choice. You either let me out of here, immediately, without harming me in any way, or you go to prison for the rest of your life."

"One choice."

"Help!"

Kruse took a step forward, to shut him up, and Laflamme fell to his knees. He put up his hands and closed his eyes.

"You've taken everything from me, Monsieur Laflamme. I'm not afraid of prison or death. I'm not afraid of anything. You tell the truth—and believe me, I know the truth—and you walk out of this room and back into your life."

"If I tell you the truth, my life is over."

"The state will protect you."

"In prison?"

The man's face was at the perfect height. Every cell in Kruse's body wanted to crush it. "My wife was an art historian. You probably didn't know that."

Laflamme closed his eyes and kept them closed.

"A philosopher. A professional."

"Please, Monsieur Kruse. Your view on all of this is naive. All I tried to do was stop an extreme political party, a party that would destroy modern France and the European Union, from—"

"Justice was one of her areas of interest. Are you listening?"

Laflamme pulled out his wallet and photographs of himself with a woman and two small children, in a garden, 1970s colours. "I'm just a man like you. I have a family. Believe me, I understand your anger."

"She wanted me to be something else, someone else. An unsolvable problem, but we tried. One of the things she made me do was read. Read books I would have read in university, if I had gone. Plato, for example. A man has to understand Plato, in a superficial way, to survive at a dinner party with art history and philosophy professors. I read *The Republic*, and skipped a lot of it. Boring. Then I read *Gorgias*, which was much better. Do you know it?"

"Please let me go."

"Monsieur Laflamme: focus. Do you know it?"

"No."

"Who's the hero of Plato's dialogues?"

"Socrates."

"Our Socrates didn't like the criminal justice system, such as it was in Greece. It wasn't effective. Do you know why?"

"Powerful people never got in trouble."

"That isn't it."

"Jean-François de Musset was a Trojan Horse, Monsieur Kruse, if you want to talk about ancient Greece. He would have come in, handsome and reasonable, but the monsters were with him. French Nazis, Monsieur Kruse. He had to be stopped. And if you know anything, you know by now it was never supposed to happen the way it did. A drunk-driving charge: that is all we asked of Joseph."

"I'll turn on the tape recorder in a moment. Socrates thought all

punishments, even capital punishments, were a level below the ultimate punishment."

"What is that?"

"The ultimate punishment, Monsieur Laflamme, and the ultimate
evil, is to commit a crime and get away with it. Do you know why?"

"Yes."

"Tell me, Monsieur Laflamme."

After ten or twelve seconds of silence he extended his hand and Kruse
helped him to his feet. Laflamme corrected his posture and fixed his tie.
"Turn on the tape recorder."

• • •

Annette was nearly finished her article. All she needed was a source
who wasn't a member of a Corsican crime family to verify it, with
some quotations. Kruse called her from a public telephone in the hotel
attached to the Palais des congrès; he had transcribed sentences from
Laflamme's confession and repeated them to her.

When he finished saying the words and she finished writing them,
her voice broke up.

"You're okay, Christophe?"

"Yes."

"I'm so sorry, for all of this."

"So am I."

She had several photos of Lily, to use as an illustration. *Le Monde*
would have first crack at it, but if they didn't give her what she
wanted—a full-time, senior reporter's position—Annette would shop
it elsewhere. The story began in Toronto, with a threatened marriage
and its lavender-scented solution: a year in the South of France. Neither Joseph nor the Mariani family were named specifically; Joseph had
agreed to speak candidly, but only as an anonymous source. Laflamme
confirmed everything, claimed he acted alone.

After he phoned the quotations in to Annette, there was nothing left to do and he had nowhere to go, so he stayed for the last few minutes of the apéritif and sat at the media table for dinner, apologizing for forgetting his business cards in the hotel room. Laflamme was gone. All five hundred of them had killed Lily and Evelyn and soon the whole country would know. He sniffed and sipped their champagne, cut into their salmon. The mayor was scheduled to introduce his *cher compa-triote* Charles Aznavour, but a gentleman from the other half of the coalition, the Union for French Democracy, said the mayor had been called away on an urgent matter.

"Fuck," he said, out loud, in English.

His dinner companions, gentlemen and ladies in suits and dresses that had not been purchased at a second-hand shop, stood up with him. What had happened? Was he suddenly ill? Could they help in any way?

Kruse ran out of the hall and into the cool night. The driver of the first taxi he spotted, in front of the hotel, appeared to be sleeping with a newspaper opened on his face.

"Are you available?"

The newspaper moved with his voice. "Always."

"How long will it take to get to Rue Santeuil?"

The driver, a bearded man with a thick accent, turned around and looked at him. "You're a soldier."

"No."

"You look like a soldier, uncomfortable in a business suit."

Kruse opened the door. "How long, Monsieur? I could take the metro."

"Twelve minutes."

It was long enough, as the driver spoke, to return to what he had been imagining: Evelyn walking up the broken path to the old yellow farmhouse behind the château, through spiderwebs, turning her ankle on a loose bit of rock, her dead daughter's fairy wand in her hand.

She knocks on the door and Pascale answers. Women know what men do not know. Pascale allows her inside the vast foyer. Evelyn has taken something from her. Jean-François has taken something from them both. He is in the bedroom and calls out to them in the foyer and swears he does not remember, not a thing.

They do not knock. Two of them, one with long hair and another without a nose, both of them dressed like businessmen, like mayors, like priests, like generals, like fathers. Evelyn hides but she is not good at that, and these men do not speak. They walk in and Pascale screams and Lucien cuts her and says things to her dying body. They go into his bedroom and Evelyn runs out the front door. She is too frightened to be careful.

"Evelyn!" one of them calls, from Jean-François's bedroom, where his blood smells fresh, "Darling!"

• • •

The ugly courtyard in front of the Sorbonne was deserted. He could see his champagne breath as he exited the taxi, whose driver was from Afghanistan and longed to be in London or New York, where a man could go from poor to rich in only a year or two. He could not marry and raise a child in this country of whores and faggots because a man does not own his wife and child in France—the state owns everything. *La* France, yes? *La?* Even the men are womanly. It is illegal to touch your own wife, to smack your own child if he is misbehaving. What sort of life is that, Monsieur?

Kruse did not give the driver a tip.

No one answered when he pressed the call button for the apartment. He pressed it again, and then he pressed all of them and waited for someone to buzz him in. A French elevator would never feel right. They were always too small, like mousetraps. At the top of the stairs he crept to the door and listened while he coaxed his heart and his breaths to slow. The voices of two men and a woman, not Annette. He could not make out what they were saying, not even the tone.

The door was locked. He tucked in his shirt, adjusted his brown tie, and knocked. The footsteps were heavy. One of the fighting systems he and Tzvi had folded into their work was Wing Chun, developed by a Chinese nun in the eighteenth century to circumvent other more aggressive, more masculine arts. The great innovation, in Wing Chun, is deflection: you use an opponent's brute strength and overconfidence against him. Kruse prepared to deflect whomever or whatever opened the door, and then to attack. He had planned to teach Lily.

It would never end, as Joseph had warned him.

A tan woman in an expensive white dress opened the door, and her perfume blew over him. She was forty and severe, with a head full of blonde hair that was too big for her tiny body, like a Hollywood star. "What do you want?"

Over her shoulder he could see a man in a suit, standing in the front of the room. Others were sitting but he couldn't make them out in the dim orange lamplight. "Is Annette here?"

"She's very busy. Are you a neighbour, perhaps?"

No one spoke in the apartment.

The woman closed her eyes for a moment, waiting for an answer. "Monsieur, to be frank, this is not a terrific time for a visit."

Kruse stepped into the apartment and shoved the woman aside. She squeaked with indignation. He saw Annette but not Anouk. The large man who had been standing, with a communications device in his ear, approached Kruse with his hand straight out, to push him or warn him, something. His grip was strong, on the front of his suit, part lapel and part white shirt. Kruse looked for a moment at Annette; she appeared stunned. Was Anouk sleeping?

"This is a private conversation, Monsieur." The man began to shove Kruse toward the door.

Kruse allowed himself to be shoved. He looked around the body-guard. "Are you okay?"

Her eyes were red but no one had hurt her, not yet.

Kruse removed the big hand and torqued it and guided the big man to the floor by his wrist. The man squealed through his teeth. "Shh," Kruse said, as he locked the man's face to the white tile floor with his new black shoe. "The baby's sleeping."

The woman had backed into the apartment and one of the other men stood up. Whoever they were, they had come with one thug and he was on the floor. They were not accustomed to this, not the guard, not the woman, and not these men. Despite what the hotelier had said about Joseph, that he was an aristocrat, he was a pretender. Joseph vibrated with the business of his family, even if his suit fit perfectly and he spoke like the minister of culture. This woman and these men who stood up, soft around the belly, looked at him as though he had vomited.

"Christophe." Annette stood up, from the half-shadow she had been sitting in. She lifted her own hands, slowly, and bent her knees as she approached him, as though he were an untamed animal. "They aren't here to hurt us."

Kruse released the man on the floor and he rolled away, cussing to himself. Annette put her hands on his chest and looked up at him.

"Who are these people, Annette?"

One man remained sitting, at the window with a sliver of the Eiffel Tower. Finally he stood up, tall and thin, and Kruse recognized him before he spoke. He wore the shiny grey double-breasted suit he had been wearing during his speech. What remained of his hair was combed back over his head.

"Monsieur, allow me to congratulate you." He extended his hand.

Annette stepped aside and the mayor of Paris lowered his head.

"And to express my sincerest apologies, on behalf of all of us."

Kruse looked down at his hand but did not take it. "All of us?"

"France." He folded his rejected right hand into his left and gently rocked on his black shoes. "I will not incriminate myself, Monsieur Kruse, just to do so. I found out about this recently, I assure you. This very night. But I imagine you know, by now, why the men and women who orchestrated this terror—the destruction of your family—were motivated to act. We can go back in time, not long ago, to distrust and hatred, to empires of blood. Or we can move into the future together, with new ideas of what it means to be French, to be European."

"You killed my daughter, Monsieur. You killed my wife."

The mayor did not speak. He did not nod. But he did not back away from it. "What has happened here, from the beginning, is shameful and murderous. It is anti-democratic, a stain on the republic. You are correct in that, perfectly so, and the responsibility for making amends rests with me. Your family, Jean-François de Musset and his wife . . . there is, I realize, no way to give back what we have taken from you. The man you confronted today, at the conference, set all of this in motion on his own."

"Your senior adviser."

"Yes."

"Say his name, Monsieur, for Annette's story."

"Philippe Laflamme. He has worked for me since 1962, since the Pompidou years. There is a danger, in politics, of feeling immune. Ideas are like bunkers. You hide in them and you forget, over time, who constructed them, upon whose land they were built. Monsieur Kruse: he has been dismissed in disgrace."

"That isn't enough."

"Of course not." The mayor gestured at Annette, still standing close enough to touch Kruse. "This is what we have been discussing, Monsieur Kruse. Making amends. The right decisions for the republic. In the spirit of solidarity and for the good of France I do hope you will speak to us—as Madame Laferrière has spoken to us—of a different sort of future together."

"Listen, Christophe, to what he is proposing. Not for me or for you, but . . ." She motioned toward Anouk standing at the opened door of the bedroom, not in pyjamas but in a red flannel nightdress. Her black curly hair was whorled. The bodyguard remained on the floor, sitting with his back to the wall, massaging his right arm and his wrist.

"Monsieur Christophe."

"Anouk."

"You came to say good night?"

"I did."

She realized that a room full of adults was looking at her and retreated shyly into her bedroom. Kruse asked the others to wait, and followed her.

NINETEEN

Boulevard Haussmann, Paris

ANNETTE AND ANOUK STOOD ON THE SIDEWALK IN THE WET SNOW, pointing at the animatronic table of ravens enjoying the Réveillon de Noël. The ravens turned to one another, lifting and lowering glasses of red wine with their wings. A French carol that sounded like a Catholic hymn, only partially lifted by light-toned bells and twinkles, played as the robot birds celebrated. In her free hand Annette carried two large white bags from Printemps. They had taken dinner in the tea room of the department store, under the pretty cupola, and now they moved slowly along the window displays of Galeries Lafayette.

Kruse felt him before he arrived, crossing the street from the old opera house, the Palais Garnier. It was the third time in a week.

"Do they know you're spying?"

If he did not speak to him, perhaps he would go away. "Spying" was not at all the right word.

"You're obviously not doing the best job of forgetting about them."

"Go away, Joseph."

"You worry about Annette and Anouk. I worry about you."

Kruse walked out of the light from the opera house and Joseph lit a cigarette, following along.

"One of these days, Christopher, you might invite me to your pretty new apartment for a glass of wine."

"You drink too much."

"Only when someone's being skinned. It almost never happens these days." They stood together and watched Anouk and Annette across the street, moved in the salt and slush to keep up with them. "How's the girl?"

Kruse had vowed—and tried—to remove himself from their lives, for their sake. "She's fine for now, I think. Nightmares."

"Of course."

"But she's never had her own room before. I think she crawls into bed with Annette most nights."

"She starts at a new school in January, doesn't she? The mayor's alma mater."

"Brigitte Bardot went there as well."

"And Sartre. From Rue Santeuil to a private school."

"What do you want, Joseph?"

"It's not what I want. It's what they want."

"These people have what they want: they bought her story. They bought her."

"And you, Christopher."

"They bought my silence. They didn't buy me."

"For the good of the republic." Joseph put his hand on his heart, lifted his chin like a veteran on Armistice Day. "You're deluding yourself, my friend."

The crowds in front of the Christmas window displays had thickened. A tourist bus had emptied into Boulevard Haussmann and cameras flashed off the glass. The word for "window shopping" in French is *lèche-vitrine*—"window-licking." No matter how French he became, that would always be peculiar.

"They don't have what they want, Christopher. They have what they wanted. And they never stop wanting, which is a business opportunity."

"For you?"

"And for you. You've come up in conversation."

"At gangster meetings?"

"I'm not talking about gangsters. I'd never involve you in petty gangsterism. As much as I find it charming, it's not for you."

"Only one thing matters. If they leave Annette and Anouk alone, they can forget about me."

"They don't want to forget about you. You didn't really think they would. The republic is always a moment away from the next disaster. Men like you. Men like us . . ."

Annette and Anouk stepped into a moving crowd in front of the next window of ravens.

"This work we're doing, Christopher, I know you'd like it. And if you want Annette and Anouk to be safe, safe for always, there is one rather perfect way."

It was so busy in front of the window that some people were moving out onto the boulevard, a dangerous place. Even in the light snow, scooters deked around cars. Buses and slow-moving, top-heavy white vans careened into the lane. Anouk and Annette were in the middle of the mob in black coats and scarves, jostling and flashing in front of the ravens. The birds twirled on a royal floor, under a chandelier, to a creepy, slowed-down version of "Have a Holly Jolly Christmas." Mother and daughter were separated, no longer holding hands.

Kruse abandoned Joseph to his cigarette and sprinted across the street, shoved his way into the crowd. He picked up Anouk and carried her out, her soft cheek touching his. He kissed her twice before her mother arrived and put her down and made her promise to be more careful. She complained, not really complaining, that his chin was scratchy. They held hands.

Annette escaped with her bags and met them under the red department-store awning. He pretended and Annette pretended it was a coincidence. They pretended not to know what they knew, to have seen what they had seen. Maybe they could step into a brasserie far from this mad sidewalk, for a cup of hot chocolate or a glass of pineau des Charentes, Annette's favourite. She knew of a place on Rue de la Michodière. He glanced inside the bags: some boxes, an owl *doudou* peeking out of yellow tissue paper. At a store near his own place, he had found a porcelain tea set for Anouk: it was white with delicate violets. He had already bought and assembled a small table with four matching chairs and had set them up in a corner near the fireplace, over lacquered parquet. On a soft floor, a girl can drop as many teacups as she likes. They will not break.

ACKNOWLEDGEMENTS

WALTER AND PATRICIA WELLS, OF VAISON-LA-ROMAINE AND PARIS, were marvellous cultural ambassadors—and friends—as I researched this novel in France. My beautiful wife, Gina Loewen, and my inspiring children, Avia and Esmé, allowed me to drag them around the hexagon for a year.

The Canada Council for the Arts helped make that year possible. So did John McDonald III and Allan Mayer (though they didn't know it) and my mother and brother, Nola and Kirk Babiak, who watched over my phantom life in Canada.

Thank you to the brilliant Jennifer Lambert and Jane Warren and others at HarperCollins Canada for their intelligence, their hard work, and their patience. Thank you to Randall Klein and Mark Tavani, for their ideas and encouragement.

It feels measly and ridiculous to simply thank Martha Magor Webb, who worked so hard with me on this novel.

Someday I will design and perform an opera for you, Martha. Or something.